Vicky

Scott's lips were only inche...

Rani had only to reach up ... her lips and receive what instinct told her Scott was offering. She closed her eyes and did so.

His mouth was as soft as she remembered, but this time the contact lasted longer, reached deeper. Her arms slipped around his waist, and she parted her lips, her nostrils recording the scent of him.

If she'd been a few years younger, without a divorce behind her, she might have reacted as a teenager would have, excited because a man she respected had paused long enough to acknowledge her presence.

But Rani had been married. She knew the difference between kisses that acknowledged the chemistry between a man and a woman and kisses that explored the depth of that chemistry. The kiss that she and Scott shared was meant for exploration....

VELLA MUNN
is also the author
of this title in
Love Affair

RIVER RAPTURE

When Michon volunteered to chaperon a group of
teenagers on a trip down the John Day River, she
knew her appearance worked against her.
Employed by an exclusive department store in
Oregon, Michon felt pressured to look
model-perfect all the time. But the real Michon
ached to be set free. In fact, Michon hoped this
trip would reveal her true self, and in Chas
Carson, the magnetic owner of Carson River
Tours, she finally found someone she thought
could help her.

The Heart's Reward

VELLA MUNN

A Love Affair from

HARLEQUIN

London · Toronto · New York · Sydney

First published in Great Britain in 1986 by
Harlequin, 15–16 Brook's Mews, London W1A 1DR

© Vella Munn 1985

ISBN 0 373 16096 8

18-0186

Printed and bound in Great Britain by
Richard Clay (The Chaucer Press) Ltd,
Bungay, Suffolk

Chapter One

Being stuck behind a large truck loaded with sheep wasn't how Rani Lassen would have chosen to spend a summer morning, but since there was no chance of passing on the narrow, curving country road, she'd decided to make the best of the situation. By the time the truck reached its destination Rani had managed to name a half dozen of the sheep and was imagining that one of the largest was winking back at her.

She was almost sorry to see the right-hand blinker start flashing on the battered but sturdy truck. It wasn't until she herself had started to signal in order to pass that she spotted the large metal sign above the entrance to the farm that was the truck's destination. SOL VALLEY DOGS FOR THE DEAF. That was the address she'd been looking for. It was here that she hoped her life would take a step in the right direction.

Rani touched her brakes and waited for the truck to pass under the sign. It didn't make sense that sheep would be coming to a dog-training center, but then not much about the whole project made sense to her yet. She added that to her mental lists of questions she'd have to ask Scott Barnett, whoever he was.

A minute later the dust from the truck settled and Rani started to ease her car forward. She almost slammed on the brakes and pulled a U-turn when she read the sign on the high, solid metal gate that had been pulled back to let traffic through. WILD ANIMALS. PLEASE KEEP GATE LOCKED.

What was she letting herself in for? Rani asked, but that didn't stop her from driving past the entrance and pulling over to the side of the gravel road. What she could see from within her car was impressive. She was at a farm all right, complete with ranch house, two barns and a half-completed building situated on a slope above the ranch house that, although it was early morning, workmen were already in the process of roofing. She stepped out of a VW Bug that hadn't been waxed for over a year and scurried around to the right side of her car. The tailgate on the sheep truck was being lowered and Rani didn't think she'd be particularly popular if she was in the way when the sheep started climbing out.

Hot, moist air hit Rani's hair and the back of her neck. The day was going to be hot, but not that hot. She froze, afraid to move. The sensation faded and she dared to breathe. She was trying to convince herself that she'd imagined the whole thing when the blast of air hit her again; there was no imagining the grass smell that accompanied the warmth. Cautiously Rani turned around and looked up, up into the eyes of a llama. The fact that there was a wooden fence between Rani and the creature didn't immediately calm her nerves.

"Hi," she managed above the crazy pounding of her heart. "Would you happen to be the welcoming committee?"

Obviously the llama was above carrying on a conversation with a mere human. The animal's enormous eyes zeroed in on Rani. It slowly cocked its head first one way and then the other, its lips curled back in an expression of disdain. Finally the llama snorted its disgust and turned its attention to the chickens clucking around its feet.

"Well! Excuse me!" Rani snorted herself, giggling now at her momentary fright.

Once Rani had assured herself that the sheep were being driven up a hill to a pasture, she turned her attention back to the llama and the other creatures around him. In the next corral were several pygmy goats, two of whom couldn't have been more than a few weeks old. Dean would love this! Rani hoped that Scott Barnett would allow her to bring her three-year-old son out to see the animals.

Rani jumped at the sound of a harsh whirring behind her and whipped around to confront her attacker. One more fright like this and she wouldn't be in any shape for a job interview. Her "opponent" turned out to be a large male peacock with its fan-shaped tail spread out behind him, spectacular feathers making a dry, shaking sound as he pushed them to full extension. "Tough guy, are you?" she asked the peacock. "Or do you think I'm some strange lady you can add to your harem with a little courting dance?"

The peacock, like the llama, apparently decided Rani wasn't interesting enough to command his attention and took off in a flurry of sound after a cat that had ventured too close.

Rani laughed, the sound catching on the early-morning breeze that blew freely through the farm complex. The breeze carried with it a mixture of smells, predominantly hay and clover. Working for the Dogs for the Deaf program in Sol Valley definitely wasn't going to be a typical job. That suited Rani just fine. She'd never held a nine-to-five job in her life and had no intention of starting now if she could possibly help it.

Of course she wouldn't be able to start anything, or even think about it, if she didn't find this Scott Barnett and get him to concentrate on her long enough for her to tell him why she felt she could handle the job as assistant director of the first program in this part of the country designed to train dogs to work with deaf people. From guard-dog trainer to guide-dog trainer shouldn't be that much of a jump. She'd observed Seeing Eye dogs being trained and hoped that would be a point in her favor. The problem, Rani admitted, wasn't how to adjust her techniques with the dogs, but what had happened in her life in the past year. She was now divorced, raising a child who needed special attention. It wouldn't be easy to devote a fair share of her energies to the job of assistant director. But she had to work. There wasn't a choice in that department.

Rani was still torn between wanting to watch a camel with a blackbird perched on his hump chomping on hay and looking for someone who knew where she was supposed to be when she noticed a teenage boy leaving the sheep truck and coming toward her. She couldn't really call his gait a walk; rather, he moved with the energy of a yearling colt. His gray-blond hair trailed in loose waves around his neck and made Rani guess that his mother was probably nagging him to get a haircut. Rani hadn't had much contact with teenagers in recent years, but she found herself warming to the boy even before he spoke. His arms, although well muscled, seemed too long for his body. At five feet ten herself, Rani could appreciate the problems that went with being all arms and legs.

"Can I help you?" the boy asked in a voice that had gone past the squeaks of adolescence and settled deeply in his chest. "You're not with the sheep, are you?"

"No, I'm not with the sheep." Rani laughed. "Actually I hope to be with some dogs. How many animals are here, anyway?"

The boy shrugged, giving Rani a glimpse of broad, strong shoulders that would frame a well-proportioned man in a few years. "I never thought to count them," he said. "The slave driver who runs this place keeps me too busy for that. Nothing but work. He doesn't know from nothing about child labor laws. Let me guess. You're here about the assistant director job for the deaf program, aren't you?"

"Yes. How did you know?"

The boy threw back his head in a self-assured gesture. "I know everything that goes on around here. Or at least I'd like to convince people that I do. I'm Chad. I take it you want to see the boss?"

Rani introduced herself and then nodded. "That's the general idea. The information the employment agency gave me was pretty sketchy. I must admit I'd rather wander around the ranch than be interviewed. Ah, do you know if there are many others applying for the position?"

Chad laughed. "One—if you could consider him an applicant. This isn't the kind of work just anyone can jump into. The other guy's working for the county pound. But he knows zip about training animals. If you can get your pet to come when you call him to dinner, you're ahead of him in the running."

Although she hadn't changed her initial opinion of Chad, Rani found herself hanging back from telling the teenager any more than she had to about herself. At twenty-seven Rani had been around long enough to learn that it wasn't always prudent to say much to strangers. "Is Scott Barnett here?" she asked.

"He was a few minutes ago. Who knows where that man's wandered off to? He can't be trusted to stay in one place long enough to take a breath. Thinks the place can't run without him. Maybe he's at the training cabin. We're trying to get it set up as a model house so the training can start in a couple of weeks." Chad turned quickly as if, like a colt, he'd stood still as long as his muscles would allow. "Come on."

If she hadn't had long legs herself, Rani would have been left behind as Chad started up the gravel road leading to the partly completed structure. As it was, Rani had to lower her head slightly and concentrate to keep up with her guide. She was chiding herself for having worn sandals which allowed gravel up under her instep, when a deep rumbling cough to her left drew her up short. She'd heard that sound before—on a TV commercial for a new car that featured a mountain lion or some such animal spread on the car's hood.

Intense black eyes stared at Rani. The small ears were pricked forward, but Rani's attention was drawn to the big cat's open mouth, the large teeth less than five feet away. She froze, too overwhelmed by the animal's presence to record the fact that he was in a large caged run that gave him room to roam but separated him from the rest of the compound.

Chad seemed to sense that he'd lost his company. The teenager turned around and came back to where Rani was still standing motionless. "That's Gaspar. He runs the show."

Rani found her voice. "Gaspar?" Now that she'd convinced herself that those teeth weren't going to get any closer, she was eager to cover up her momentary fright. "That's a heck of a name for a creature like that."

"His stage name is El Grande, but Gaspar suits his personality a lot better. That's the name of one of the three wise men, but I'm afraid our friend here is a little lacking in the brains department," Chad explained. Before Rani could react, Chad reached through the bars and was rubbing the big cat behind an ear. "Too hot for you is it, fella? You'd like to take a nap, but those sheep have you all stirred up, don't they? Forget it. That's not going to be your dinner."

"You can touch him?" Rani asked, leaning forward but not taking a step. She still wasn't convinced that El Grande, or Gaspar, would pass as a household pet. "I'm not sure about those teeth."

"His mouth is open because it's hot and he's panting. Gas is one of our star performers. He gets a curtain call every time Hollywood needs a mountain lion, panther, cougar or puma. Versatile, aren't you, Gas? You don't care what they ask you to do as long as we're not late with dinner."

"What's going on here? You aren't giving away our trade secrets, are you?"

Rani, whose nerves still hadn't fully recovered from

discovering the big cat so close, started at the sound of the unexpected voice. It was then that she saw the man coming toward them from the far end of Gas's run. She supposed she should say something, but for the moment at least she couldn't organize her words enough to come up with something intelligent. Fortunately neither the man nor the boy seemed to notice.

"We've been looking for you," Chad explained. "You didn't forget you had an interview for that assistant's job, did you?"

"When I need a personal secretary you can have the job. I know you think I'm already senile," the man was saying. "But until I'm ready to admit that myself, weren't you supposed to be getting those sheep into their pasture?"

"Gee. Slave all day. Work my fingers to the bones. And do I get a word of thanks? No. Can't even get minimum wage around this place," Chad challenged before taking off on his long legs.

Although they hadn't been formally introduced, Rani had gathered enough from the short conversation to figure out that the tall man with curly, gray-blond hair a shade darker than Chad's was the man she'd driven fifteen miles out into the country to see. Rani stuck out her hand, noting with resignation her long, long wrist, and introduced herself. "You said anytime this morning would be all right. I hope I'm not too early for..." Her words trailed off as her fingers were enveloped by a hand capable of keeping El Grande in line.

"Yeah. Fine. It's hard for me to pin myself down timewise. One of these days I'm going to get organized. But don't hold your breath." Scott Barnett looked down at the woman in front of him. Her hair was tangled on the left side, proof that she'd driven with her window down. That pleased him as did the fact that she seemed to be taking her surroundings in stride. "I hope you don't mind," he finished up.

"Of course I don't," Rani replied. "That's quite some watchdog you have there." She nodded her head in Gaspar's direction. "I practically bumped into him before I saw him."

Scott finally remembered to release her hand, but its soft warmth continued to register on his emotion. "Not many people go looking for a cougar next to the road," he explained. Usually it irritated him when he had to stop everything to explain to visitors about his menagerie, but talking to the woman was turning into a pleasant experience. "Gas likes company. I put his run where he can keep an eye on the action; otherwise he pouts. And Chad was right. If we let Gas have the run of the place, we'd wind up missing some of the sheep. Look, maybe we better go inside. We're going to get interrupted if we try to have an interview out here." Scott thought about putting his arm around her shoulders in order to guide her to the ranch house, but decided that would be pushing a brand-new relationship a little too fast.

Actually Rani was content to stand where she was. The breeze blowing in from the mountains was unbelievably pure and she hadn't seen enough of the farm complex to understand everything that was going on, but she was, after all, here for an interview. With regret she denied her desire to remain in the shadows of the evergreens, oaks, even blackberry bushes that provided landscaping for the farm. "If I get the job, would I be responsible for the program's finances?" she asked. "I'd like to know more about that."

"So would I." Scott laughed, approving her direct approach. He indicated by gesture that they should start toward the ranch house. Unconsciously he altered his stride to match hers. Because she was tall, she came closer to being able to keep up with him than most women could. As they walked, Scott explained briefly that a retired public relations expert had agreed to volunteer his time toward fund-raising projects.

Rani tried to concentrate on what the animated man was saying about using the media to spread word of the project's work, but her thoughts centered on her hand and the impact Scott's fingers had left on it. She couldn't remember when she'd stopped hoping she'd be a petite creature who would slip her dainty foot into a glass slipper. Cinderella she wasn't; getting past her teen years had helped her accept what couldn't be changed.

Scott had to be well over six feet tall, she decided. She wondered if his height ever caused him awkward moments but decided it probably didn't. Although the V-neck pullover he was wearing was called into maximum service, Scott handled his broad shoulders and big hands comfortably. He'd probably long ago made his peace with the wildly curly hair that had been bleached by long contact with the sun. The flesh around his eyes was permanently creased from squinting. That plus a few lines around his mouth put him in his mid-thirties.

They were inside and Rani was blinking to help her eyes adjust to the darker interior before she took note of his eyes. They were green, a smoky green that seemed to continue forever. "Have you read my résumé?" Rani asked after he'd hurried her through a huge, masculine living room and into a bedroom that had been converted into an office.

"Yep. I've got it here somewhere." Scott nodded at a comfortable recliner and took the large chair behind the hardwood table strewn with letters, papers and a stack of books in danger of toppling over. "I don't know if I can find it in all this mess, so why don't you fill in the spaces? I remember you said something about having trained German shepherds for the police. That's why I thought you might be what I need. It shouldn't be that hard to make the mental shift from thinking about protection to service."

Rani settled into her chair and crossed her long legs. She could still feel a pebble caught in her sandal, but the thought that it might drop onto the floor didn't bother her. Although what she'd been able to see of the house was in fine repair, housekeeping apparently played second fiddle to whatever else went on at the ranch. The chair she was sitting in was almost too comfortable for her to be able to concentrate on the fact that she was being interviewed. Rani hadn't been sure a white blouse with short puffed sleeves tucked into the light-blue culottes was dressy enough even though she was coming out to a ranch, but her prospective employer was wearing faded jeans and boots. Training shepherds hadn't called for many dressy outfits. Maybe she wouldn't have to spend money on clothes, money that had to go toward meeting Dean's medical expenses.

"Do you think you'd have trouble switching from shepherds to mutts?" Scott was asking. "You aren't hung up on purebreds, are you?"

Rani didn't know whether Scott Barnett was joking

or not, but she found herself bristling slightly. "I like shepherds, yes," she admitted. "But my father was a vet. I grew up handling everything from Mexican hairless to Great Danes. And a great many mutts, too."

"That's good." Scott leaned back in his chair, waited for it to stop complaining and went on. "We probably won't be training any purebreds for the program. Because this is a nonprofit organization I've made arrangements with the humane society to donate animals that meet our criteria. The humane society doesn't get many purebreds. We'll be working with small dogs for the most part because most people don't have houses large enough to accommodate large ones. The dogs we choose have to be energetic, intelligent and good-natured. They have to be eager to please and attached to humans. I don't care who their great-grandparents were."

"Will I be doing any of the training?" Rani asked. "I'm not sure what an assistant director does."

"Neither am I." When Rani gave him a confused look, Scott laughed and continued. "I've been working with animals all my life, but this is the first time I've taken on anything like this. I'm flying by the seat of my pants. I hope you're adaptable."

Rani thought about the recent changes in her personal life and nodded. "I'm adaptable." She started to add to the comment and then remembered what Chad had said about the boss being a slave driver. "I need to know about the hours I'd be working," she said. "It looks as if something's going on here all the time."

"There is." Scott leaned forward and placed his elbows on his desk. The movement gave Rani a closer look into his green eyes. They seemed to stretch so far that they might be reaching his soul. "Are you a clock-watcher?"

Rani shook herself free from his eyes and tried to answer truthfully. "No. It's just that—well, the truth is that the young man I was talking with said something about a rigorous pace. I'd like to know how much that would involve me."

Scott threw his head back and groaned. "Do you have children, Mrs. Lassen? That gangly character out there is my son. I've decided there's nothing like having a teenage son around to keep me aware of my faults—or at least his version of my faults."

"Your son? I should have guessed."

"Please don't tell me we look alike. I don't think I can handle that." Scott groaned again and ran a hand through his curls.

"I'm afraid so," Rani said, smiling. "He's going to be tall. His hair isn't as wavy as yours, but the color is almost the same. How old is he?"

"Fifteen, going on twenty-three." Scott's thoughts caught for a moment on the years he'd lost with his son, but he refused to let it pull him down. It was what was going to happen from now on that counted. "Sometimes he has all the sense of a two-year-old, but I understand that's part of being a teenager. Back to my question. Do you need to know what hours you'll be working? I'm afraid I can't be specific about that. The program simply can't run like an office."

"I understand." Rani was certain that Scott's eyes hadn't left her face since they sat down. She found that both disturbing and strangely comforting. She liked people who met her eye to eye. Zack hadn't really looked at her from the moment they'd sat in a doctor's office and heard the words that hit her like hammer blows to the heart.

Rani shook off thoughts of Zack and finished her comment. "I'm a single parent. I have a three-year-old son and not the most satisfactory child-care arrangement in the world. I'm sorry if that's going to cause a problem, but—"

"But nothing. I'm a parent, too." Scott nodded to himself. He'd been right about Rani Lassen. Personal responsibility and the people in her life came before her career. That was the kind of person he wanted to work with. "We can work things out. As long as the job is done, I don't care what hours you work. And if you want to bring your son out here, that's okay with me. It's just that this place might not be all that safe for a little kid."

"I'd like him to see the farm. Dean's pretty good about doing what I tell him to do. There was a time when he had to be restricted," Rani explained. So they were both parents. It gave her an unexpected bond with the man sitting across from her. But she still didn't know what her job would consist of. Feeling uncomfortable because she knew so little, Rani asked questions about the program. Scott filled in the blanks with words that said this was much more than just a job with him. He explained that the country had only a handful of Dogs for the Deaf training centers. Those simply weren't able to keep abreast of the need. Scott had visited those programs, talked to the directors, done research on deaf education and the most pressing problems of the deaf. He felt he was now ready to set up his own center.

"It's quite an undertaking," Rani admitted. "Not

many people would be willing to sacrifice themselves to something like this."

"It's no sacrifice. I don't know if this is going to come out right, but I've done all right for myself; I figure it's my turn to do something for other people. Naturally I'll go on doing what I do to earn a living. That's why I need an assistant. My job calls for me to fly to Hollywood every time I turn around. I don't want the program to suffer when I'm not around."

"Hollywood?" It was the second time today she'd heard the word. "I'm afraid I'm confused."

"You are? Why do you think Gas is here? Do you think I keep raccoons and deer and a timber wolf around here because I'm eccentric? Those animals all earn their keep."

"They do?" Rani winced as she said the words, but it was too late to take them back.

Scott shook his head and momentarily closed his eyes. "I know I keep a low profile around here, but I didn't realize it was that low. I happen to be the largest supplier of animal actors in this part of the country— the whole country for all I know. Hollywood needs four-legged actors for commercials, movies, TV. That's where I come in. That's what pays the mortgage on this ranch and keeps Chad in name-brand running shoes. It's a pretty good living if I do say so myself, and it keeps me out of three-piece suits."

"Then why are you starting the deaf program?" Now that Scott had opened his eyes gain, Rani was looking into even more depth than had been there before.

"My father was deaf."

"Oh." Rani swallowed, wondered frantically if the

conversation was going in a direction Scott didn't want it to. "I didn't know," she wound up lamely.

"No one said you had to. Look, I don't know if you've ever been around a handicapped person before or not. I have. Deafness isn't something people can look at and identify, but it's just as hard to deal with as not being able to walk or see. Maybe harder, because deaf children can't hear speech and thus can't learn how to talk. They're going to school while their friends are still learning to ride tricycles. The coping never lets up. I can't change that for them, but I can make coping in the world easier by supplying some of them with a dog who responds to their needs." This time, instead of running his fingers through his hair, Scott tugged at the curls around his forehead. "I'm sorry," he said softly. "I didn't mean to jump on my soapbox. It's just that I'm excited about this program."

"So am I," Rani said. She didn't add that she knew every bit as much as Scott Barnett about the meaning of the word *handicap.*

Chapter Two

Rani was unable to identify the exact moment when she realized she was no longer in a job interview and Scott Barnett was using words that made her realize he'd hired her. While they were still sitting in the small office, Rani gave her new employer a brief sketch of her work background. She spoke of what it was like to grow up as the daughter of a small-town vet. Their house had been less than a block from where her father cared for pets, farm animals and 4H livestock, which meant Rani was assisting in operations, accompanying her father to farms, even cleaning cages when other girls were still playing with dolls. She'd been accepted to attend the veterinary program at the university in Davis, California, but in the middle of her third year there she'd met Zack Lassen.

"I know I'm not the first woman to choose a man over college," she said honestly. "Zack wanted me to drop out of school because he was working in Sacramento and didn't like the idea of us being separated. I finished my junior year. We were married a week later."

"Do you regret not finishing your education?"

Rani started at the probing question. Scott dominated the small office; she couldn't sidestep his question without it turning into an embarrassing moment. "I can't really answer that," she admitted. "My parents were very disappointed. At least my father was. Mom is one of a dying breed. She never wanted more than a wedding ring and four walls. She thought I was settling into happily ever after when I got married. Zack and I had a good marriage for a couple of years. He had a contract with both the county's and the city's law enforcement departments to provide them with dogs. Zack and I trained dogs for tracking, defense and attack, drug detection—whatever the police needed. I was working with animals all the time because we were also training dogs for private owners, people with small businesses that needed guarding. There wasn't much time to think about what direction my life would be going in if I had still been in college."

"Do you think you'll ever go back?"

Rani's bitter laugh vibrated in the room. "I have a child to raise, Mr. Barnett. He comes first." Rani stopped talking as a thought hit her. How had she let the interview go this far without asking the most important question of all? "What about health insurance? What kind of program do you have for your employees?"

Scott Barnett named one of the major carriers and then frowned. "It's that important to you? You don't have some health problem you aren't telling me about, do you? You're really going to have to be physically active to handle this job, I'm afraid."

Rani stuck out her hands. "Do these wrists look like they belong on a ninety-pound weakling? I'm healthy as a horse, as they say. My son," she faltered. "Dean was in an automobile accident last year. There are still some residual problems. He's on medication and under a doctor's care." It hurt to give voice to something she was still trying to accept, but her employer had to know what the demands on her time and energies were.

Scott gave her a puzzled look. For a moment she feared he was going to ask for more information. Instead he pushed his chair back and rose to his feet. "How about I give you a tour before I take off? I'd like you to see the facilities we're getting ready for the dogs. You might have to select the first ones we use if a certain baby-food company decided to go ahead with plans to use pygmy goats in their ad. I'd be in Hollywood then."

Rani followed after Scott, her mind on how close his shoulders came to touching both sides of the door they passed through. "What do goats have to do with baby food?" she asked.

"I have no idea." Scott's laugh rumbled back to her. "If they want to foot the bill for those expensive little buggers, who am I to argue? They're cute. I guess they're supposed to grab the audience's attention."

"They're adorable," Rani admitted as they reached the front porch and she squinted against the summer sunlight. On her way here she'd been wondering why anyone would have a business out in the middle of nowhere, but the ranch was a constant wave of activity. The sounds of hammers from the half-completed building on the hill above them blended with the sounds of the still-agitated sheep. The goats and the llama had come close to the road so they could watch a tractor being backed out of the barn just beyond the house. "I was watching the goats when I got here. I'm not sure I should let Dean see them. He'll want to take the babies home with him."

"Those con artists are experts at escape. They're almost more trouble than they're worth," Scott said in a tone that told Rani he would put up with a lot of inconvenience before getting rid of the pint-sized creatures.

The conversation switched to what still needed to be done before the actual dog training could begin. No small matter was getting the dogs completely checked out by a vet who'd offered his services. Rani scrambled after Scott as he plowed his way up the hill to the unfinished cabin. She was slightly out of breath by the time they were looking at the roof. Scott was standing a foot away, but Rani could sense the heat coming from his body. True, the day was working its way to ninety plus degrees, but she couldn't be sure that was the only reason she was aware of his nearness.

The fact that she noticed surprised and shocked Rani. True, he was a big man, one who could make her feel feminine, but she hadn't expected to feel any reaction toward a man. Zack and his desertion had altered her world. Normal man-woman responses no longer touched her the way they once had.

Besides, Rani reminded herself, Scott had a son. There was probably a wife around somewhere. The image she retained of Chad Barnett struck Rani as incongruous with what she now knew of the father. Scott must have been barely out of his teens when his son was born. And yet despite early parenthood and the responsibilities that went with it, he'd become successful in the highly competitive world of Hollywood.

Scott was speaking. "We want the dogs to learn their

skills while in a normal home environment. Most of the mutts haven't had the opportunity to form attachments with humans, let alone be inside. That's why I'm having this house built. It'll have a kitchen, bedrooms. In fact if I can get an appliance store to donate a few kitchen appliances, someone could actually live in the house. Not that that's likely to happen. Some ten dogs will be trained in the house, and there aren't many people who would be crazy about trainers and handlers traipsing in and out all the time. But I want it to sound like a house so the dogs get used to that."

Rani turned toward Scott. "What exactly will you—we be teaching the dogs?"

"To respond to sounds," Scott said, his eyes sparkling. "To bring the world to their masters. It's a long process. It takes the dogs months to learn all the skills they'll need. Basically they have to identify separate sounds and let their owners know what's going on. They have to identify the telephone ringing, the doorbell, alarms, crying if the deaf person has a child. Each situation will be different depending on the needs of the people we accept to receive a dog. In fact, it'll take more time to screen the applicants than it will to select the dogs."

Rani held a hand up to stop Scott's rapid speech. "You said the dogs will be expected to tell their masters when the telephone rings. How will they do that?"

"By running between their master and the phone, pawing at the deaf person if necessary. Because telephones can be fixed with special devices such as amplifiers or teletypewriters, most deaf people don't have to be cut off from that form of communication. A telephone can be a lifeline to independence. You wouldn't believe how many young couples are afraid to have a child because one or the other of them can't hear a baby cry. A trained dog can free them of that fear."

Rani shook her head, still trying to absorb it all. "I'm just surprised programs like this didn't start a long time ago. There must be a tremendous need."

"There is. And I don't have an answer to why there aren't more centers except that it's an expensive process. The dogs have to be trained, applicants interviewed. Trainers go with the dogs to the deaf person's home and spend several weeks there getting the dog and the new master used to working with each other. All that takes money. Okay." Scott grinned down at her. "That's enough of my soapbox for today. I'm going to be late if I don't get a move on. I'm supposed to be interviewed for the evening news on one of the local stations. They're giving us coverage in the hope we can get donations. After all, your salary has to come from somewhere."

Fortunately Scott didn't give Rani time to wonder whether she was supposed to apologize for being a paid employee. He placed an arm over her shoulders and turned her back around toward her car. "Don't mind me. Actually your salary is a drop in the bucket compared to what we'll put out for the dogs. Believe me, you'll earn every bit of it."

Rani tried to nod, but it was hard for her to concentrate on the gesture with his arm around her. For an instant, but only for an instant, she struggled with a primitive desire to lean against him. Standing alone had kept her awake more nights than she wanted to think about. She was tired, not just physically but emotionally as well. Zack should be around to help with their child.

But he'd bailed out, and she'd had to handle everything on her own. It was easier than it had been at the beginning, but the road still wasn't smooth.

"When do you want me to start work?" she asked when they were standing beside Rani's VW.

"How about this afternoon? Seriously, do you think you can make it the day after tomorrow? And your little boy can come out here if that's easier on you." Scott opened her car door and then stepped back, his head cocked. "How do you get into one of those things? I'd have to be pried loose."

"It's all in knowing which muscles to move when," Rani explained. "Actually there's more legroom than I thought there'd be."

"Being tall has its drawbacks, doesn't it?" Scott laughed. "That's why I hate motels. My feet hang over the edge of the bed. At least we don't have to worry about putting on weight. There's so much of us to fill up."

Rani found herself laughing. Most people expected her to apologize for her height, but here was a man who saw it as an advantage. "You're right. I haven't been on many diets in my life."

Scott was staring openly at her. "I should hope not. I could wrap my hands around your waist."

Rani flushed but said nothing. It was the last thing she expected from a man she'd just met. In truth she knew why Scott's remark had thrown her off balance. Rani simply didn't understand men. She had thought she knew Zack, but obviously she'd been wrong. After that experience it didn't make sense to try to get inside a man's head.

Finally Rani said something about being on the job

the day after tomorrow and coaxed her little car to life. As usual it complained about being thrown into reverse but finally gave in. Scott was waving at her when she drove off.

He was still waving when his son joined him on the gravel drive. "The lady's gone, Dad," Chad pointed out. "You can stop grinning."

"What—I thought you had those sheep to attend to." Scott pulled his eyes off the car disappearing down the country road and focused on the son so much like himself that sometimes he wondered if they were two separate people.

"It doesn't take all day to put a few sheep in a pasture. And yes, I'm on my way to water the animals. Did you hire her?"

Scott nodded. "She's worked with animals all her life. And she believes in the program."

"And she's a lot easier on the eye than that guy from the pound, isn't she?" Chad jabbed his father. "Is she married?"

"No," Scott said more quickly than he wanted the word to come out. He'd wanted to know that from the moment he saw the woman standing next to Gaspar's run but hadn't known how to bring up the subject. Fortunately she'd supplied the answer. "She has a little boy," he said vaguely. "He was in an accident." Scott didn't add that he felt Rani Lassen wasn't at the point where she could talk about her child's health. It was something he'd seen in her big hazel eyes, a deep weary pain.

It was the same kind of pain he'd felt when, at twenty-three, he'd had to say good-bye to the youth standing beside him, not knowing when, if ever, he'd become a full-time father again. Thank God he'd had his second chance. Scott was once again around to give dimension to his life. "Are you coming to town with me?" he asked because he didn't want to start thinking about how long he'd waited to have custody of the boy.

Chad shrugged. "I guess. I have to register for school. I'm not looking forward to September."

Scott ran a big hand through his son's loosely curled hair. "Let's get you a haircut while we're there."

"Only if you get one." Chad focused on the tight curls covering his father's forehead. "You want to look your best when she shows up."

"Mrs. Lassen doesn't care whether I have a haircut or not." If Chad hadn't been living with him since school let out, Scott might have taken offence at his son's teasing, but he'd had two months to get used to the way a fifteen-year-old boy thought. "She has enough on her mind trying to juggle a small child and getting ready for a new job." Besides, he added to himself, she hasn't been divorced very long. She's not thinking about men.

Scott Barnett was wrong. Rani was thinking about him. As she drove through fenced acres holding dairy and beef cattle, Rani was trying to figure out why a man whose business was in Hollywood would be living a state away and fifteen miles from a town of any size. True, he needed room for his operation, but there must be land in southern California that would be closer to the action. Rani wondered if his wife objected to living on an isolated ranch. Rani wouldn't mind, but then she'd grown up spending much of her time on farms and ranches.

Rani rolled down her windows, turned on the radio

and let her mind drift. The daily ride out to the ranch would take time, but she wouldn't really mind. Sol Valley's name didn't come about by accident. In fact it had a reputation for being fog-free no matter how dismal the rest of the county became in the winter. Maybe she could find a place to rent out here where Dean could run free. True, it would take him away from his grandparents, particularly his grandmother, who had agreed to look after him while Rani worked.

That would be a problem. Rani wouldn't feel right turning Dean over to just any babysitter, and most day-care centers were hesitant to take a child who needed regular medication.

Dean was settling down to lunch in his grandmother's kitchen when Rani walked in. Dean gave her a smile that allowed a bite of hot dog to pop out of his mouth, but he retrieved it and popped it back in. "Your hair's messy," he observed with a young child's candor.

"And you have catsup on your cheek." Rani leaned forward and planted a kiss on the red stain. "How has my wild Indian been?"

"All right," Susan Chapman offered. "I was going to try to give him his medicine if you didn't come after lunch, but I was rushed, what with getting your father ready for his physical therapy. Thank goodness for good neighbors. Bill offered to take him today."

Rani nodded. Her father's stroke last year had altered what was to have been a peaceful retirement for her parents. He had changed his eating habits and was taking better care of himself than he ever had before, but he still needed a lot of help from his wife in order to get around. The physical therapy alone took up three days a week. Rani could hardly blame her mother because Dean hadn't had his Dilantin yet. "I know you didn't think you'd be back in the baby business again," Rani said. "I'm sorry it turned out that way."

"Don't apologize." Susan squeezed her daughter's hand and stepped aside to let her take over supervision of Dean's lunch. "I'm glad you agreed to come here when you and Zack separated. I'd be worried sick if you were alone in Sacramento."

Rani laughed, a little bitterly she knew. "Zack got the business and the hospital bills. There wasn't much to keep me there." She could have fought for her share of the business they owned jointly, but when she returned from six weeks in Nevada, Rani realized she couldn't bear to stay in Sacramento where she might bump into Zack or their friends and have to answer questions she didn't have answers to. Where else could she go except to the town where her parents had retired? Maybe for the first few weeks Rani had been like a wounded creature trying to recapture the security she'd had as a child.

That feeling hadn't lasted. She'd stayed with her parents for a week and then used some of the money Zack sent her to rent an apartment.

While she tended to Dean's lunch and nodded absently at Dean's chatter about a superhero cartoon he'd seen, Rani told her mother about her morning. Susan hadn't wanted Rani to go looking for a job. There was Dean to consider. Zack should be legally forced to provide much more support than he was. But Rani had always worked, and even if she hadn't, she knew Zack couldn't afford to support her. Zack had all he could do to finish paying off Dean's hospital bills and keep the business going.

Rani cleaned Dean's face and lifted him away from the table. "You, young man, will never be allowed in a good restaurant. Your table manners leave a lot to be desired."

Dean laughed as his mother planted her nose on his and kissed him Eskimo style. He was still grinning when Rani reached for the Dilantin. Susan excused herself and wandered off into the living room, her feet dragging. As Rani handed Dean a glass of water she closed her eyes, sighed.

It wasn't going to work. Her mother simply was too burdened to be asked to be responsible for handling the medication that gave Dean freedom from seizures. If Susan accidentally missed a dosage, the essential saturation of Dean's body tissues might be lowered. Dean hadn't had a seizure in three months. Rani wasn't going to let them start again.

Scott Barnett had said she could bring Dean with her. Maybe that was the only way she could devote herself to her job without worrying about her son. Rani led Dean out of the kitchen. "I think we'll be going, Mom," she said as she went into the living room. "Dad will be tired when he gets home. He's not going to appreciate a grandson who needs a nap. Mom? I might take Dean out to the ranch with me. Mr. Barnett suggested it."

Susan smiled. "He'd like that, dear. Are you sure you'll be able to keep an eye on him and work as well? I know there'll be all kinds of animals for him to play with. Be sure to take some pictures. I'd love to see them."

Rani nodded and left her mother to her soap opera. There was no denying it. Susan was relieved to have her grandson off her hands. It wasn't that she didn't love Dean, but she wasn't a young woman. Doing what had to be done for her husband was enough.

"You'll like the ranch," Rani told her son as they were getting into her car. "How would you like to see a lion?" She gave a fair imitation of a lion's roar. "Does that sound like fun?"

"He can't bite me," Dean announced. "I'll punch him in the nose and knock his teeth out. See my muscles."

Spurred on by Dean's animation, Rani continued. "There's a teenage boy there. Maybe he can show you how to play football. He's pretty big. He could put you on his shoulders and bump your head against the sky." Rani reached over and tapped Dean on the head to demonstrate. As she did so, her smile froze. Zack used to carry Dean on his shoulders.

Rani concentrated on driving. "Do you remember your daddy?" she whispered, noting that Dean was drooping in his car seat. "He was around when you went to bed one night, but he wasn't there in the morning. There weren't any big fights. Just that one with the lawyer around to act as referee. Do you remember the little apartment in Nevada? Daddy paid for that because he wanted to get the divorce over as quickly as possible."

Rani didn't want to hear her voice anymore. She simply didn't know how she felt about Zack these days. His desertion had been so swift, the end to a marriage a sharp knife descending so cleanly that she didn't know whether she was bleeding or not.

She wondered if she was in shock. She'd only seen Zack once since he'd walked out, and that had been in the lawyer's office. She'd been relieved and frightened and white-lipped with fury during that meeting, but so boiling with emotion that she honestly didn't know what she and Zack had said to each other.

It was easier to think of the good times. They'd had a normal marriage when Zack had had control of his temper. The lovemaking had been good, and the period when she was pregnant a second honeymoon. Zack was delighted when he learned he'd fathered a son. Being the father of a baby was hard on Zack's nerves, but fortunately Dean was happy-go-lucky and didn't cry much. It wasn't until he started walking and getting into things that Zack's lack of patience became something Rani could no longer dismiss.

Stop it! Rani warned herself. The past couldn't be changed. It shouldn't even concern her anymore. She had a new job, a boss she already liked, and a rare opportunity to expose her son to experiences most children never even dream about.

Chapter Three

Dean was fairly bouncing in his car seat and chattering excitedly when Rani drove out to the ranch two days later. Almost from the time he could focus his eyes, Dean had been enchanted by living things, the furrier the better. It was going to be difficult to keep him out of the corrals and Gaspar's run, but Rani would have her son with her. That was worth the extra work. She'd been able to have him with her, tucked securely in a backpack, while she and Zack worked with the dogs. When he started walking it was a circus trying to keep him out of the way, but before long Dean had learned that *no* was serious business. Now he probably took it for granted that children went to work with their mothers.

This time the front gate was closed, which meant Rani had to get out of the car, unfasten the gate and push back the heavy barrier herself. She parked in front of the main house, lifted Dean out of his car seat, and hoisted him onto her hip. His active body was packed securely inside blue coveralls and a shirt; Rani had used her employer's attire as a guideline and donned her usual faded blue jeans and a pale-blue blouse she hoped struck the right contrast between serviceability and whatever image it was an assistant director was supposed to project. She'd tried to tame her hair, but as usual the thick neck-length auburn mass looked as if she'd been driving in a convertible. She'd put on a light touch of makeup, especially eyebrow pencil to aid her sparse brows, but had nibbled off her lipstick long before reaching the ranch.

So this was what first-day-on-the-job nerves felt like, Rani acknowledged. She'd tried to call Scott Barnett last night to tell him Dean would be accompanying her, but he was out and she wasn't sure Chad had remembered to relay the message.

Because she was certain the day would be fast-paced, she'd arrived early in order to take Dean around the ranch and satisfy, at least a little, his curiosity. She couldn't help but laugh when Dean spotted the baby pygmy goats cavorting in the early-morning sunshine and dragged her over so they could watch together. His expression sobered when he realized a camel was staring down at him from its great height. He then asked a half-dozen questions about the peacock Rani decided must be in charge of taking stock of whoever came to the ranch.

"Let's go see the mountain lion," she suggested when she felt she could drag Dean away from the corrals without risking tears. "There's a few things you have to realize about him."

"I'm tougher than any old lion," Dean proclaimed. "I'm going to teach him how to roll over."

Rani didn't know what to expect of Dean's reaction to a big cat, but some instinct made him hold back, clinging to her hand as he stared wide-eyed at claws and rippling muscles, teeth and massive shoulders. Rani took a cautious step toward the cage, reached out and quickly drew her hand back, yelping as if she'd been burned. "Don't touch him," she admonished. "Do you understand? I don't even want you to get close to him."

"He's big, Mommy. Will he bite me?" Dean didn't appear to have any intention of touching the mountain lion, who had started pacing, staring at the main house instead of his visitors. There was a certain air of anticipation in Gaspar's actions that caused Rani to turn toward the house herself.

Scott Barnett was leaving the front porch, walking up the incline to the big cat's run. He was bare-chested, hair glistening wet and tightly curled. A pair of faded jeans clung to his hips. His feet were jammed into tennis shoes without socks. "You're early," he said as he ran his fingers through his hair to lift the curls to the drying influence of the breeze coming in from the surrounding mountains.

Rani started to say yes, but the words literally froze in her mouth. She'd known she was looking at a big cat when she watched Gaspar. Until this moment she didn't realize the ranch possessed two big cats. Was it the impact of taut flesh stretched over muscle, the way his jeans rode low, the way he spread his legs to balance his body? Something pounded in Rani's chest and filled her temples with a mindless throbbing. She sucked in her breath without being aware of it. But she was aware of the sudden hardening of her nipples, the rush of warmth deep in her belly.

Rani lifted her head, needing the cooling effect of the breeze. She tried to remember what muscles were needed for a smile, but her thoughts refused to leave the image of a totally sexy man.

"I take it that's your boy."

Rani blinked, sucked in the cool air and worked her throat muscles. As she introduced her son to her boss she tried to get Dean to shake hands, shaking her head because her preschooler chose this moment to turn shy. "He isn't around too many men," she said by way of explanation. "His pediatrician is a woman and Grandpa is a bald man who always has candy tucked in his pockets."

"I'll have to remember that." Scott leaned over but not so close as to intimidate a little boy. "I can come up with the candy, but I'm afraid I'm a long way from bald." He raked his fingers through his hair. "Chad says I should use his hair dryer, but I never take the time. Besides, I guess I'm too old and set in my ways to see myself using a hair dryer."

"You aren't old," Rani managed.

"Wait until your boy's a teenager. Then tell me about feeling old."

"I'm three," Dean proclaimed, speaking to Scott for the first time. "I'm going to have a lion when I grow up."

"Am I too early?" Rani asked when she realized Scott wasn't going to argue the point with Dean. "I interrupted you."

"No," Scott reassured her. "I've been hung up on the phone for an hour. I decided I'd better grab a shower before the day got away from me. Why don't the two of you come inside? I'll get you a cup of coffee. How about some hot chocolate, Dean? We need to put some meat on your bones if you're going to work with the lions."

Rani walked beside Scott, Dean bouncing beside her, as they walked back to the house. She'd lost some of the sensation that her employer was a big cat, but her reaction still shocked her. True, he was bigger than most men, but through her work with German shepherds she'd come in contact with dozens of policemen, many of whom went to pains to project their masculinity. None of them had ever elicited that kind of response.

Rani wondered if her reaction was due to the fact that she had gone from sharing a marriage bed to sleeping alone and was much more primitive than she imagined. On the other hand, Scott was already reaching her son on his level. It was possible, very possible, that she was warming to that quality in him.

Giving a quick mental yank to her emotions, Rani tried to concentrate on what she needed to ask her employer about the day's schedule. He was explaining that the phone call had been to confirm that he would be going to Hollywood on Monday to accompany his four-legged actors. He'd be leaving her with a considerable stack of applications from deaf people that had started to arrive even though the dogs had yet to enter training.

"It's sad when you think of how much need there is," Scott said as he poured her a cup of instant coffee so black she wasn't sure she'd be able to swallow it. He didn't continue until Dean had his hot chocolate. "There was one article in the newspaper a couple of weeks ago when I got the nonprofit status. The applications started coming in right after that. I'd like you to study them and work at some kind of priority list. The final list will be selected by a committee I'm forming made up of social workers, medical personnel, that sort of thing.''

Rani nodded and lowered herself onto the leather couch in the living room. She held Dean's cup and patted the space beside her to let him know he should join her. Scott had disappeared to, as he put it, cover his bones. There was something about the living room that seemed out of place, but at first Rani couldn't put her finger on it. The carpeting was thick and lush, probably no more than a couple of years old. The drapes were pulled back to let in the morning sun, but because the windows were dusty, the day's full promise wasn't reaching the interior. The coffee table in front of her was filled with sporting and business magazines and portions of two nights' newspapers. All the furniture in the room was bigger than average, sturdy and masculine.

Masculine. That was it. From the rock fireplace in the far corner to the boots resting beside the front door the entire room was masculine. There was no woman's touch.

Now that Rani thought about it, she realized that Scott had never mentioned a wife. Because he had a son living with him, she'd assumed a man and his son wouldn't be living alone without a woman to keep them dressed and fed. But no law said a man couldn't raise his son.

It was men like Zack who ran from the responsibility of parenthood.

No, that wasn't fair. Not many men, or women

either, knew the load a doctor's words had dropped on Rani and Zack Lassen. Zack shouldn't be condemned because he couldn't live under that weight.

Dean squirmed and started to rock back and forth on the couch. His restless wiggling said that his little body had been still long enough.

"Not much for sitting, are you, young man?" Scott asked as he reentered the room. He was wearing a T-shirt that covered his bronzed flesh but didn't deny his muscles. His hair had been pushed into some semblance of control. "Do you want to see where your mother is going to be working?" He reached out a hand in Dean's direction but wasn't surprised when the boy didn't take it. "He's cautious, isn't he?" Scott observed, aware of how closely Rani was watching the interplay between himself and her son.

Rani nodded. "He's seen more than his share of strangers lately. You know how it is with kids. They're more comfortable with the status quo than with change. He's still taking stock of what's happened lately."

"I'll go slow. We'll get along all right, won't we, Dean? Did your mother tell you that *I* have a son? He's almost old enough to drive, but he likes to be around animals. And play football! Do you know how to throw a football?"

Dean nodded, eyes glowing. "I can throw it a mile. I can throw it over this house."

"I'd like to see you do that," Scott replied. He stopped, surprised by the intensity of emotion he felt for the boy. Maybe it came because he was a father and had room in his heart for all children, and maybe it was because he wanted to reach out and offer his hand to Dean's mother.

For the next half hour Rani had little time to think about Scott's easy understanding of what it was like to be three years old and around strangers in a strange room. Scott took Dean's boasting in stride and didn't point out the holes in Dean's tall tales. Since her last trip to the ranch Scott had received applications from five people who wanted to work as dog trainers. Because of the program's budget constraints, Scott wanted to hire only two trainers. He hoped that between them and Rani, the initial ten dogs would receive adequate training. "I don't know if you've ever interviewed people before, but you probably have a good idea of what personalities work well with dogs. I'm putting you in charge of hiring the help you'll need."

Rani nodded but said nothing. She wasn't sure why people always thought she was capable of handling everything that came her way. Part of it, she realized, was because she was tall, but height alone didn't mean a woman could hold up her end of a dog-training business or hire people who would meet her employer's specifications. She could only hope she wouldn't disappoint him.

And Rani didn't want to disappoint Scott Barnett. There was something about the way he ran a successful business and was venturing into a new undertaking that made her want to live up to his expectations.

That wasn't all there was to it. There was something deep inside her that made her want Scott to turn toward her with words that told her she was more than just an employee.

The revelation shocked Rani. Scott hadn't said anything to indicate she was anything more than his assistant manager. Just because she hadn't been able to shake herself free of the memory of what she'd felt when she first saw him this morning didn't mean he'd been aware of his impact on her.

While they were still looking over the applications, one of the carpenters came in with some questions and Scott had to leave. Rani made some preliminary notes about each of the applicant's qualifications and was reading the rough draft of a press release Scott had written when the phone rang. Feeling somewhat self-conscious, Rani answered it. It was the humane society with the message that there were several dogs at the center who might meet the program's needs. Would it be possible for Mr. Barnett to come out and look at them? Rani wasn't sure but promised to call back with the answer in a few minutes.

"I'm going to see about getting a phone line between the office and the training cabin," Rani told Dean as they were hiking up the hill. "I thought your mommy was in pretty good shape, but a few more trips like this and my calves are going to knot up."

It took Rani several minutes to locate Scott. He wasn't at the cabin with the carpenters but was a few yards behind it with Chad marking distances off on a flat area and pounding stakes into the ground. As Rani caught her breath Scott explained that the dog kennels and runs would be built where they were standing.

Dean had grown tired of listening to grown-up talk and gave Rani a bored look. He trotted over to tug tentatively on one of the stakes and then marched over to Chad and planted himself in front of the teenager. "My name is Dean," he said. "What's yours?" To Rani's surprise her son wrapped his arms around Chad's neck when the older boy picked him up.

"Would you look at that?" Scott mused. "I had to bribe the little guy with hot chocolate to get him to look at me and my son's already got him eating out of his hand."

"When you've got the touch, you've got the touch," Chad said, cocking his head in a superior attitude. "Can I show him the work we're doing on the cabin? I'll keep an eye on him."

Rani nodded, feeling somewhat deserted as her son let Chad carry him off without a backward glance at her.

She sensed Scott grinning. The man stepped closer and patted her lightly on the shoulder before speaking. "Little boys have to grow up, Mama. They don't always need your apron strings."

"I know. It's just that Dean's all I have." The words were out before Rani could test their wisdom.

"Give him his freedom." Scott was still standing so close that Rani could smell the faint scent of his aftershave. "I believe that letting kids test their independence is the greatest gift we can give them."

Rani tightened inside. "I wish it were that easy," she explained. "He was so sick for a while. I wasn't sure things would be right for him. I'm afraid it's going to take me a while to relax and not hover over him."

"You'll get there," Scott said softly. It wasn't the first time he'd felt her need to have someone reach out and touch her; this time he didn't try to deny the impulse. He took her shoulders in his hands and turned her toward him. "Look at me. Okay, I'm your boss, but I'm also a human being, a parent. If you need someone to talk to, I have pretty broad shoulders." He didn't need to ask himself if he was letting himself in for more involvement than he wanted. He wasn't.

Broad shoulders. Shoulders like a mountain capable of handling any weight dropped on them. Rani stared up at Scott, found the open corridor through his smoky green eyes and for a moment took a few steps into that corridor. There was something deep in him that spurred her on, something the woman in her hungered to learn more about. That plus the way his hands on her shoulders were making her feminine nature respond stripped her of thoughts of single parenthood and earning a living and reminded her that she was capable of another role. The role of a woman.

Then she blinked, and in that brief space of time the hold his eyes had on her was broken. "I—thank you," she whispered, keeping her head low so she wouldn't be looking into his eyes again. "It—this thing with Dean really threw my life out of balance. I need time to adjust to it."

Scott still wouldn't release her. "Let me tell you something," he said softly, his breath rippling along her hair. "Chad's mother and I were divorced when Chad was three. He was the most enchanting little boy in the world. I felt toward him in a way I thought I'd never feel toward anyone. He was part of me. I had to walk out of his life. What that did to me inside wasn't something I adjusted to in time. I'm not sure you're going to be able to adjust, as you call it, either."

The conversation was reaching too close, tearing through Rani and reopening still-fresh wounds. She pulled back until Scott could no longer hold on to her without hurting her and took a calming breath when his hands were no longer touching her flesh. Stumbling over her words, she forced her thoughts onto why she'd come up the hill. "Do—are you going to have time to go out to the humane society today? Do you want me to call them back and try to arrange another time?"

Scott glanced at his watch. "If we don't go now, there isn't going to be another time."

"We?"

"Yes," he said almost sharply. "You're going to be choosing most of the dogs. If we go out together this time, I hope we'll come to a meeting of the minds on what makes a good candidate for training."

"Of course." Rani was surprised to hear the control in her voice, the outward return to business. "I'm used to looking for aggressive qualities in dogs. I hope I won't let that get in the way of other factors we need to consider. Oh." She stopped momentarily and then plunged on. "What about Dean? Will he be in the way?"

"Why don't we leave him with Chad? I think you've got a ready-made babysitter on your hands," Scott offered.

"Oh, no," Rani said quickly. "I can't ask that of Chad."

"Don't shortchange my kid," Scott pressed. He sensed that they were on the edge of a breakthrough. Rani had said she knew she had to loosen the apron strings. What better way to start, then, with his son? "Look at it as a maturing experience for Chad. He relates to animals. He needs to try his devastating personality on little children."

When they located the two boys, Chad was holding a nail while Dean was trying to pound it into a board. "He's going to make a good carpenter if I don't lose a finger first." Chad laughed and quickly agreed to keep an eye on Dean until the adults returned. Rani dismissed her last argument against the plan. If Scott felt Chad was mature enough to look after a three-year-old, it wouldn't look right if she objected. Now that Dean's seizures were under control, there was no reason why he couldn't stay with a fifteen-year-old. She was still struggling with the impulse to warn Chad not to let Dean get too close to the animals when Scott saved her the trouble by pointing that out.

"Chad's always been a sucker for little kids," Scott said as they were getting into the pickup with Sol Valley Animal Ranch written on the side. "He just hasn't had the opportunity to be around them enough. I was worried about his being out here without other kids, but he's so busy I don't think it bothers him. Besides, once school starts he'll meet other teens in the valley. I hope he goes out for football. It'd be a good way for him to meet some kids."

Rani had little to say. She was thinking about large hands on a steering wheel, eyes down to slits as they stared into the morning sun, booted feet maneuvering the large pickup through its gears. She noticed that Scott hadn't put a shirt over his T-shirt for the drive into town and decided that dealing with Hollywood hadn't affected him as far as personal attire was concerned.

"Is that what you'll be wearing next week?" she asked. "No purple shirts with lavender ties?"

Scott laughed, his voice warming her. "I do make a

few concessions when I hit Tinseltown," he admitted. "I have a few pairs of slacks I keep for just that purpose. But that's only for business meetings. No one expects me to accompany a giraffe in a suit."

As Rani listened, Scott told her of a trip he'd made last year with a giraffe to be used in a jungle movie. Scott's new shirt bought for the trip had wound up minus a sleeve when the bored giraffe decided to see what fabric tasted like. "I asked my accountant if I could deduct the shirt as a business-related casualty, but he didn't think the IRS would buy that."

"I've never thought of animals in movies as a business before," Rani admitted. "How did you get started?"

As they waited their chance to pass a carful of older people out for a sight-seeing drive, Scott explained that he hadn't deliberately set out in life to supply animal actors, but that his first job after school in a feed store gave him the opportunity to meet the man he eventually bought the business from. "I was going to save money for college, but things got in the way. Before I knew it, I had a family to support. College was out of the question. Fortunately by then I was apprenticing with the animal trainer and coming up with ideas on how to expand the business. At least one thing I was doing during those years turned out well. I can't say the same thing about my personal life."

Rani didn't know what to say. She realized that Scott was making reference to his marriage and to what he'd said earlier about having to leave Chad when the boy was three. But Rani wasn't going to pry. When and if Scott felt like telling her more, she'd listen.

She watched as Scott pulled around the slower-moving car and stepped on the gas. There was so little she knew about him. True, she knew he loved what he was doing and obviously enjoyed having his son around, but she knew nothing of what went on inside the man. She wanted to know if there was a woman in his life, what of a personal nature he wanted for himself.

Scott was still telling her about his adventures while trying to convince animals that there were certain standards of behavior expected of them when they reached the humane society complex. As they got out of the truck, Rani paused to glance at a large cage under a tree housing a half-dozen puppies. Scott's hand was on her elbow before she realized it. "We're not here after puppies," he admonished with mock severity.

"Sorry." Rani laughed, tearing herself away. They walked side by side toward the office, their steps matching, Scott's hand still on her elbow. Was it an unconscious act or did he want his hand there? Rani lowered her eyes and glanced over at him. His profile was bland, giving her no access to his eyes. Good, she admitted. Stay away from those eyes. They make you forget everything else.

Although the humane society director was trying to convince Scott that at least six dogs had the combination of intelligence and eagerness to please that the program was looking for, it took Rani only a couple of minutes to eliminate four of the dogs. One was more interested in the other dogs than in the visitors, another hung back, a third's eyes lacked sparkle, and the fourth she rejected was already fifty pounds and still growing. But the two who were licking her fingers had potential. She looked up from her squatting position and nodded at Scott. He nodded back.

"We think alike," Scott said a few minutes later

when, with the necessary paperwork completed, they were loading two excited dogs into portable kennels in the back of the pickup. "I figured you'd have to have an instinct about dogs to have worked successfully with them before."

"Dogs are easy to figure out," Rani explained. "Humans are the complex creatures."

Scott gave her a hand up into her side of the truck. "That sounds like the voice of someone who has learned from bitter experience," he said as he was getting in.

Rani frowned. "I'm sorry. I didn't mean for it to come out like that. I don't like it when people go on about how hard their lot in life is."

"If you don't mean it, don't say it."

Rani looked sharply at him, but Scott's eyes revealed nothing of what he might be thinking. "It's a little early, I know, but if you'd like I'll buy you lunch," he said.

Rani glanced at the watch on Scott's wrist. "It's after eleven," she said in alarm. They'd been at the humane society longer than she realized. "I have to feed Dean. Please, can we start back?"

Scott shrugged, his shirt protesting the movement. "I take it your answer is no. Having a child ties a woman down, doesn't it?"

"Maybe you'd like it better if I put him in a kennel with the dogs," Rani snapped, not understanding her anger and yet too wrapped up in it to be able to analyze it. "I could give him water and dry food and exercise him once a day. Is that what you want?"

"Hey, back off, will you." Scott's voice was as intense as hers. "I didn't say that. I was just making an observation."

"An observation I don't like." Rani forced herself to stop. "I'm sorry. I shouldn't have said that. But Dean's father decided his son could get along without him. I resent it when someone tells me a three-year-old boy can get along without his mother as well."

Scott sighed. "It's obvious I'm going to have to watch what I say around you. You're sensitive when it comes to the subject of parenthood."

"I have my reasons." Scott had started on the road back to the ranch, but Rani was too caught up in their conversation to take comfort in that. "I take being a parent seriously. I don't have much patience for a man who lacks the self-control to accommodate a small child's spontaneity."

"I'm not that person," Scott said through taut lips. "Don't lump me with your ex-husband. I'm raising my son now. Don't I get a gold star for that?"

"What?" Rani turned toward Scott. At that moment he glanced at her, just long enough for her thoughts to hang up in his eyes. "I shouldn't be arguing with you. You're my boss."

"Being your boss has nothing to do with it. We're discussing basic philosophies. I've never had patience with women who hold out their motherhood status as if it entitles them to sainthood."

Silence. Now that Scott was back to concentrating on driving, Rani could think without his green eyes getting in the way. She couldn't even put her finger on what was behind the sudden argument except that she'd been lashing out at Zack at the time. The situation she was in now had nothing to do with Scott. She had no business blaming him. But he'd jumped on her, let her know that being a single parent didn't make her a martyr.

True, he didn't know the whole story. He couldn't understand that there was more to it than a simple divorce. Scott understood that there was something wrong with Dean, but she hadn't told him enough to know the added responsibility she'd taken on now that she was raising Dean alone. And he couldn't know of the guilt she felt.

Rani cast about desperately, trying to think of a safe subject for them to discuss, but the sharp words spoken in the truck prevented her from concentrating. She liked much of what she'd seen about Scott so far. And there was no denying that she was reacting to him in a physical way. She hadn't wanted to fight, but it had happened.

Neither of them spoke until they'd returned to the ranch. Even then they spoke only when necessary, trying to figure out where the dogs would stay until their kennels were built. "I'll get my workmen started on that this afternoon," Scott said briefly. "It'll slow down the work on the house, but if I can get the fencing delivered it shouldn't take more than a day to have things set up."

Rani nodded. She didn't comment when Scott asked her to keep the two dogs in the office with her for the afternoon to determine whether they were used to living indoors. "I'll get Dean now," she said once the dogs were inside. "I hope you don't mind."

Scott said nothing. He gave her a look she couldn't fathom and then left her alone. She stared after him as he headed up the hill, her eyes recording the way his calf and thigh muscles tightened in order to carry his solid body along.

Rani clenched her fists together at her sides. This

was going to have to stop. She had no business looking for the male animal in him, especially after the disastrous way their morning had turned out.

A half hour later Rani was in Scott's kitchen trying to coax Dean into finishing the last of the sandwich she'd packed for him. Chad had followed them into the house and stood around for a few minutes, but when Dean showed more interest in his new friend than food the teenager agreed to leave Rani and Dean alone. "So you like Chad, do you?" she asked Dean. "Did he entertain you while I was gone?"

Dean wiggled, trying to get out of the chair she'd put him in. "I'm not hungry. I want to go out with Chad," he protested.

"Sorry, little man," Rani said with a sigh. "Mommy has to give you your medicine first. And you're going to need a nap in a little while." She was handing Dean a glass of water for his medication when Scott walked in.

For a moment he stood watching, leaning against a kitchen wall, his eyes making Rani feel uncomfortable. "Does he have to take medication all the time?" Scott asked. "Chad said Dean told him he broke some bones in an accident and had to stay in the hospital. Is that what that's for?"

Rani shook her head. "It has to be done" was the best she could manage. She hadn't thought ahead to this moment, tried to decide on the words she'd use when and if her employer saw her treating her son.

Scott didn't move. He continued to watch with an intensity she couldn't fathom. She'd never been able to get her mother to watch the simple procedure, and Zack had walked out on her before she and Dean had become adept at what they were doing. This was a particularly lonely period for Rani, a block of time when there was nothing to think about except Dean's injury and her unwitting role in exposing him to something that almost cost him his life. "We've had to test a lot of combinations of medications to learn what works with Dean," she said when the silence stretched on. "The doctor might need to make adjustments as Dean grows."

"Oh. What's wrong with him?"

Rani looked up. "It—" she faltered. The words weren't that hard to say. "Never mind," she managed.

"I'd like to know." Ten minutes ago Scott had been telling himself that he was going to keep his distance from Rani until she'd gotten over whatever was eating her, but here he was. Now he was glad he'd listened to his heart and not his head.

The soft, caring quality carried in Scott's whispered tones pulled Rani's thoughts toward him. She met his eyes, acknowledged their power over her. She started to shake her head, denying reality, but Scott took that moment to push himself away from the wall and step toward her. His hands reached the back of her neck, strong fingers warm against her taut muscles. "You don't want to say it," he whispered. "Why? Is it so terrible?"

"No. It really isn't." From somewhere deep inside Rani found the strength to speak. Or maybe it was his fingers on her neck that provided that strength. "He looks fine, doesn't he? He looks like every other child."

"I wish you'd tell me about it."

Rani closed her eyes. She'd known the meaning of

the word for months now. It shouldn't be hard to say. Giving a name to what her son had gone through recently wasn't any more of a mountain to climb than those first terrible hours when she didn't know whether he was going to live. Scott's warmth was reaching a spot deep inside she barely knew existed. That warmth was unlocking the chain she'd wrapped around the words since she first learned their ramifications.

"Do you know what epilepsy is?"

Scott frowned. "Of course I've heard the word, but I know I don't know enough."

"Not many people do. Because it doesn't show, most people don't know who the victims are."

"Victims?"

"Scott?" Rani took a deep breath. "Please, this is new for me. I'm still learning that it's all right to start breathing again."

For a moment Scott let silence hang between them. He knew that Rani had necessary steps to take but that the steps couldn't be rushed. He decided to give her time to get her feet under her. "I have to go back outside. When Dean's down for his nap, I want you to join me."

He was going to walk out of the room, take away the warmth in his fingers. "Why?"

"Because we have to talk. Please, Rani," he said, feeling closer to her than he believed possible. "Whatever the reasons behind Dean's epilepsy, it's eating you up. You need to talk to someone. Me."

Rani wondered if she could do that. Maybe, finally, she could find the words to explain what had gone wrong with their lives. But there was more to the story than an auto accident. There was another word. Guilt. Rani didn't know whether she could tell this caring man that.

Scott left without asking her for a commitment. As she went about cleaning up, Rani focused on the impact left behind by his hands on her neck. Rani had made love to Zack countless times and yet none of those lovemaking sessions had touched the nerve now awakening inside her.

Now wasn't the time to ask why that was. Scott was demanding a certain honesty from her. "You need to talk to someone," he said. He was offering himself as that someone.

A part of Rani hoped Dean would find it hard to fall asleep in strange surroundings so she could delay the inevitable, but obviously his morning with an active teenager had worn him out. He was asleep on a couch in the office before Rani had finished reading him a story. For a few minutes she wandered around the room, shuffling papers, making minor changes in the press release. But she was too restless to concentrate on the effectiveness of the release. She wasn't going to be able to think of work until some other emotions had been brought into the sunlight.

Rani walked outside. In the time she'd been in with Dean, the day had warmed another five degrees. She felt the sun on the top of her head, the moisture building along her temples. Maybe Scott wasn't around anymore. There was much for him to be involved with on the ranch.

But he was waiting for her. She spotted him over by the llamas' corral and waited on the front lawn in the shade of an oak tree as he crossed the dirt road and joined her. "Is he asleep?" Scott asked, dropping cross-legged onto the lawn. He reached up, took her hand and pulled her down next to him. "He doesn't complain about taking his medicine."

"Not anymore. He was fussy the first few times, but now he thinks that's what everyone does after meals." Rani was staring down at her hands, thinking about nails kept short for working with dogs—when she was still Zack's wife.

"What does the medicine do?" Scott pressed. "I gather it controls the epilepsy, but that doesn't tell me very much."

"No, it doesn't, does it? Are you sure you want to hear about this?"

"I'm asking. What makes you think I don't want to?"

Rani stopped fighting. She lifted her head and met Scott's eyes. Her hands were trembling, but she'd gone too far to back down now. "Dean's father never wanted to talk about it. He denied its existence. He—I think he wanted to keep Dean locked in the house so no one would ever know."

"I'm not Dean's father. And I'm asking you. Look." His voice softened. "I know this is hard for you. I'm reading your body language like it's an open book. But if you don't tell me I'll just get the information somewhere else. You can save me a lot of extra work—"

"All right," Rani interrupted, "I'll tell you. Dean isn't marked or cursed or any of the horrible things people used to believe." She kept staring at him, mouth working, trying to collect her thoughts without emotion getting in the way of fact. If only his eyes weren't so powerful.

"Take your time," Scott soothed. He took her hands, stilling their trembling with his strength. "Listening to you is the most important thing I have to do today."

His honest concern was helping. And because what she needed to say had been so much in her thoughts in recent weeks she was able to concentrate on that instead of the contact that was taking place.

"Dean and his father were in a car accident. Zack wasn't hurt, but Dean wasn't in his car seat. He—the broken bones healed, but his brain took longer to recover. He—the force of the impact left him susceptible to seizures. He hasn't had any for several months, but he isn't ready to be taken off the Dilantin."

"Okay." Scott drew her closer, then continued, "What happens now?"

"He'll outgrow it." It was easier to speak than Rani had thought it would be. "As long as he takes his medication he doesn't feel any effects from the injury. But it didn't have to happen."

"What do you mean?" Scott pressed. Because he was afraid she might start trembling again, he gripped her hands even tighter. "It was an accident."

"Accident!" Rani spat out the word. "If Zack had been thinking— Never mind. I don't want to talk about that."

"Not talking about it isn't going to help, and you know it. There's a lot of things you're not saying, like whether the divorce and the accident are related."

"No." Rani sighed. "I'm not saying that. My marriage is over. Zack walked out."

"Dean's father left you alone with an injured little boy? The bastard!"

Rani stiffened, freed from her prison. "It isn't that cut-and-dried."

"It is to me." Scott's voice was grating on her nerves, but there was no way to stop him. "Maybe I couldn't stay married to Chad's mother, but that didn't mean I ever wanted to stop being involved in his life. Any man who would turn his back on his child—"

"Stop!" Rani warned. "It's none of your business."

Scott's eyes were boring a hole through her. "You're right. It isn't any of my business. I'm your boss. Nothing more. It's time for me to butt out, that's what you're telling me, isn't it?"

"No. Scott, I don't know what I'm saying," Rani managed, hating the tears she heard in her voice. But she wasn't going to cry. She hadn't since the day she'd learned that Dean would eventually recover. "This is a very emotional subject for me. I can't help it if I'm not handling it the way you want me to."

For a moment they sat in silence on the lawn with only the mountain to observe them. Then Scott leaned toward her and gently brushed his lips against the side of her head. "I understand," he whispered. "I probably wouldn't be able to talk either if it was happening to me. I just hope things will get easier for you as time goes on. Look." He drew back slightly but still didn't release her. "What if we leave it like this? When you need to talk, I'll be here."

Rani dropped her head, body shuddering. No one had said that to her. Not the doctors, Zack, her parents. With a single sentence Scott brought new sunlight into her life. She no longer felt so alone. "Thank you," she whispered from the depths of her emotions. "You're right. There are a lot of knots to untie."

"You're welcome." Scott lifted her head by placing the palm of his hand under her chin and pushing up. This time his lips found not the side of her head but her lips.

Chapter Four

Scott should have been concentrating on what Chad was telling him about how much room he thought each dog needed in its run, but the ranch owner's mind wouldn't leave what had happened less than an hour ago. There had been more than a handful of women in his life since his divorce, and he'd felt something for each of them. But it was different this time. It could be nothing more complex than sympathy for the mother of a child who'd gone through a lot. She was tall and self-confident when it came to doing her job, but just because Rani Lassen could juggle a career and a pre-schooler didn't mean there weren't times when the woman didn't need someone to lean on. Maybe it was the contrast between her outward appearance and what he knew she'd gone through that made her hard to shake.

She was feminine. There was no doubt about that. Scott wouldn't be surprised if she was unaware of how well her soft, faded jeans molded to her rounded hips, flat stomach and long slender legs.

He wasn't sure that was how an employer was supposed to think about a new employee. He'd employed many people over the years, a few of them women. But none of them had been single, near his age, with a below-the-surface vulnerability that kept pushing at him, making him want to take over some of the burden.

He wasn't sure she'd let him. If Rani was suspicious of men because of what her ex had done to her, Scott could understand that. But he couldn't understand how a man could walk out on a woman like that, a little boy. There was something about the way Rani carried herself, that told the male inside Scott that being a mother hadn't made her forget what it meant to be a woman.

"Look," Scott's teenage son interrupted, "why don't you go pack for the big city or something? I'll take care of housing the dogs. Obviously that isn't what you're thinking about."

"What?" Scott turned toward his son, noticing that he barely had to look down to meet another set of green eyes. "You think you can run things in that department, do you?"

"Better than you," Chad shot back. "I swear, you left your brain somewhere else today. What's gotten into you?"

Scott changed the subject. "Are you sure you don't want to go with me? It might be the last chance you have to see your mother before school starts."

Chad shook his head. "I'll call her. You were right about that. I never did belong in the city."

As Chad walked away, his father's eyes remained on him. For years Scott had had to content himself with occasional visits, all the time telling himself that he was doing right by letting his son stay with his mother. But the teenage years and the effect the city life was having on Chad finally combined to make both parents take a long hard look at what was happening. As a result Chad was now living with his father on a ranch miles from drugs, alcohol and fast cars.

It felt good to be able to look at the boy whenever he wanted and to be able to take pride in what he saw. Yes, Chad was going to turn out all right. He couldn't help wondering whether Zack would be able to experience that sense of pride or whether he'd carved too deep a valley between himself and his son.

Rani had little time to ask herself such questions. Before the day was over, she was aware of how large the scope of her job would be. Now that there was a telephone listing for the program, the phone was ringing several times an hour. Agencies such as the ASPCA and the county planning commission would have to put their stamp of approval on the program and expected Rani to be at their disposal. A few neighbors called to have rumors settled. People with unwanted dogs called trying to get her to take them. In between handling these things, Rani had to keep an eye on two curious dogs and an equally curious preschooler who was improvising a strange game of chase in which all three participants were it at the same time. While he was still around, Rani received a call from Scott's accountant. Before she knew it, it was nearly six and Dean was restless from hunger.

Rani switched on the automatic answering machine and turned the dogs over to Chad. "Will you tell your dad I've gone home?" she asked. "Dinner's waited as long as it can for this character."

"You can eat here," Chad offered. "Dad's a decent cook and I can open a can of soup."

Rani shook her head, smiling because she felt as if she'd known Chad all his life. "I don't believe dinner is one of the fringe benefits. He can call me tonight if there's anything that won't keep."

The sun was dipping toward the mountains as Rani walked to her car. She could see Scott at the far side of the barn measuring food into feeding troughs for some of the animals. Red lights from the setting sun glinted off his curled hair, pointing out its pale highlights and softening his outline. Rani knew he was intent on his work and unable to see her, which gave her a moment to study the man. Her lips still retained the memory of their kiss, but she was no longer asking herself why he'd kissed her. It was enough to understand that it had happened, that her new employer had reached out and offered her someone to make contact with when what she carried inside threatened to overwhelm her.

But if Scott had meant his kiss as purely paternal, he was the only one who saw it that way. Rani's reaction was a much more primitive one. She was going to have to be very, very careful around Scott Barnett. Surely he wasn't interested in taking on any more responsibility than his life already had. He was raising a teenager, running a business, starting a program designed to help deaf people. The last thing this remarkable, broad-shouldered man needed was an assistant director who had a long way to go before she could forget the role both she and Zack played in Dean's accident. Someone's guilt was an emotion no one else should have to get involved with.

Rani's body was occupied with the task of driving, but her mind had fastened on something else. Epilepsy. She didn't think she'd said the words more than two or three times since she'd learned the broadest ramifications of Dean's head injury, but she'd been able to say it around Scott. What was happening? True, it had been painful to give Scott the answers he wanted, but she'd been able to do it. His hands, strength, warmth had been enough to bring the pain to the surface and to allow her to give voice to feelings even her parents didn't understand. She felt strangely cleansed as a result of the experience.

Scott didn't call that night, but he was waiting inside the office when she and Dean showed up the next morning. He was wearing a suit, his hair cowed into a semblance of submission. "Meeting with my lawyer," Scott groaned as he tugged at his tie. "I'd rather go to jail than put on a suit. I swear, there's more paperwork involved in starting a nonprofit organization than a conglomerate. Red tape is going to be the undoing of the free enterprise system."

Rani laughed and nodded at Dean who wanted to go look for the two dogs. She felt out of place in her jeans and cotton blouse. "Is the meeting something I should go to?" she asked. "I'm afraid I didn't dress for it."

"No, you're going to have enough to do here today. I'll give you a blow-by-blow when I get back. Look, I've been thinking. This running back and forth every day is going to cost you a fortune in gas."

"I know," Rani said, grimacing. "It's a good thing I have an economy car."

"That's not the only consideration," Scott went on. "You're spending a lot of time commuting. I've been thinking about the training cabin. I was serious about it being able to accommodate someone living there."

Move out here? "I don't know," Rani stammered. "I appreciate the offer, but—"

"You don't want to live here? I think it makes a lot of sense."

"Please." Rani tried to stop him. "Give me a little time to think about it."

"Is it because of what happened yesterday?"

"What?" Rani blinked and tried to concentrate.

"Did you say more than you wanted to about your past? What do you think I'm going to do, blackmail you? I'm not."

"I know that," Rani protested. "I'm not ashamed of anything that involves my son."

"Is it because I kissed you?"

Scott had asked the telling question. "I don't know," she stammered. "Scott, we hardly know each other. I didn't expect it."

"Don't you ever do anything simply because you feel like it?" Suddenly Scott was tired of being serious. "Blame the weather. It seemed right for a kiss yesterday."

Rani started to smile, but the gesture was stopped. He was so close. It might only be a trick of the imagination that made her wonder if he'd taken a step, or it might have been because she wanted it to happen. "It didn't mean anything," she whispered, wondering at her ability to lie.

Scott's probing eyes told her that he didn't believe the lie. This time there was no doubting the fact that he was coming closer, eating up the distance between them. "Don't say no to what I suggested," he said, his eyes holding her captive. "Dean needs security. He can get it here."

"Scott! I don't know."

"Think about it," he whispered. "Just think about it." He reached out and pulled her into the circle of his arms. Rani responded to the feel of his suit against her bare arm, the scents of after-shave and freshly cleaned fabric.

Scott's lips were a tiptoe away. She would only have to reach up, present her lips and receive what instinct told her he was offering. Rani closed her eyes, lost herself in masculine arms and lifted her height to reach his. His lips were as soft as she remembered, but this time the contact lasted longer, reached deeper.

Rani's arms went around his waist as she balanced herself in her sandals, her body held securely in arms that seemed powerful enough to protect her against the world. She opened her lips, breathed through her nostrils and recorded the scent of him.

She didn't stop to ask herself whether Dean was still in the room or if his son might be around. Scott had no hesitancy about kissing her, and because she identified that in him, she felt secure enough to match his mood, his actions. Rani didn't try to ask herself whether their kiss had a meaning that went beyond that moment. She'd been left alone by Zack. Her body was hungry for proof that she was still a woman.

Scott sighed, his body shuddering a little as he released his breath. He felt as shaken as he had when at eighteen he'd decided he was in love for the first time. "I didn't know that was going to happen," he whispered, in awe of the emotions ignited in him. "I didn't mean to jump at you earlier."

"That's all right." Rani lowered herself onto the balls of her feet but didn't ask to be released. "Scott,

I'm not sure moving here is best for Dean. I need time to think about it." Even as she said the words she was asking herself whether it was Dean she was thinking about. It could be that she was already wondering where a kiss could lead to if they were together day and night. "You—don't you have a meeting?"

"What? Yeah." Scott released her and turned half away. "I guess I do. I'd rather talk to a monkey. Monkeys don't chatter as much as that lawyer," he muttered as he left the room, his legs feeling almost as numb as his brain.

Although the day was even busier than yesterday, Rani kept coming back to what she'd felt while in Scott's arms. Between phone calls and paperwork she asked herself where this employer/employee relationship was going. If she'd been a few years younger, without a divorce behind her, she might have reacted as a giggling teenager would, excited because a man she looked up to had paused long enough to acknowledge her presence.

But Rani had been married. She knew the difference between kisses that acknowledged the chemistry between men and women and kisses that explored the lengths and depths of that chemistry. The kiss she and Scott shared was for exploration.

Scott hadn't returned by the time Rani had given Dean his lunch and medication. The boy was down for his nap when Rani heard the ranch pickup pull into the gravel drive. A minute later the front door opened and Scott hurried into the wing of the house that contained his and Chad's bedrooms. Rani was on the phone when Scott, back in jeans and T-shirt, entered the office. He waited until she'd hung up before speaking. "I think we've got it all worked out," he said quickly. "My pilot has another commitment, so I'm going to have to leave earlier than I thought I would. I'm sorry, but it can't be helped. I've got a delivery truck due in a few minutes, so there isn't time to explain how messed up things are right now. The lawyer will be sending us some forms in a day or two. He explained what they are for, but I wasn't listening. Other things on my mind. Yell if there's anything you don't understand. Someday, I hope, we'll be able to carry on a coherent conversation." With that explanation he was gone.

Rani didn't have the chance to say more than a half-dozen words to Scott before he left for Hollywood early Monday morning. She'd worked part of Saturday, but both Scott and Chad were at the north end of the farm's acreage and she and Dean had had the main complex to themselves. She'd gone home Saturday afternoon and spent Sunday with her parents. Chad was holding down the fort when she arrived on Monday.

"He left just after dawn," Chad explained. "We keep a plane that's been modified to handle just about any animal at the county airport. Dad's pilot had another flight to make later today, so they took the animals to the airport last night and left as soon as it was light."

"How long is he going to be gone?" Rani asked. She was wearing a pale-green summer-weight sweater her mother had knitted to go with her eyes.

Chad shrugged and turned his attention to enticing Dean to share his toast with him. "We never know about these things. Maybe a week."

"And you stay here alone while he's gone?"

Chad gave her a look that said he wasn't a kid and

explained that he'd been staying by himself for years. "My mother works. I've been letting myself into the house after school since I was in the second grade."

"Oh" was the best Rani could offer. It was none of her business, but she could never see herself allowing a teenager to stay alone at an isolated ranch for days, especially if that boy had responsibility for the well-being of valuable exotic animals.

Chad had taken Dean into the kitchen with him but returned a few minutes later to hand Rani an envelope. "Dad said to give you this. He said I was to keep my big nose out of it."

The note was short, written in a hurried, bold scrawl. "If you want to, the sheets on my bed are fresh. I'll probably be gone all week. I left Chad the checkbook if you two need groceries."

Rani read the note again. He was turning his house over to her, giving her access to his checking account. Did he already trust her that much?

Of course she wasn't going to stay. She had her own place in which to live. But as Rani went about filling out the forms that had arrived from the lawyer, her mind refused to leave the issue of clean sheets. Maybe Scott felt Chad was competent enough to spend the better part of a week alone except for the people who swarmed over the ranch during the day. But that didn't mean Rani could drive away every afternoon and not spend the evening worrying about whether the lanky teenager was eating more than toast for dinner.

In the end it was work as much as a sense of responsibility that kept Rani at the ranch that week. The retired public relations man who'd volunteered his services in fund-raising drives had a multitude of ideas but wasn't able to get himself into gear until midafternoon. As a result he didn't call or show up until late in the day and then sucked Rani into his enthusiasm so much that hours would pass before she realised she'd let other work slide while discussing ways of interesting dog-food companies and social organizations in the program. Dean slept next to Rani in Scott's bed Monday night, but the next morning she made a flying trip to her apartment for a spare mattress to put on the floor so Dean wouldn't have to nap in Scott's bed or in the office. She felt uneasy about having the two boys together all the time because she wasn't sure if Scott had told Chad about Dean's epilepsy and she hadn't been able to bring herself to tell Chad that his little friend had had to be treated as if he were a cracked egg not that long ago.

As it was, she wasn't even in the room when Chad went in to check on Dean. Rani's knowledge that the time for an explanation was now came when Chad entered the office with Dean in tow. "What is he talking about?" Chad asked. "He said he used to fall down a lot and it scared him."

Rani took Dean from Chad and ran her fingers through his tousled hair. She felt frozen and yet released from prison. "Dean had some unusual problems as a result of his accident," she said, knowing she was just touching the surface. "He hurt his head. It took longer to heal than the rest of him."

Chad leaned against a wall of the office, his green eyes as relentless as his father's. "What was wrong?"

It was easier this time. "Dean had epilepsy. It's possible that there is some residual effect, and that's why he needs to continue taking medication for a while.

When he had it, there were times when he'd pass out or have a seizure."

"Oh." Chad looked puzzled. "Have I been playing too rough with him?"

"Oh, no," Rani reassured him. "Dean isn't fragile. Besides, he's crazy about you. He'd be crushed if you didn't let him play cowboy on your back."

"Oh," Chad repeated. For a moment he watched Dean without speaking. Rani held her breath, wondering if she'd destroyed some special bond that had formed between the two boys.

"Are you done with him?" Chad asked.

Rani released Dean, biting her lip as her son turned toward his new playmate and not her. "All systems are go," she said.

"Good." Chad swung Dean onto his shoulders and leaned forward so he could go through the doorway without bumping Dean's head. "Guess we'll mosey on down to the corral. Got some broncos to bust."

They were gone. Rani turned toward the window so she could watch the two as they headed toward Gaspar's run. Zack had been afraid to touch Dean from the moment he learned about epilepsy. Chad didn't question, didn't hold back. Dean was his little friend. That was all he cared about.

Rani closed her eyes and pressed her forehead against the glass. She was crying, but they were tears of release. How beautiful friendship could be!

On Friday night Scott called to say that the filming of advertisements using the pygmy goats had been a success but that he didn't expect to be back until late Saturday. "The goats kept trying to eat the diapers, which kind of put the advertiser in a bad mood, but he's the one who wanted the buggers. I talked to Chad," he finished up. "He told me you've been staying at the ranch. Good. I'm going to owe you some overtime."

Rani fell asleep early that night despite the tug of anticipation she felt at knowing Scott would be back. They'd talked several times during the week, but their conversations had been short and concerned with work. There was a great deal she needed to tell him about the fund-raising campaigns already underway, but money talk wasn't what filled her with excitement over the thought of seeing him again.

She wanted to know if his eyes were really as green as she remembered them, if his lips were still as soft.

Rani woke, for the moment not sure where the line between dreams and reality lay. Someone was in the room with her and Dean. But the knowledge didn't frighten her. Even with her eyes closed, she found the presence a comforting one. Chad?

It was Chad's father. Rani turned onto her back and pushed hair out of her eyes. It was still dark outside, but she could make out the substantial form dominating the space above her. "What are you doing here?" she whispered, mindful of her son sleeping nearby.

"I live here," Scott whispered back.

Rani slid her shoulders under the covers, sleep still tugging at her. How perfect it would be to stay where she was, watch the big man shed his clothes, join her on the bed.

What was she thinking of? Before Rani had to answer her question, she sat bolt upright. "I—you weren't due back until this afternoon," she stammered.

"I lied. Actually my pilot convinced me that the plane was safe for night flying. God, it's good to be back." He lowered his frame into a chair near the bed and stretched out his long legs. "I must say, it's been a long time since I've walked in to find a woman in my bed."

Rani pulled the sheet up around her. How much of her thin nightgown could he see in the dim light? "I'll get up," she whispered. "Could you just leave for a minute?"

"No, I don't think so."

"Scott!" Rani grimaced, glanced over at Dean's mattress and lowered her voice. "This is crazy. I don't want you to read anything into my being here."

"Darn. And just when I was starting to enjoy it. Well, how do you like my bed?"

"Very well," Rani admitted. "I've been keeping the window open at night. It smells so good out here."

"It's just what Dean needs. Puts color back in his cheeks." Scott leaned over to unlace his boots, but his eyes didn't leave her or the thin covering over her shoulders. "I told you the air's much better out here. That's why I could never live near Hollywood."

"We'll be going back home tonight," Rani said quickly. She wasn't about to get caught in an argument about where she should be living. She stammered around for a minute, trying to tell Scott everything that had happened in his absence, but he only pulled off his boots and again sprawled in his chair.

Finally he spoke. "I don't care about any of that. For your information, it's five A.M. I didn't close my eyes all night for wondering if my pilot knew what he was doing. Later today I have to drive a truck out to the airport to pick up the goats. Right now all I want is to get an hour's sleep."

Rani scrambled out of bed before stopping to think about how much of herself she was revealing by her action. She stood away from the bed, her long, lean body outlined by the thin yellow nylon fabric of her nightgown. Her hair was even more rumpled than usual, her hands nervously clenching and unclenching at her sides. "I—here. It's your bed."

"You're uneasy," Scott said without moving. "I didn't mean to make you feel as if you've been kicked out."

"It's your bed. You can do whatever you want in it."

"Whatever I want?" There was no mistaking the teasing quality in Scott's voice. "That opens a lot of doors."

"Don't," Rani warned, blushing at the way her words came out. "I don't feel like playing games."

"Why not? There's been an awful lot of seriousness in your life lately. I think you need to let your hair down once in a while. Or out, as the case may be. Your hair doesn't behave any better than mine." His eyes roamed down her body, letting her know that he was seeing almost everything there was to see. "I happen to remember a kiss. It was just the first chapter—or at least it could be."

"Scott, please," Rani moaned nervously. The conversation had taken a turn she wasn't ready for.

"Please what? Rani, you haven't been out of my mind all week. It didn't matter what I was doing, what I was supposed to be doing. Even when the goats were nibbling at the cameras and diapers, I kept seeing your big hazel eyes and that mop of hair that's enough for two people. Don't blame me for wanting to be with you now."

"Scott, I don't know what to say."

"Don't say anything," he warned, coming to his feet before she knew he was going to move. "Why do you think I agreed to fly at night? Because I wanted to get back here, see you." He'd taken her hands so she couldn't escape and was backing her against the bed until she had nowhere to move. "How has your week been?"

Full of thoughts of you. "Busy," she sidestepped, torn between the part of her that said she should leave and the woman deep inside that wanted to stay. "That public relations man wants you to consider taking one of the dogs to meetings and groups once it's trained. He says we have to show what we're doing, not just tell people. Scott, I told Chad about what Dean had gone through. He knows about the epilepsy."

"Oh."

"I would have felt better if you'd been the one to tell him. I hope you don't mind."

"Of course not," Scott reassured her. He'd thought about telling Chad himself but decided in the end that letting Rani handle it herself would help her healing process. He hoped that had been accomplished. "I'm more concerned with how we're going to handle what's happening here." His eyes found hers and wove their familiar web around her.

"What's happening?" she whispered.

"I don't know, but there's something here. Something I've never felt before. Do you know what I thought about all week?"

"No."

"I kept thinking about making love to you. Those

goofy goats reminded me of you. Everything did."
Scott laughed softly. "Does that make sense? I hired
you to get this program off the ground. I wasn't looking
for a woman who wouldn't get out of my thoughts. But
it happened."

"I'm sorry," she said, wondering if she really was.

"I'm not." He leaned toward her, trapping her between him and the bed. "I kept thinking about what
happened when we kissed. You wanted it as much as I
did, didn't you?"

Rani tried to tell him he was wrong, but the words
wouldn't come. She felt herself start to tremble, her
body assaulted by the presence of a male force too close
to ignore. "This is crazy," she managed. "We hardly
know each other."

"I can't agree." He sounded almost angry. "I know
your world revolves around that little boy. You know
that Chad gives me more pleasure than anything else
that's come my way in life. Those are the important
things two people need to know about each other. It
gives them a common bond."

"Chad loves Dean."

Scott didn't let her finish. He silenced her with his
lips, cut off all thought except the pure unadulterated
joy of finally tasting what her lips had been hungry for.
Rani didn't try to fight him. Her compliance came not
from fear of waking her son, but because her body had
no other need, her mind no other thought than to join
with the man whose hands were testing the distance
between her nightgown and the flesh beneath. Rani responded to the freedom he'd given her hands by placing them on his shoulders, pressing her fingers against
the strength that was being offered her.

Scott lowered himself onto the bed, taking her with him. Their lips were still fused together, fingers searching with an intensity that bordered on pain. Rani felt the sudden pounding of her pulse as it consumed her chest, her temples, the veins in her wrists.

Scott was home. He was in the room with her, letting her know that their earlier kiss wasn't something he regretted. Had she been so lonely that the only response that made sense was to surrender her separate self to him? It wasn't a question she could answer. She honestly didn't remember his being in her thoughts that much during the week, but now she realized he'd always been there, simmering beneath the surface, teasing her subconscious at night, making her ready for this moment.

She didn't know him, not really. He was right when he said they shared a bond through their children, but that wasn't the bond that drew men and women together. What opened her lips and sent her tongue on a road to exploration was the primitive beating of a woman's heart brought to life by a man she respected, looked up to, was physically aware of.

Scott's fingers were playing with the thin straps holding her nightgown on her shoulders. The teasing way he slowly pushed them toward the downward slope of her shoulders made her shiver with anticipation.

She gripped his arms with punishing strength as the flimsy top of her gown slid to the rise of her breasts. Scott pulled the fabric out and then down to free her aroused nipples. "Now," he sighed, his voice seeming to come from deep within him.

"Now what?"

"I've wanted to do this since I first saw you." He pushed her gently away, eyes focusing on her breasts.

"Scott?" She was embarrassed, unaccustomed to having her body discussed. "Did you really wonder what they were like?"

"Oh, yes." He laughed at himself. "About that, and about what your hips and thighs and throat looked like." He was still holding her away from him but now he used his right hand to push the useless fabric low on her hips. "I was right about your waist. I can put my hands around it."

"That's because you have big hands." Rani could barely make her throat muscles work, but she felt she had to say something, to keep on top of the emotion that threatened to spill over and swallow her. He was her boss—she should be thinking about that. Instead her mind refused to go further than where his lips were. He'd dipped his head to taste her shoulders, the swell of her breasts, her nipples. When the teasing of his tongue forced her to arch away from him with an inhuman moan, his lips and tongue found the outline of her ribs beneath the thin covering of flesh.

Rani had no thought of resisting him. She laid her body back against the bed and brought Scott with her, moaning as he leaned over her, his lips exploring every inch of exposed flesh. The nightgown still clung to her hips, but she was unaware that she was anything but naked. In her heart nothing stood between him and what she wanted him to do to her.

"I don't understand," he groaned. "It's never happened this fast before. What are you doing to me?"

Rani had been raised believing that lovemaking between a man and woman came after months, years even, of getting to know each other. It didn't take place between two people who were little more than strangers, who should still respect each other's privacy. But they weren't strangers. His lips were learning everything there was to learn about her body. Her fingers and tongue were bold on his flesh, her rapid panting breath telling her that she'd gone past the point of modesty. This—this stranger—had walked into a dark bedroom a few minutes before. Now they were clinging together, now they were going to make love.

No! It couldn't happen! She couldn't let it!

"Scott, please," she groaned, sudden desperation resulting in her nails digging into his shoulders. "It can't happen like this!"

"Why?" His voice was animallike.

"I—what if I got pregnant?"

Scott took several ragged breaths and heaved himself away from her. "God, I didn't think," he groaned.

She rolled away from him, oblivious to her naked state. "It can't happen," she sobbed, no longer thinking of her sleeping child. "Scott? Please leave."

Chapter Five

"Don't apologize," Scott was saying. "I'm the one who should be sitting here with a red face. When I walked into the bedroom and saw you sleeping—well, birth control was the last thing on my mind."

Rani's hands tightened around the coffee cup Scott had handed her a minute ago. She was trembling inside the man's bathrobe she was wearing. The early-morning light was touching the kitchen table where they sat, but she shied away from it, wanting the anonymity of night back again. She felt rather like a teenager who has just left the backseat of a car. Grown men and women have things like birth control well in hand. They don't have to scramble out of bed with muttered apologies because the woman was unprepared. "Please," Rani asked, "can't we just leave that alone. I was asleep when you came in. I wasn't thinking. Things happened too fast."

"You were thinking all right," Scott challenged. "Do you think I'd take advantage of a woman? You wanted it as much as I did. I don't think you can deny that."

Rani shook her head. "I wasn't thinking," she repeated. "I've never had a man walk into a bedroom before and— All right, I wanted to make love to you.

But it's better this way." She dipped her head. "Things are happening too fast between us."

"Maybe, maybe not." Scott's knuckles were white, and if Rani hadn't been so caught up in her own emotions, she might have worried that he was going to shatter his coffee cup. "I didn't know there was a timetable to be adhered to when it came to relationships."

"You know what I mean!" Rani shot back. "My God, I've only been working for you for a little while. And I haven't been divorced long." She ducked her head so Scott couldn't see the flush that sprang to her cheeks. "Finding a man I'd be attracted to was the last thing I expected at this point in my life. That's why I wasn't prepared."

"Then you admit you're attracted to me."

"Yes, but—"

"But nothing. That's what really matters. There'll be another time for us. When you're ready."

Rani looked up. How considerate he was. Zack's idea of lovemaking had always been to reach for her whenever he had the urge. Usually she was willing, but even when she wasn't, Zack went ahead anyway. "I appreciate that," Rani said slowly. She thought for a moment about the advisability of continuing, but Scott had seen her naked a few minutes before. Was what she had to say any different from physical nakedness?

"What has happened to my life since Dean's accident has been like a one-two punch," she admitted. "By the time Zack and I decided that everything had changed between us and nothing was ever going to be the same, I was like one of the walking wounded. The last thing I was thinking about was having a man in my life."

"Why?" Scott's hands released his coffee cup and gripped her before she had time to prepare for the capture. "You're an attractive woman. You're intelligent with a lot of enthusiasm and energy for life. I'd think you'd be looking for ways of putting your life back together."

"It is back together," Rani said. "I have my son. I don't have to worry about and react to Zack's temper anymore. That's all I really want out of life."

"Zack's temper? What are you talking about?" Something cold had entered Scott's voice.

"I don't want to answer that. Please." Rani tried to pull away, but Scott wouldn't give her her freedom.

"Sorry." Scott was determined. "I'm not letting you get off that easy. You've been carrying a hell of a burden caring for and supporting Dean alone. Do you think I'm really going to walk out of here without knowing why you thought you were going to go through the rest of your life as a nun? Look, something almost happened in the bedroom a few minutes ago, something good. I don't think you can deny that. Okay, so you don't want to get pregnant. That I can understand. I can wait until the risk isn't there anymore. After all"—his smile lacked warmth—"we're not husband and wife. But I guess I just assumed that an attractive single woman would have that department accounted for. Now you're saying something about Zack's temper. Is that why you're so turned off where men are concerned?"

"I'm not turned off men." Rani tugged until Scott was forced to release her hands if he wanted to avoid injuring her. She pushed herself to her feet and walked to the kitchen window where she could watch the ranch animals responding to the new day. In the distance a couple of lambs were chasing each other in reckless abandon around their grazing mothers. God, to be that free! "I don't know," she laughed without knowing why. "Maybe I am, or I was there for a little while. Zack has always had a temper—I knew it from the day I married him and maybe even before—but I knew how to avoid that temper. We were terribly busy because of the business. I worked hard to keep our lives orderly and the house looking nice. Those things pleased Zack. Also—" Rani paused, remembering. "There were a lot of good times in our marriage. Zack worked hard to control his temper. But"—Rani turned back around to face Scott—"he didn't have enough patience when it came to a toddler's curiosity for life."

"He lost his temper around Dean? Is that how the injury happened?" Scott looked as if the room had suddenly become too small for him.

"No," Rani reassured him quickly. "At least not the way you're thinking. Zack didn't strike Dean. He never did that. I would have divorced him a long time ago if he had." Rani ran a hand over her eyes. "I don't know why I'm trying to defend him now. God knows I was his accuser enough times. I wouldn't leave it alone until finally Zack walked out on his son and me."

"Wait a minute. Back up." Scott held up a restraining hand. "You said Zack didn't strike Dean. What happened?"

Rani didn't know how long silence filled the darkened kitchen. At last, when she couldn't be sure whether Scott was still in the room, she opened her eyes. He was still sitting at the kitchen table, unwavering green eyes upon her. "Zack and Dean were alone in our car when the accident happened. Zack wasn't concentrating on the driving. He ran into the back of a large truck.''

"Was Zack hurt?"

Rani shook her head. "A few bruises, that's all. But Dean wasn't in his car seat." She clamped her lips against the anger she always felt when forced to think about that. "He was thrown against the windshield. For three days we didn't know whether he was going to live."

"He hit his head. That's where the epilepsy comes from?"

Rani nodded. She found the strength to pull away from Scott's eyes and turned back toward the window. "There's more. For too long I wasn't sure whether Dean would have any kind of future. The news I had to hear was a long time coming. It hasn't been easy for me or Dean."

Rani heard the scrape of Scott's chair, but her mind didn't focus on the sound until she felt him against her. His arms surrounded her shoulders, their strength pulling her against him until her back was nestled warmly against his chest. Because she didn't have to look into his eyes, her heart still maintained some degree of freedom, but her control wasn't enough to risk being challenged. She didn't speak; instead she kept her eyes on the lambs cavorting in the pasture.

Scott's voice was a barely audible whisper, but the deep sounds were reaching her, vibrating against the side of her face. "The accident spelled the end to your marriage. Was that your idea or Zack's?"

"Both of ours. I couldn't look at him without wanting to bury my fingers in his face, and he couldn't take it anymore, either. I'm sure he felt guilty, although he never admitted that. Scott?'' Rani had to take several deep breaths before she found the courage to go on. "Dean wasn't in his car seat because he was trying to get away from his father. Zack had given Dean some chocolate and it melted and got on Zack's sleeve and the car. Zack—you have to understand Zack's temper to understand this—started yelling at Dean. I don't know what he said, but I have a pretty good idea. I've seen him lose his temper enough times. Dean always tries to get away when his father yells at him.''

"So Dean climbed out of his car seat to get away from his father. Yeah, I would say Zack must feel guilty.'' Scott was gripping her tightly, his muscles relaying his mood. His emotions at the moment were so intense that they shocked him. If Zack had been in the room right at that moment, Scott wasn't sure he could have kept his hands off the man.

"You don't know Zack,'' Rani was saying. She hated the bitterness she heard in her words. "He always had an excuse for his anger. It was always someone else's fault when things went wrong. Even now he says there wouldn't have been an accident if Dean had been behaving himself.''

"I can't believe it.'' Scott forced his words to remain calm, but inside he boiled with emotions born of what he felt for a three-year-old boy. "That's an incredibly immature reaction.''

"Why do you think I divorced him?''

"I think the man lost all claim to his child.''

No. She couldn't do that. Rani's heart recoiled from what Scott was saying, but her body wasn't strong enough to join the rebellion. She stood, body sagging, mind flitting aimlessly, until at last she remembered how to speak. "I can't do that. He's still Dean's father."

"Dean's father almost killed him. Rani?" Scott turned her around until she was forced to face him. His hands on her shoulders were both comforting and possessive, giving her no opportunity to escape the conversation she hated with every fiber within her. "Rani, answer me something. You don't have to, but it might help my understanding. When you learned that Dean had epilepsy, what was Zack's reaction?"

Rani might have laughed if she wasn't so close to collapsing. "What epilepsy? He denied it. Can you believe that? He refused to acknowledge that anything like that had happened to his son. He—he'd talk about the accident and the broken bones, but he refused to admit that Dean could have suffered a brain injury."

Scott shook his head. "Because he'd have to admit his guilt. I've heard of burying your head in the sand, but this takes the cake."

"Can you blame him?" Rani asked without thinking. "Would you be able to admit you'd done anything to jeopardize your son's life?"

Scott stared at her for a moment before answering. "I wouldn't want to," he whispered. "But denying it wouldn't make the condition go away. I'd just hope I'd learned something from the experience, learned to control my temper, and I'd work like hell to regain my family's respect."

"Well, that didn't happen to Zack." Scott's face was only inches away from hers. He was pressing her against the cold kitchen window. Maybe he was using the window to keep her from collapsing. "He was turned toward Dean, yelling at him, when the accident happened. He was so angry that he'd forgotten his responsibilities on the road. That's how much of a temper Zack has." The cool window, Scott's arms, were all that kept her from flying out of the room. "Dean was lying unconscious in a hospital room and Zack was telling me it was Dean's fault. The accident didn't change anything for him. I shriveled up inside when he said that. I no longer had any feeling for him."

"Then why didn't you give him his walking papers right then?"

Rani laughed angrily. "I couldn't think any further than that little boy lying on that white bed. What I felt toward Zack wasn't important. It wasn't until Dean started to heal that I started to feel anything again."

"That's when you told him to take a hike?"

"I didn't have to." Rani let Scott absorb her with his eyes, suck her into that warm place that existed deep inside him. "Zack left us. He didn't want anything to do with us."

Scott shook her, his fingers digging into her flesh. "I don't ever want to hear you say that again. Zack didn't leave you because he didn't want to have anything to do with you. The bastard ran off because he's a coward."

"Don't," Rani moaned. "Scott, you're hurting me."

"Then listen to reason." Scott stopped shaking her and his fingers became less punishing, but he still held her tightly. "I don't know Zack. And I hope I never have to meet the man. But my gut reaction is that he took off because he couldn't face reality. If he had stayed, he would have had to admit sooner or later that he couldn't blame a three-year-old boy for what had happened to him. Zack bailed out because he's a coward. And because he knows he can't handle the guilt. You have every right to hate him.''

Did she hate Zack? She was furious at him for deserting her and their child, but more than that, she felt relief because he was out of her life. She remembered all too well his physical and emotional withdrawal in those punishing weeks while they waited to see what kind of future Dean would have. Rani had had enough to handle learning what controlling epilepsy meant and coming to grips with her own sense of guilt. She hadn't been strong enough to be Zack's rock as well, to be supportive and understanding and wait for the day when he would admit that it was he and not their son who was responsible for what had happened to him. If he hadn't found her supportive enough, if he'd left because she wasn't there offering understanding, being someone he could cry with, yell at—it had happened. She wasn't going to accept that burden. Her own guilt was all she could handle.

"He's gone," she managed. "I don't even think about what things might have been like if he had stayed."

"Good." Scott propelled her back to the kitchen chair and eased her into it. She heard his deep sigh. "I thought you were going to explode in my arms there for a minute. I've never seen anyone get that white and stay on his feet."

"I'm sorry." If she had wanted to flee this man she could no longer remember why. Scott was letting her pull out all her emotions and expose them. It might alter their relationship, but at the moment she needed him so much that the form that alteration might take didn't matter. "Did any of what I said make sense?" she asked.

Scott nodded. So much had happened in the space of a few minutes. It would take him time to let everything sort itself out in his mind, but one thing was clear. He'd felt her heart beating, heard things she probably hadn't told anyone else. That made her more precious to him at this moment than he could have dreamed possible. "Don't think about it anymore."

"I can't. I have a headache."

Scott left her long enough to bring her a glass of water and a couple of aspirin. "What we've been talking about has been enough to give anyone a headache," he said. It would feel so good to see the light return to her eyes. "Are you going to be all right?"

Rani nodded, wincing because the movement caused her pain. "I want to cry," she whispered. "I can feel the tears building up until I think my head's going to burst. I didn't cry when Dean was in the hospital. I was too scared for tears. The only time I cried was when I finally heard that his head was going to heal itself."

"Cry now," he said gently, once again warming her numb fingers against his chest. "Tears are nothing to be ashamed of."

"If I start I might never stop."

"I'll be here to make sure you do." He slid his chair next to hers and sat on the edge of it, their knees touching. "Rani, you aren't alone any more. I want you to understand that. Whenever you need to talk or cry, I'm here."

Could she believe that? Could she go on living and not wanting to cling to him? "Thank you."

"Don't thank me. Believe it. I'm not just your boss.

What's happening between us is something I don't want to stop. I hope you feel the same way. Rani, I want to be here when you need me and have you here when I need you." His lips gently brushed her hot forehead before he spoke again. "You have my world all turned around. I'm not about to let you slip out of it now."

"Scott? Thank you."

He nodded, smiled slightly. "There's something else I want you to think about. Listen to me. I sound like a seventeen-year-old kid." He stopped her when she tried to interrupt. "Would you think about something? I understand your reasons for not wanting to get pregnant at this stage of your life. Rani, will you go to a doctor about birth control?"

Rani refused to concentrate on the possibility that what had almost happened in his bedroom this morning might be repeated. She was too full of unshed tears, colliding emotions, thoughts of her hands on Scott's naked chest. She felt as if she'd been physically beaten and was only now beginning to assess the damages to both her body and soul. Make love to Scott? The thought caused her blood to race, but whether in anticipation or fear she didn't know. That was something that would have to be faced once her emotions had recovered from the assault they'd received this morning.

Once again Scott brushed her forehead with his lips. "I'm not going to get that sleep I was talking about, and I know you're not going to be able to sleep either. What if you go lie down on my bed while I take a shower?"

At Rani's startled look, Scott smiled, released his grip on her hands and ran his fingers through her tousled hair. "I can see our minds are going in the same direction. I knew there was something I liked about you. Unfortunately, I'm suggesting you lie down. You can get up when your head feels better.''

Rani wanted to tell Scott that there was no way she could make herself stretch out on his bed again, but the thought of resting her head on his pillow until the heavy pounding went away won over her half-formed protest. She let Scott pull a sheet over her and rested with her arm over her eyes as the sound of the shower blocked out the outside sounds of lambs insisting on breakfast. It wasn't long before she was thinking of nothing except soft pink mouths opening for mother's milk.

She was still lying with her arm blocking out the light when she heard Scott pad barefoot into the bedroom. He was running through drawers and closets, covering himself with the trappings of civilization.

"I'm going to get myself some breakfast," she heard him say. "You need to eat, too."

"In a minute," she heard herself say. "May I take a shower?"

"Haven't you been doing that all week?"

The challenge in his voice made her pull her arm away and open her eyes. She could see the teasing in his green eyes, the slight lift to his lips. The air in the room suddenly seemed less heady. "I confess," she said, making herself smile to match his mood, "you have a much nicer shower than I do."

"It's yours whenever you want it," he said and left the room.

Rani was dressed and drying her hair in the bathroom when she heard a familiar laugh coming from another part of the house. Dean had gotten up while she was in the shower. Where was he now?

She found the answer in the kitchen, where Dean was playing with cereal in a chair made to accommodate him with the help of several pillows while Scott was fixing breakfast. "He said something about being starved," Scott said as she entered the room. "What was that? Waffles. Hash browns and bacon. Scrambled eggs. Hold the coffee."

"You didn't have to do that," Rani said as she started to set the table. "I usually get him cleaned up before I give him breakfast. He's used to waiting."

"That's not the story he gave me." Scott winked. "Said he was hungry as a bear and twice as mean. He picked out his own clothes. I hope you have no objection to one blue sock and one red."

Rani laughed. "That sounds like his style. I'll get our things out of the room this morning. You didn't have to dress him."

Scott shrugged. "It isn't the first time I've dressed a child." His smile turned serious. "The truth is, I didn't get to do near enough of that when Chad was little. I was off trying to earn a living much of the time. I missed too much of his first few years."

"That's the way it is in many families," Rani pointed out, relieved to have the conversation on a safer topic than what they'd been discussing earlier this morning. "Women get most of the work of taking care of a baby."

Scott placed eggs on their plates before speaking. When he did, his voice was somber. "It's a rotten arrangement. Maybe I would have understood what

Chad's mother was going through if I'd spent more time taking care of a baby. She kept saying she needed more than diapers and four walls. Insisted on getting it. I couldn't understand that. I thought all women wanted to be mothers and damn little else. She misses Chad some now. That's understandable. But she's also enjoying the chance to experience things she couldn't when there was Chad to consider. She has always had a hankering for the night life."

Rani felt uncomfortable listening to Scott talk about the mother of his child but didn't know how to circumvent the topic. Her headache no longer consumed her, but her mind still had trouble following a straight line. "We had the dog-training business, so I was never really a full-time mother with nothing else going on in my life," Rani explained. "I don't know how I would have felt about that."

"Chad's mother didn't like it. That's why she's always worked even when I offered to support her. She's very independent. She tried to tell me, but I didn't know what to do. In those days I wasn't much good at communicating."

"Scott, you were young. Weren't you barely out of your teens when Chad was born?"

Scott laughed, bitterly it seemed to Rani. "You're right about that. There we were, a couple of kids ourselves, trying to play house. We didn't do a very good job. I wanted an old-fashioned wife, she wanted to flex her muscles. The house fell in around our ears. Chad's the one who got the short end of that."

"I wouldn't say that," Rani pressed. "He impresses me as a squared-away young man. He left the big-city life behind. You have every right to be proud of him."

"You think so?" Scott stopped eating and stared at Rani. "I hope so. There was a while there when I wasn't so sure. Chad was skipping school, running around with older kids who had dropped out of school. His mother was trying to fulfill her own needs. It had gotten to the point where Chad was raising himself." He took a bite of toast before continuing. "About the only thing his mother and I agreed on was that something had to be done to change Chad's life around. Moving him here was a radical move, but I think it's going to work."

Rani got up to get a washrag to clean Dean's face with, but that didn't stop her mind from dwelling on the picture Scott had painted for her. "How does his mother feel about this?" she asked, shocked at her boldness in asking such a personal question, even though Scott had already supplied a partial answer. "I mean, it must be hard for her after having Chad with her all those years."

Scott's shrug was casual enough, but there was no denying the harsh edge to his voice as he answered. "She'd had Chad for years. She said it was my turn. She didn't know how to deal with a teenager."

"Scott, I'm sorry. It's none of my business."

"Of course it is. I wouldn't change having Chad with me for anything. I just wish it had happened earlier."

"That's because you don't have to pay me minimum wage. Talk about slave labor."

Rani laughed as Dean yelled a greeting when his friend came into the room, but she felt uneasy knowing that Chad had walked in on a personal conversation. At least they hadn't been discussing anything as personal as birth control, Rani admitted to herself, blushing, as she offered to fix Chad breakfast. She was still at the stove when Scott excused himself, saying that he wanted to check on the progress in the training cabin before going back to the airport.

Rani watched him leave, eyes recording his lean length beneath his uniform of jeans and T-shirt, remembering how he looked in a darkened bedroom after she'd stripped him of his clothing.

When she turned away, she wondered if she'd be making that doctor's appointment.

Chapter Six

Rani sat cross-legged on the floor, Dean leaning against her, as she watched Scott, under the supervision of Marcus Wesner, put Marcus's demonstration hearing-ear dog Pepper through his paces. Marcus and Pepper had flown in the night before and were now giving Scott a hands-on opportunity to learn what a well-trained dog was capable of. Scott had met Marcus when he was doing research on the Dogs for the Deaf program, and Marcus had agreed to bring Pepper to Sol Valley.

At the moment Scott was pretending to be asleep on the couch. Pepper was lounging beside him, his head resting on his forepaws. At a signal from Marcus, Rani activated the system that rang the front doorbell. Instantly Pepper was on his feet. The dog trotted to the door, whimpered, and then trotted back to Scott. He kept nudging Scott's arm and licking his face until Scott got up and went to answer the door. Pepper's diligence was rewarded with a dog biscuit and a pat on the head. "Never let up on the rewards," Marcus reminded both Scott and Rani. "Dogs need positive strokes to have a reason for learning a skill."

From the moment she had met the soft-spoken trainer, Rani had been impressed by his practical approach. Training dogs was a business, and making their responses automatic couldn't be rushed. The dogs weren't pets. They had a definite role in life.

"You're going to have to guard against overzealous media people," Marcus pointed out when the short, liver-colored dog paused to cock his head in the direction of activity outside the training cabin. "Reporters are the worst. I don't know why it is, but people can't keep their hands off the dogs. Let them know from the beginning that you're trying to develop dogs who are loyal to their deaf owners, not dogs who'll go off with anyone who hands them a bone."

"What about my son?" Rani asked. Despite Scott's protests, she and Dean had been staying at her apartment since his return, but that still meant Dean would be around during the day. "I thought he'd be bored by the training, but he's been fascinated by what goes on. Is he going to be too much of a distraction? Should I keep him away from the cabin?"

Marcus leaned against the same wall Scott was now lounging against and rubbed Pepper behind the ear before answering. "I don't think so. He'll imitate you. If you're businesslike in your dealings with the dogs, he'll understand," he said slowly. "In fact it'll be good for dogs who'll be going into homes with children in them. Just make sure your son doesn't interrupt the dog's concentration when the animal's in the middle of a training session. Ideally dogs shouldn't be trained for any more than a half hour at a time. They can't concentrate for longer than that."

Rani nodded. She'd learned about dogs' concentration spans when she was working with attack and guard dogs. She was relieved to hear that she wouldn't have to keep Dean out of the training cabin, since she suspected she'd be spending a considerable portion of her working day there. A major reason for Marcus's visit was to instruct her in the training methods. Thanks to her background she was a fast learner. In the week since Scott had returned from Hollywood she'd interviewed several potential trainers, and she and Scott had agreed to hire two of them. Another three dogs had been accepted from the humane society. Barring any unforeseen delays, actual training should begin in a matter of days.

Scott was asking Marcus about the setup of the now nearly completed training cabin. Scott had had to delay yet another flight to Hollywood to accommodate Marcus's schedule, but from the way he was asking about minute training details, Rani would have never known that he had anything on his mind except the training of dogs for deaf owners. It was almost as if he could switch portions of his brain on or off depending on the demands of the moment.

"I'd like to see the cabin completely furnished," Marcus pointed out. "You want the dogs to become accustomed to working in a setting as close as possible to the one they'll eventually be part of. Put in a refrigerator so they can get used to its humming; hook up the water pipes. The outside can remain tar paper, but give the dogs the feel of the real thing."

Rani made a note of that and then asked Marcus a few more questions about the process his training program used to screen potential candidates for dogs. She was feeling overwhelmed by the letters and applications the center was receiving almost daily from people all over the country.

"It might seem like more work to you at the beginning," Marcus offered, "but what we wound up doing was expanding our board to some eight people from all walks of life. Let them take over the screening process, with you making the final decision. I agree. It isn't easy. There's nothing we'd like better than to give a dog to every hearing-impaired person, but it simply isn't possible. A deaf person living alone generally takes priority over one living in a family setting. Age isn't nearly as much of a criterion as the need to function independently."

"I know." Rani sighed. "It's just that the need is so great."

"I couldn't agree more," Marcus replied. "But until there are more centers like this in the country, all we can do is the best we're capable of."

"Do you see what I have to put up with?" Scott interjected. "I think Rani would put a collar on herself if she thought that would help. It isn't easy to be objective."

"Are you trying to tell me you're doing any better than I am?" Rani challenged in a teasing tone. She wasn't the only one in danger of losing her mind trying to keep straight such criteria as health and economic considerations and the availability of public facilities. "Next thing I know you're going to have the pygmy goats in the kennels with the dogs."

"Do you think they can be trained to fetch? Probably if you were the one doing the coaxing."

Rani's heart warmed at Scott's words. Because they were living life in the fast lane these days they hadn't touched, kissed or had a personal conversation since that very special morning, and yet the memory of those precious moments had seldom been out of her mind. Scott's eyes told her he hadn't forgotten, either. It didn't make things any easier to know he would be leaving for Hollywood the day after tomorrow.

She wondered if she'd have the time or the courage to tell him that she'd been to a doctor and was now taking birth control pills. If she did, she'd be admitting that she was ready for a deep relationship, a love affair even.

But giving her heart to Scott would mean having to tell him something that might destroy the promise that was there. Guilt lived at the corners of her conscience. When the final tally was made, she knew she was a participant in the accident. True, she had been at home when it happened, but Dean wouldn't have been in the car if she'd asserted herself that day. As had happened too many times in the course of their marriage, Rani had allowed herself to be submerged under the barrage of words Zack used to control the ebb and flow of their life together.

The problem, Rani now realized, was that she'd allowed Zack to control her with his temper. She was getting a taste of freedom now. She was learning to be responsible for Dean without the tug-of-war that had existed when she was married.

She wasn't sure she dared expose her will to that of another man again. One round under the guise of marriage left her to face the role she had played in her son's accident.

"Mommy! Are you going to be here forever?" Dean squirmed, pushing at his mother's hands to be released.

"I think someone has listened to all the grown-up talk he can for one day. The dogs are going to be just like that. They'll let you know in no uncertain terms when they've had all the schooling they can take for one day," Marcus observed. As he allowed Dean to come over to get acquainted with Pepper he asked Scott questions about the ranch's primary business. Rani was surprised to realize how much she already knew about the animal-actor business. She wasn't doing the ranch's books, but she'd handled more than her share of telephone calls from advertising agencies, publicity agents, even those in charge of a movie's casting. It was impossible to separate the dog program from the other things that were taking place here.

Things like a little boy and a man falling under each other's spell and the woman who'd brought them together wondering if the simple word *guilt* would shatter that spell.

Rani jumped when the phone in the training cabin rang. She glanced briefly at Scott, flushed because his eyes were on her, questioning her reaction as she hurried to answer it. The relative of a deaf gentleman in his eighties wanted to know if there was an upper age limit to those who could be considered to receive a dog. As Rani answered the question she turned her back on Scott so she could concentrate on business and not green eyes. By the time she'd finished her explanation that age wasn't usually a factor, Scott and Marcus were getting ready to leave the cabin.

"I want to show Marcus some of our other four-legged residents. See if I can get Gas to do something impressive," Scott explained, his eyes daring her not to answer his honest gaze. "Before I forget, there's something I want to talk to you about before I take off again. Marcus and I are going to go into town for dinner tonight. Why don't you join us?''

Rani hung up, turned from the phone and took a calming breath. Was she being asked to respond as Scott's date? Even as her mind clicked off the possibility that she could get her mother to watch Dean for several hours, she couldn't quite bring herself to make this simple commitment. "I don't have much in the way of dressing-up clothes," she stalled.

"It can't be anyplace fancy," Marcus interjected. "When I travel with Pepper I don't bring along any suits."

Scott's comment was even more direct. "Don't turn us down," he said.

Rani shied away from what she read in Scott's eyes, but the same kind of courage that allowed her to face her son's long recovery gave her the strength to answer. "I'd love a meal out. Where do you want me to meet you? I'll have to go home and change and drop Dean off first." There. Now he couldn't accuse her of turning him down.

"We'll pick you up." Scott's voice was still as matter-of-fact as it had been. "We can drop Dean off on our way to dinner."

Rani was ready long before she expected the men. She'd hurried through the afternoon's work so she could leave early. Then she'd worked up a sweat cleaning the neglected apartment and thrown together a quick dinner for Dean. Now he was asking nonstop questions as she applied a touch of hair spray to hair that had chosen tonight to become charged with electricity. Her hazel eyes glowed with a light that didn't

come from the blue shadow accenting them. Finishing
with her hair, Rani glanced down to find Dean grinning
up at her from under the hood he'd made of her floor-
length softly gathered blue suit. The cotton skirt was
set off by an aqua cotton blouse that buttoned high on
her long neck but was thin enough to need the rows of
gathering from shoulder to waist to keep it from revealing too much of her breasts.

The outfit was much too feminine for a purely business meeting, but when Scott told her the name of the
restaurant they'd be going to, instinct had opted for a
womanly touch. Scott might stick to jeans and a white
T-shirt, but tonight Rani wanted to feel like a woman.
Even Dean noticed the difference. "You're pretty,
Mommy," he said. "You're the prettiest mommy in
the world, even Hollywood."

When the doorbell rang, Rani ran her tongue over
her lips, nervously tucked her blouse into the waistline-
revealing skirt and smoothed the soft fabric over her
hips. A date? Maybe that's what this was.

Marcus whistled when Rani opened the door, but
Scott's only response was to stare at her with an intensity that made her wonder if her blouse was too revealing despite the gathers. For a moment Scott stood in
the doorway, fingers pulled unnaturally close to his
palms. Finally she saw him swallow. "You look beautiful," he whispered.

Rani averted her head to hide the blush she could
feel crawling up her neck to her cheeks. "Thank you,
sir. You and my son are exactly what my ego needs,"
she said lightly. "You look pretty handsome yourself.
And you don't smell like hay tonight."

Scott wasn't wearing a suit, but he had changed into

a summer-weight sport coat and a dress shirt that accented his healthy tan. Rani could tell that he'd spent time bringing his curls under control and warmed at the thought that maybe he'd gone to that work for her sake.

"Isn't anyone going to tell me how good I look?" Marcus asked, his innocent comment breaking the tension that had built up when Scott came close enough for Rani to feel the warmth radiating from his body. "What say we deposit this young fellow and go get something to eat?" Marcus asked.

Rani held out her hand for Dean to take and draped her free arm through Marcus's. "I couldn't agree more." She laughed. "After all, it isn't every night that I get to eat in the company of two handsome men."

Tonight Scott was driving a silver car with bucket seats, a leather-wrapped steering wheel and an expensive stereo tape deck. She had to laugh at the low mileage and decided the car seldom had a function on the ranch. Despite Rani's qualms Marcus insisted on sitting in back with Dean, leaving the seat next to Scott free for her. Rani turned half around to make sure Dean was comfortable. As she did, her knees brushed Scott's thighs. He might have only been reaching for the stick shift between them, but his fingers came into contact with her legs. For a moment his palm rested on her knee, something electric flashing from man to woman. Rani caught her breath, too overwhelmed by her reaction to find the strength to move her legs. "This toy is something I bought during a low point in my life," Scott explained. "Now, of course, Chad can hardly wait to run up the mileage on it for me."

From the back seat Marcus was teasing Scott about

the expensive toy he was driving and asking Dean if that's what he wanted when he grew up, but if Scott was thinking about anything except his hand on Rani's knee, he gave no indication. She felt his breath touch the side of her face as he turned in her direction, but she couldn't trust herself to return the look. Every inch of flesh in her body had come alive under his touch. She couldn't remember having ever wanted anything more than she wanted to experience his hands on her.

When she thought she would wind up screaming if she didn't dare to take the breath her lungs needed, Scott brought the car to life and eased out into the night. Rani sat unmoving next to him, her knee now free of his touch. She was breathing again, but there was nothing natural about that. It took every bit of concentration she was capable of to remember how to pull air into her lungs, to think of something except the hot wash of emotion that had heated her body to the boiling point.

Rani hadn't come close to finding her previous self-control by the time Scott stopped at her parents' house and she hurried in to deposit Dean. Scott was concentrating on what Marcus was saying when she returned, but she knew she wasn't imagining the electricity that flowed from him to her. No matter how many times she tried to tell herself to concentrate, she hadn't been able to contribute anything to the conversation by the time they'd reached the restaurant. She accepted Scott's arm as he led her into the dark interior, her head held high as she realized that several heads turned in their direction as the tall man and his companion entered.

"I feel like a fifth wheel," Marcus observed once

they'd been seated at a window table. "Maybe I should start wearing high-heeled boots if I want people around here to notice me."

"Being tall has its drawbacks, especially for a woman," Rani said in an effort to take her thoughts away from Scott. "People think I can handle everything that comes my way. Just once I'd like to be five feet tall and have someone think I need help changing a tire."

Marcus laughed. "I can't believe you can't get anyone to change a tire for you. Especially if you dress like that. I must say, you look completely feminine tonight. If I weren't happily married I might make a pass at you."

Rani blushed but recovered quickly. "You could anyway. Just to keep your hand in. Would you like me to grade you on your effort?" She glanced at Scott. He hadn't spoken since they sat down. Instead his eyes were roaming around the room, glancing at the menu, everywhere but on her.

Even after they'd ordered and their dinner was brought to them, Rani still didn't know why Scott was so moody. At least he'd started talking. He and Marcus discussed the training program a little more and then the conversation drifted to tales of how Scott went about locating and training animals for TV and movies. "I have people coming out of the woodwork who have tried to raise a wild animal only to give up in despair when a fawn becomes a doe ready for mating season or a wolf cub starts looking at the family cat with a hungry eye," Scott explained. "They've had the animals illegally, of course, and don't like it when I point that out to them."

"Most of the animals aren't dumped on your doorstep, are they?" Marcus asked, obviously fascinated.

"I wish. It'd certainly cut down on the time I spend scouring the country."

Rani nibbled on her salad and formed mental pictures of Scott traveling to places she'd only read about in his quest for talking parrots, a young cheetah, a monkey who wasn't tempted to bite a high-strung actress. "I've never been able to form any real attachment to monkeys," Scott admitted. "When they decide I don't live up to their expectations, they can make things miserable for me. I guess I just don't speak monkey. But they're dirty; they're bundles of energy; they can be foul-tempered. Give me a shy little lady bison any day. They don't make any bones about wanting me to get close enough to their hooves in order to give me the old heave-ho."

"What do you expect of a woman?" Marcus laughed. "Present company excepted, of course."

Rani didn't want to think about the women Scott must have met while he flew about the world unencumbered by a wife or children, but she couldn't help it. She wondered if having his son come live with him had necessitated a change in his life-style. It didn't make sense that he would be interested in a divorcee with a small child when he could have just about any woman he turned his green eyes on.

"Don't tell me you're on a diet?" Marcus asked as she ignored her baked potato. "From what I've seen of the way Scott works you, I don't see how you'd have time to eat."

"No diet," Rani admitted and then cast around for an explanation that didn't include what having Scott so close was doing to her. "You know how it is with us mothers. Can't get the old maternal instinct to shut down. I don't leave him with his grandparents much, and he's at the age when he has a thousand reasons for not going to bed."

Marcus patted her hand. "Don't worry about him. I'm sure the little guy is doing just fine. He impresses me as someone who gets along well with people."

"He does." Then before she took time to weigh the wisdom of what she was going to say, the words were out. "My son was recently treated for epilepsy."

Marcus frowned. "I'm afraid I don't know much about that."

"Neither did I a year ago," Rani admitted. "I've learned a lot."

Scott spoke. "Dean's epilepsy developed as the result of a blow to his head. Seizures occur when a group of brain cells become abnormally active. In Dean's case trauma led to the abnormal activity."

Rani jumped and turned toward Scott. She was sure she hadn't said that to him. "You sound just like Dean's doctor," she managed.

A smile that didn't reach his eyes touched Scott's lips. He'd been skating around Rani and what he felt for her all evening. He'd thought he'd be able to keep his distance, to let silence take over for the words he didn't have, but that was before this opportunity to reach her presented itself. When he was done, she might understand how much her world had become his. "I've been doing some research. There were some things I wanted to learn but didn't feel like asking you. Marcus, Rani's husband deserted her when he learned what was wrong with their son."

Rani felt her jaw muscles clamp together, but that wasn't enough to keep her from speaking. "I'm sure

Marcus doesn't want to hear about my personal problems," she said through clenched teeth. "We're supposed to be relaxing tonight, not talking about something that took place a long time ago."

If Scott was aware of her anger he didn't acknowledge it. To her surprise he gave Marcus a thoroughly adequate description of what forms epilepsy took, at the same time showing Rani that he had indeed done considerable research on the problem. "I happen to believe Rani's a very brave woman," he finished up.

"I'm not brave. I'm a mother," Rani said, meeting Scott's eyes straight on for the first time. "It goes with the territory."

"Mothers don't have a corner on caring. A father can be just as responsible," he said, eyes unwavering.

"I didn't mean that." Rani wanted to back down from the strength she heard in Scott's voice, but she didn't dare. "You know I admire what you're doing with Chad."

"That's not the point I'm making." Scott turned toward her, his strength more inescapable than before. "I don't expect a gold star because I want to provide a decent environment for my son. What I'm saying is, I don't have much use for men who abdicate their responsibility."

Rani froze. So that was what this argument was about. Scott was talking about Zack, not about himself. "That's my concern," she said, emotions held firmly in check. "You don't have to concern yourself with whether my ex-husband has abdicated his responsibility or not."

"There's no question about it. He bailed out."

With a wrench Rani freed her eyes from Scott's and attacked her neglected potato. How had the evening taken this turn? If she'd had any idea Scott was going to bring up her ex-husband, she would never have come here. The fact that he'd taken this moment and this method to bring up something she'd been trying to forget upset her more than she would ever let on. Of course she was angry with Zack. She wouldn't be human if she wasn't. But it wasn't Scott's business. He wasn't even involved in the situation.

When Rani felt she dared speak without lashing out, she pointedly turned the conversation back to what the three of them had in common. She ignored Scott's silence as she asked Marcus about how he'd become interested in training dogs and offered a few observations about why she was looking forward to working with deaf people after trying to satisfy policemen and people interested in protecting their homes and businesses. "You wouldn't believe the men who have this macho thing about guard dogs," she pointed out. "There were times when I knew we were training dogs to be extensions of some man's overblown ego. I like the idea of meeting people who need dogs in order to function normally, not because there's something they feel they have to prove to the world."

"That's too bad," Scott said. "I was going to ask you about a guard dog for the ranch, but since that's the way you feel—"

"Wait a minute," Rani interrupted. She was still angry at Scott for what he'd said before, but at least he'd broken his self-imposed silence. "I didn't say that all guard dogs are bought to satisfy someone's ego. There are times when guard dogs serve a very worthwhile purpose." She paused, thinking about what Scott had said. "Maybe having a guard dog would be good for the ranch."

"It might be. That's what I wanted to talk to you about at dinner." Rani blinked. Yes, Scott had said something about there being something he wanted to discuss. Between her primitive reaction to him in the car and their subsequent argument that had completely escaped her mind.

"I'm sorry," she whispered. "I should have asked you what you wanted to speak to me about earlier. If you want me to train a dog to guard the ranch I'll be glad to, but a sign that says Lion on the Premises might be just as effective."

"You're right," Scott said lightly. "Dumb idea. What do we need with one more mouth to feed? Could you teach Gas to growl?"

"I don't see why not," Rani countered. "You could show him how it's done."

Marcus's deep sigh took Rani's mind away from thoughts about Scott that whirled in endless circles without ever drawing a straight line. "You don't know how relieved I am to hear the two of you talking again." Marcus sighed again. "I thought I was going to have to referee a fight."

"Hardly." Before she could react, Scott had taken her hand and was holding it tightly in his. He lifted her hand into the air and then brought it to his mouth to place a feathery kiss on her fingertips. "I refuse to fight with a beautiful woman on a summer night in a setting as relaxing as this one. Truce?"

Rani met the challenge in his eyes. "Truce," she said, willing her hand to remain passively in his.

Could he guess at her reaction to their decision to call a truce? She'd been on the brink of tears since they'd exchanged heated words, shaken because she had no way of knowing how intensely she'd react to an argument with this man.

If only they'd met when they were both innocent youths, unscarred by previous relationships. If only she hadn't lost her confidence in being able to sustain a working relationship. As Rani continued to look into Scott's eyes, she drew a parallel between what she was wanting tonight and what Scott's son might soon experience. Once, a thousand years ago, she'd been a young girl, a virgin, "in love" for the first time in her life. That summer romance complete with vows of undying love and copious tears when September brought an end to passion had been as unreal as a dream of turning into a princess simply by placing her foot into a glass slipper. And yet she'd had her summer romance. The memory would always remain special, the marking of a girl's journey toward womanhood.

Was it so wrong to want that innocent summer back again, to place Scott there with her, block out divorce and cares and responsibility? And guilt. Yes, it was a child's dream, but for a few minutes at least Rani let green eyes swallow her and made Scott her bronzed teenage hero.

By the time dinner was over, Rani still hadn't completely shaken off the wish to turn back the clock. She was aware that Marcus was saying something about needing to get back to his motel room to check on his dog, but she was only vaguely aware of getting into Scott's car and driving to the motel. She said her good-byes to Marcus and settled back in her bucket seat, letting the music from Scott's stereo seep through her.

"Are you tired?" she heard Scott ask.

Rani opened her eyes and focused on the strong face next to her. "No," she managed. "I was just thinking about something that happened a long time ago. Do you ever wish you were a teenager again?"

"And have to go through all that searching and self-doubt again? No, thank you." He laughed. "It's a lot easier on the emotional system now that I know who I am."

"Do you know who you are?"

"Oh, yes." The car was back on the road again, but he took one hand off the steering wheel and ran it lightly through his thick hair. "There isn't much I'd change about my life. I don't have many regrets about the way it turned out. There are always goals we don't achieve, but I don't believe in wasting my life thinking about that."

"That's good." Shouldn't she be responding to his touch? If she was, it was in a deep, settled way, not like the electric charge she'd felt earlier. Maybe she was much more tired than she realized. Maybe it was the company. "Earlier, when you and Marcus were talking, you said you'd been all over the world. Don't you miss that kind of freedom?"

"What freedom?" Scott shook his head. "I was working all that time. I knew I had to satisfy certain contracts or I'd be out of business. Charging all over the world isn't much fun when you're trying to meet deadlines."

"I didn't think of it like that," Rani admitted. "It sounded very sophisticated to me, completely different from what I've done with my life. I suppose people always wonder about others' life-styles."

"We all do what we have to," Scott said, effectively putting an end to her thoughts of jet-set romances and passionate flings in exotic locations. "I'm just relieved that I don't have to go anywhere except Southern California anymore. Getting my son away from the street gang he was in there was the best thing I could have done for him."

Rani smiled. "This conversation is much nicer than the fight we had earlier. How did that happen? Poor Marcus. He must have thought he'd blundered into a street fight."

Scott's fingers were still exploring her hair, a movement she was becoming more and more aware of. "You didn't like my bringing up your ex like that, did you?"

"It wasn't the time or the place."

She was right. Scott hadn't felt right about what he'd revealed to Marcus. But Scott believed that Rani had endured too much at Zack's hands. Tonight his anger and resentment had boiled out before he could stop it. "I'm sorry," he said softly. "It won't happen again. But I can't understand a man who would do what he did. Wait," Scott warned when she tried to speak. "I'm speaking from experience. I have reasons for feeling the way I do."

"Such as?" Rani challenged.

As Rani sat with her head resting on the back of her bucket seat, her mind flitting between the feel of fingers on her scalp and his deep voice in the dark interior of the car, Scott told her things that she knew were painful for him.

"Do you know what it feels like to be chopped into pieces? I was trying to build on the business, establish the ranch. The divorce was just over and I still felt as if I'd been left in the fight ring too long." He sighed deeply. "I almost wound up in the hospital because I was trying to cram too much into each day. I was flying to Hollywood every week both to maintain my business and to try to remain part of Chad's life. I was scared, so damn scared that I'd lose contact with him."

"I didn't know," Rani whispered, her fingers on his cheek finishing the emotion her words started.

"My doctor tried to get me to slow down. He said I was digging myself an early grave. Because—well, because it took so much out of me emotionally, I wondered if it might be better for everyone if I got out of Chad's life."

"But you didn't. You couldn't."

"No, I couldn't make myself let go. Thank God." Scott's breath was a heavy gasp. "As I saw him growing up and getting involved with what I knew were the wrong kinds of people I was glad I'd kept that contact all those years. It was a lot easier to pack him up and get him away from all that. I like Chad. Do you know what I'm saying? I like my son. I wouldn't trade that feeling for all the money in the world."

Tears blurred Rani's eyes. She tried to speak, to thank him for revealing so much of himself to her, but the words didn't come out. As a mother she knew how much you love your own child. That bond went beyond words.

"I'm sorry." Scott brushed away a tear. "I said something wrong."

"No." Rani shook her head, accepting the headache that went with it. "I—I know what you're saying. That kind of love is exquisite. It's the kind of feeling parents should be able to share."

"I thought we weren't going to talk about Zack."

She only nodded and stirred herself when Scott pulled up in front of her parents' house. Fortunately her sleepy parents turned a bundled-up Dean over to her without asking about her evening.

Fifteen minutes later Dean was curled up in a ball in his bed. Rani straightened and turned back toward the living room, where Scott was waiting for her. Because she didn't want to wake her son she hadn't turned on the light in the living room. Scott was sitting on the couch, long legs stretched out in front of him. For a moment she hesitated, aware of nothing except how much he resembled a mountain lion at rest.

Chapter Seven

"I'm not crazy about this apartment," Scott said. He shifted his legs and folded his arms behind his head. He'd wondered what kind of place Rani lived in, but what he was seeing didn't tell him nearly enough about the woman who hung her hat here. The furniture was secondhand; there were two plants in the room but no pictures on the wall. He wondered if she simply hadn't had time to do any decorating or, as he rather suspected, didn't feel attached enough to the place to invest any emotional energy in it. "You have a terrific view of an alley and the back of a shopping center a block away. Is it ever quiet at night?"

"Not so you'd notice," Rani admitted. She was pleased to see he had no intention of leaving. Because sitting on the throw-covered couch would place her too close to Scott, she'd taken the chair opposite him. Although there was distance between them, she couldn't avoid looking at him, her mind settling on the length of him from feet to waist, the strength of his arms— something his dress shirt couldn't hide. "Fortunately kids can sleep through anything," she went on. "Dean seldom wakes up."

"What about you?"

Rani frowned but decided to be honest. "You know how it is when you get older. Sleep isn't as assured as it used to be."

"Because we have more to keep us awake—more to think about."

"Something like that." Sitting in the semidarkness was helping her maintain the dreamlike state she'd been in in the car.

"You'd sleep better out at the ranch. Fresh air always helps me nod off."

"I thought you weren't going to keep after me about that. What about allowing me a little time between innings?" Rani countered. She made herself a promise not to start arguing with him. She was much too content for anything to disturb her. Not even his remark about her apartment bothered her. The place wasn't what she would have chosen if circumstances had been different. She simply couldn't take offense over something that meant so little to her.

Scott laughed, a low growl of sound that was more vibration than noise. "I don't remember making any promise like that, but I *will* drop the subject. Tonight has had some very nice moments. I don't want to mar that. And I believe there's potential for what remains of the evening."

"You enjoyed the evening?" Rani asked. Absently she unbuttoned the two tiny buttons holding her blouse high on her throat and lightly rubbed the newly freed flesh. "You were so quiet there at the restaurant I thought maybe you were regretting it."

"I gave you that impression? I'm sorry. Actually I was thinking about my very attractive dinner partner and chiding myself for not having done something like taking you out before. Next time Marcus won't be along."

"I appreciate the compliment," she said in an attempt to keep the tone light. "You must have been wondering if I owned anything except jeans."

"Jeans have their place. Tonight, however, isn't one of those times. I meant what I said. You're a beautiful woman."

Instead of being embarrassed by his unexpected compliment, Rani felt her body fill with a warm glow that came from remembering what it was like to be treated like a woman. They could be moving toward a dangerous moment in their relationship, but Rani didn't care. Something warm and alive and hungry deep inside her admitted she needed that danger.

"You're awfully quiet. You didn't want me to say that?"

"No, I'm sorry." Rani stopped playing with the high collar of her blouse and tucked her legs up under her long skirt. "That isn't it at all. I'm just not used to being complimented. First Dean and then you tonight. It's a heady experience."

"I mean it." Scott sighed, was quiet for a minute. He wasn't sure it was wise to let the conversation continue in this vein, but then he wasn't sure he was in a position to turn it around, either. "You're doing things to me I honestly don't understand. I definitely don't have the home-court advantage. You wouldn't be throwing me off balance on purpose, would you?"

"Hardly." Rani laughed, aware that the potentially dangerous moment was coming closer. "I gave up trying to be anyone except myself a long time ago," she said honestly. "It's all I can do to keep up with what's expected of me."

"Maybe that's it. You're an incredibly strong woman, and yet I sense this hidden vulnerability. I think that's what I find fascinating. You keep whatever vulnerability you have below the surface where it can't interfere with what you have to do. You could lean on me, you know, ask for help. But you don't. You stand on your own two feet."

"Stop! You make me sound like Joan of Arc," Rani said, blushing. "That's a role model I could never live up to. I'm not doing anything any mother wouldn't. Dean's only three. He has certain needs, like food and clothing and whatever time it takes to make certain memories fade. It's my job to meet his needs."

"But what about your own needs? That's what vulnerability is about, having needs and admitting them."

"I know," Rani whispered, her eyes on the way her hands were curling and uncurling on the chair arms instead of resting quietly. If only she could be honest! He'd mistaken guilt and her attempts to atone for her acts as vulnerability, but she wasn't ready to tell him that. "You've made me aware of that."

"Have I?" Scott was on his feet, eating up the distance between them, placing his hands over hers to still their restless movement.

Rani looked up, found Scott's eyes and for a moment fought the power they had over her. The fight was a short one. Her mouth parted slightly and she surrendered to what she was feeling inside.

The touch of lips against lips came so slowly, so perfectly that Rani couldn't tell when the actual contact had been made. It didn't matter. She was testing him with her mouth, taking measure of the man, letting him know of the woman waiting beneath the high-necked blouse and long straight skirt. Rani closed her eyes and blocked out everything except the masculine body leaning over her. She wanted him, wanted much more than his kiss. She wasn't going to think of anything before or after this moment.

Scott lifted her to her feet and pulled her into the circle that was his strength. Rani reached for his neck, her body rising slightly as she continued the exploration her mouth had begun. His scent was sensual, more, much more powerful than any other she'd experienced. She breathed deeply, quickly, pulling his scent deep inside her and holding it tight to her heart. Her breasts tingled as though something was touching them from the inside, daring them to respond. If she existed beyond this experience she was unaware of it. She hadn't been without a man's arms around her that long, but her body was reacting in a savagely primitive way that made a lie of every other time she'd felt a male heart beating near hers. This man could consume her, fill her!

"I'm not going to leave unless you tell me to." He was talking to her, demanding a rational response.

Rani wasn't sure she was capable of that, but she had to try. "I went to a doctor while you were gone," she whispered.

She felt his body shudder and then his embrace became too all-encompassing for her to think off anything except his presence. "Thank you," he whispered, his lips not leaving hers. "I want to spend the night with you."

I know. I want it, too. She didn't have to say the

words aloud. He had to know what her answer was, because her breasts and belly and thighs and arms were telling him what he wanted to hear. She wasn't going to attempt to hide what was so obvious.

Scott's hands slid under her waistband and pulled her blouse free. His fingertips found the satin flesh covering her ribs, explored the small of her back and then rode higher to play a tantalizing game with the fastening on her bra. His fingers darted under the fabric, came out again and teased their way around to the front, where they tested the soft white mounds above the chaste covering. Rani groaned and pulled her mouth free. "You're making me crazy," she moaned as his fingers dipped under fabric and his nails gently raked the darker flesh of her nipples.

"Not as crazy as I am," he answered, his nails still working their magic.

When she was afraid she would cry out with wanting, he quickly undid the fastening and cupped her breasts, using his hold on her to pull her closer. "Perfect," he whispered. "They fit perfectly in my hands."

It wasn't enough. Rani wanted more than this basic contact. Her clothes had become an iron cage keeping her away from what the woman in her needed. Scott must have known how deep her hunger went. But he seemed to be in no hurry to satisfy that appetite. His unbuttoning of her blouse took agonizing minutes while her own fingers fumbled with his shirt. By the time he finally slipped the soft fabric off her shoulders she had to spread her legs to keep from swaying. Her knees almost buckled when he dropped her bra to the floor on top of her abandoned blouse.

Rani didn't give him time to capture her naked

breasts again. It was time to give pleasure as well as receive it. Rani leaned forward, pressing her hardened nipples against his flesh and abandoned herself to the pure ecstasy of this intimate contact. He felt so good. His flesh was cooled by the night air, but beneath the layer of skin there was warm muscle, warmth that came close to consuming her. Scott was right. She never wanted to be a teenager again. Testing the boundaries of womanhood made virginity a distant memory.

"I'm going to spend the night," he breathed. "It's too late to stop now."

"I don't want it to stop. I can't," Rani answered and cut off anything else he might say by pressing her open mouth against his. How good he tasted. Did he think her too bold? It didn't matter. Rani was beyond thinking of civilized actions. Scott was the man she needed at this point in her life. He wasn't the first, but something living deep inside said that he could become the last.

Rani had never been swept into a man's arms before, but Scott lifted her as easily as she lifted her child. She clung to him as he carried her into the bedroom and laid her out on the single bed. She lay unmoving, her arms without strength, as he sat on the side of the bed and slowly pulled off her long skirt and lavender panties.

She was naked, night air tickling its way along her body, wondering if she'd ever want clothing again. There were faint stretch marks on her belly from child-bearing, but those were badges of womanhood, marks a man would understand and accept.

Scott joined her, the long hard length of his bare legs brushing against hers. His lips sought her jawline as with tiny nips he defined the line between cheek and neck. Rani tossed her head back, savoring the sensation, quick breaths transmitting the thrill she felt surging through her as his teeth nipped lower. He was exploring her throat now, brushing his way to the swell of her breasts as her deeply sensitive fingertips traced the strong cords of muscle that made up his chest. She was bold in a way that would have shocked her had she not been past the point of modesty.

Rani heard her breath catch in a primitive sob as her nipples were covered by Scott's mouth. She stopped breathing altogether when his tongue touched the hardened tips, making her hips move restlessly on the bed. Rani thought of nothing, wanted nothing except the fulfillment that would come, but she willed herself to be patient, to experience fully every moment of the exploration leading to the pinnacle.

When it drew close, she dug her fingers into his shoulders and pulled Scott against her. Her eyes closed so nothing could distract her from the artistry of two bodies giving and receiving pleasure.

So this was lovemaking. Rani had heard the words before and thought she knew what it meant to her as a woman. But what she'd experienced in bed before had never reached the heights she was catapulted to under Scott's expert tutelage. Rani gave herself willingly, freely, eager to give as much pleasure as she was receiving. As she reached that delightful mountaintop she heard Scott's own ragged breathing and knew they were on the same path.

Scott's body was next to hers as she slowly became aware of the night air, the coverlet scratching her naked flesh. Rani turned slightly, found Scott's body in the dark and savored the taste of his wet mouth. "Thank you," she whispered and snuggled closer as his arm pulled her into the haven he offered.

Despite the night temperature she fell asleep, warmed by Scott's beating heart. Dawn was pushing the night into the far reaches of the room when she realized that Scott was trying to wake her up.

He was propped up on one elbow, a leg draped over her, his free hand gently roaming over her naked breasts. "It's time to rise, beautiful lady," he whispered against her ear. "I confess the alternative is much more pleasant, but we're not the only ones in the house and I don't think Dean's ready for this."

Rani sighed and focused on the face above her. Scott's curls were back to taking off in wild directions and he needed a shave. Grinning, Rani ran her hand over his chin. "Have you ever grown a beard? I wonder if it's just as curly as your hair."

"I'm afraid so. I tried growing a beard once. I looked as if I'd plugged myself into an electric socket. Rani? I don't want last night to be the only time."

Neither do I. And yet, close as the words were to pushing through, Rani kept them to herself. There was no denying how vulnerable, how willing she'd been last night. While they were exploring each other she had no reservations about lovemaking.

But this was morning. What she and Scott had shared was new, untested. It was better to leave things as they were, to acknowledge last night for what it was—a very, very special night but not a commitment to the future. She'd failed miserably at one relationship. She didn't dare plunge into another.

Scott was watching her, waiting for an answer. Rani

sighed. "It was special," she breathed, "but I don't know where we're heading. I have to be cautious."

"I'm willing to find out. I'm going to say it again. I want you to move out to the ranch."

"Scott—"

"Not because of what you're thinking. I'm thinking about Dean and you. I'd feel a lot better if the two of you were out of this place. Even with you here it depressed me."

"I know. I don't like it either, but I was in a hurry," Rani groaned. "Please give me a little more time. Last night was—I need time to put it into perspective. If that's possible."

Scott sat up and swung his legs over the bed. "I'm not going to give you too much time. I mean what I said. I don't want last night to be the only time."

Scott's words were seldom out of Rani's thoughts that day or for the next five while Scott was gone and Rani was busy getting the five dogs and two trainers comfortable with one another and working out a routine. Something neither Rani nor Scott had given any thought to cropped up. Because the dogs were young they had an abundance of energy. It soon became evident that recess was as important as class time. Not only that, the dogs needed the chance to get out and run in the morning before they were willing to settle down to business. Dean thought the morning romps the best part of the day, since that was something he could be an active participant in.

Once again Rani and Dean spent nights at the ranch. Scott called every evening, but because there was so much that had to be discussed about the program and the progress being made in setting up a larger board, there was precious little chance to say much of a personal nature. In addition, Chad was facing the reality of the first day of school and seemed to need reassurance from his father that all would go well for him at a new high school. In fact, Chad's unaccustomed show of nerves gave Rani the distraction she needed.

"I don't know what you're so worried about," Rani teased as she was fixing breakfast for the three of them. "One look at you and the girls at school are going to be trailing after you like puppy dogs."

"Yeah?" Obviously Chad was unconvinced. "I don't know. I mean, I don't know any of those kids. What can I talk to them about?"

"Tell them about going to school near Hollywood. Everyone'll want to hear about that. You can bet none of them have spent the summer working with exotic animals and winding up on the evening news."

"That was an accident," Chad pointed out. "I didn't know those news guys were going to come out to the ranch. They were supposed to be filming Dad, not me. Besides, the kids will probably think I'm some hotshot. No one will want to have anything to do with me."

Rani groaned and suppressed a laugh. If she had to go through this with Dean in a few years, she was going to need help surviving the child/man stage. "Have confidence in yourself, will you? You don't come across to me as a hotshot."

Chad's groan matched hers. "You're different. Why don't you go *for* me? What do I need with an education?"

Rani refused to let herself be sucked into that argument. She realized that Chad was trying to involve her in a senseless conversation because that would take his mind off what had his stomach tied in knots. In the end it was Dean and not anything she said that provided Chad with a distraction. Dean had taken a liking to a baseball cap Chad wore and teased him about it until Chad plunked the oversized hat on Dean's head. The child peered owlishly out from under the bill and then turned the experience into a game of hide-and-seek that had Chad laughing in delight as Dean's eyes appeared and disappeared from under the bill. "That's not what a baseball cap is for, kid," Chad pointed out. "Boy, do you have a lot to learn about sports."

"I can hit the ball a mile," Dean declared. "Better than you."

"Oh, yeah? That sounds like a challenge if I ever heard one. What if I throw a few of my fastballs at you? I'll fan you before you know what hit you."

At the word *hit* Rani froze. "I don't know if that's a good idea," she said nervously. "Chad, what if you hit Dean? I've seen batters on TV get hit in the head." She didn't add that the idea of a baseball striking Dean's head made her blood run cold.

"I'm not going to hurt him," Chad replied somberly. "I'd never do that. Look, I have a couple of batting helmets. What if I make sure Dean's wearing one?"

Slowly the tension seeped out of Rani. Chad's solution was so simple, so reasonable. Of course Chad wasn't going to try to fire fastballs past a three-year-old. She had to stop thinking of Dean as a child who couldn't be sent out into the world like every other child. "I'd appreciate that," she said, making herself smile. "I'm sorry. You'll have to be patient with me."

Chad reached over and patted her shoulder. "Hey,

I've been raising parents for fifteen years. I know all about their hang-ups.''

Rani laughed and let them go. It wasn't until she was alone that the laughter died. She considered Chad one of her closest friends. She was afraid it wouldn't remain that way if he learned that her lack of backbone was an instrumental part of what had happened to his little playmate.

When Rani saw Scott at the airport Friday night, Chad and Dean and their relationship weren't what was on her mind. She was waiting out by the airstrip built for private planes with the ranch pickup Scott needed when the plane taxied in. Rani had taken advantage of having Chad around to run down the road the day before to get her hair cut and was wearing the summer-weight sweater her mother had knitted for her and Scott had never seen. As the airplane door opened to discharge first the pilot and then Scott, something caught in her throat.

She wondered if he had become even more handsome since the last time she'd seen him or whether it was simply the five-day absence that made him seem bigger than life.

Scott, however, didn't need time to study her. His long legs covered the distance between them. He swept her into his arms and lifted her off her feet. He buried his face in her hair, drinking in her scent. The past five days had seemed twice as long, and he didn't care if she knew what he'd gone through. "Do you ever look good! If I see one more woman with false eyelashes— forget it. I can put all that behind me." He nibbled playfully on a lock of hair. "You got your hair cut. I like it."

He noticed! "Just a couple of inches," she reassured

him. Their kiss effectively put an end to anything else she might have said about trying to undermine her hair's determination to overbalance her face. Her hair, her special sweater didn't mean anything. This moment in Scott's arms was what she'd been waiting for since she'd waved him off five days ago. Questions, doubts, fears even would have to wait for a saner moment.

If it hadn't been for the pilot clearing his throat nearby and the young orangutan and two spider monkeys waiting in the plane, Scott might never have let her feet touch the ground again. Rani stepped aside, willing to let Scott and the pilot unload the primate passengers and settle them and their cages into the back of the pickup. She climbed into the passenger's side and waited while Scott and the pilot maneuvered the plane into the hangar.

Finally he was seated beside her. Scott started the motor and stretched out his arm to pull her close. "You don't know how much I've missed you," he whispered as they started back to the ranch. "There's so much I want to talk about, so many things we have to get settled."

"Settled? What are you talking about?" A small warning bell went off inside Rani's head. Much as she loved being near Scott, she felt instinctively that their relationship had to slow down. There was too much at stake to rush into the future.

"I don't know what I mean exactly. Look, I don't believe in one-night stands. And I know you're not looking for that, either. We want more than a short roll in the hay. What we haven't talked about is what the boundaries of our relationship are going to be."

It sounded so cut-and-dried the way Scott was putting it, as if they were going to be presented with a contract drawn up by an attorney and signed in front of witnesses. Rani wasn't ready for that. What was driving her to distraction was that she didn't know what she was ready for. She was like a runaway horse tempted by sweet apples and yet afraid that another rope might settle around her neck. "Do we have to say anything?" she asked. "Can't we take it one day at a time and see what develops?"

Scott shook his head with a gesture that left no doubt as to what his feelings were. "Not from where I see it. Rani, we aren't a couple of eighteen-year-old kids. We're responsible for the future of our children. I'm the father of a boy who's looking for a role model as he approaches adulthood. I don't want him to see his old man sleeping with a woman and nothing else."

"Please don't put it like that," Rani interrupted. "That makes it sound sordid."

"Does it? Look, Dean's only three years old, so you aren't facing the same thing I am. I see Chad falling in love in a few years. When that happens, I want him to believe that commitment goes along with physical attraction. He's not going to understand what commitment means unless his old man gives him some guidelines."

Commitment. There was that word again. Rani was commited to her son. Even in her darkest moments she'd never wavered from that. But loving and caring for her son was instinct. What she felt for Scott, what could develop went beyond instinct. And now, because of Zack, she was afraid of looking beyond today with Scott. She hadn't had the wisdom to see what Zack really was before it was too late or the courage to demand that he accept certain responsibilities, make crucial, necessary changes. What made her hope she could succeed in any relationship?

"You're going too fast for me," she admitted, averting her eyes from the answers his eyes demanded. "Scott, we haven't known each other very long. People don't fall in love that fast." Or did they? If what she felt for Scott wasn't love, it was only a whisper away.

"In other words, it's time to put on the brakes. Is that what you're telling me?" Scott sounded bitter. "I don't have much choice, do I?" After a moment of silence while he concentrated on the road, Scott continued. "Rani, there's something I want you to understand. I've been single a lot longer than you have. I've experienced just about every relationship there is for a man to experience. This time it's different. I'm not going to be content with dates and nights playing bed games. I want more. I'm not going to push the issue right now," he reassured her, "but I want you to know how I feel. I want a hell of a lot more from you than what we've had so far."

Rani pulled herself into a tight ball and closed her eyes. There was no misunderstanding what Scott was saying. Part of her ached to respond to his words. It would feel so good to place her future in Scott's hands, but her past was getting in the way. She'd trusted a man once before and he'd deserted her, jeopardized their son's life. She was left with the one thing that remained of that relationship—a very special little boy. "Give me some time. I have made too many mistakes already. I won't let that happen again."

Scott didn't pick up the threads of their conversation again. He spoke little during the ride back to the ranch.

When he did it was to ask questions related to the training program.

Rani brought him up-to-date on the preliminary training that was taking place, and as they pulled into the ranch, she mentioned that Chad was having reservations about going to school. "I've seen it coming," Scott said as they were getting out. "When he was in California he used his fists to gain acceptance. That's what his friends were doing. He's going to have to learn a whole new way of communicating." Scott laughed. "I think I got the kid out of there just in time. I would probably have had a prize fighter on my hands if I'd let things slide much longer. Either that or a kid with a permanently bent nose."

"I find that hard to believe," Rani said as she was assisting Scott in the unloading. As a way of illustrating the maturity she saw in Chad, she told Scott about Chad offering to put a batting helmet on Dean. "He certainly knows how to deal with a nervous mother."

Scott gave her a positively lecherous look. "I have ideas of my own on how to deal with you."

Chad had offered to keep Dean with him while Rani went to the airport to pick up Scott. Now the growing teenager and his small passenger were loping out of the house and toward the truck. Rani swept her son off Chad's shoulders and hugged him close. For a moment the wash of love surging over her made speech impossible. She covered Dean's face with kisses. What she wasn't ready for was the blank stare that probably wouldn't have been noticed by anyone else.

Dean had seemed a little lethargic all day. He clung to his mother as she worked with the dogs and fell asleep without finishing his lunch. By the time he woke up from his nap there was no ignoring the fact that he wasn't his usual self. Nothing his mother did pleased him. "My head hurts," he whimpered when she tried to press him about what was the matter.

"Maybe I should take him to his pediatrician," Rani told Scott when she mentioned Dean's changed behavior. "If he's getting sick, I want to start treating it right away."

"I wouldn't put it off," Scott seconded her. "Do you want me to go with you?"

Rani shook her head. "You've been gone for days. You've got enough going today to keep you up half the night." She smiled up at him to let him know she appreciated his gesture and was rewarded with a kiss that might have made both of them forget the day's schedule if Dean hadn't been in the room.

The pediatrician, who had all of Dean's medical records from California agreed to squeeze him in that afternoon. That left her with just enough time to load Dean's mattress back into her car and get the boy ready for the trip. She was glad Scott was mending a fence a lovestruck bison had tried to go through; otherwise he might have said something about her decision to stay at her apartment whenever he was at the ranch.

"I wouldn't let it upset you," the pediatrician told her after examining Dean. "Your instincts are right. He isn't getting a cold or one of those things kids are always getting. What's happening is that his body's reaction to the Dilantin he receives is changing. I'm going to want to adjust the dosage."

"What happened?" Rani remembered to ask.

The doctor smiled. "Your little boy is growing up, and because he is, his body chemistry is changing. We simply have to make allowances for that. Mrs. Lassen, Dean has come a phenomenal distance in the past few months.''

"I know that," she said. "But isn't there more I can do? I want all of this behind him."

"You can let him be a little boy. Let him experience life. He was telling me about this ranch you take him to. He loves it. In fact, it sounds like a place I'd like to go to myself. Fresh air and outdoor living is exactly what he needs after all the time he spent in a hospital. Another thing: if you're relaxed about his environment, he'll sense that.''

The doctor's words stayed with Rani as she treated Dean to an ice-cream cone and then drove back out to Sol Valley. Rani had been staying at her apartment as a way of keeping distance between Scott and her while she tried to map out the parameters of their relationship. Now she was no longer sure she was doing what was best for everyone involved. A long ride twice a day plus spending his nights where there was no place to play outside wasn't what was best for Dean.

And Dean's needs came first in Rani's heart. Living at the ranch provided him with fresh air, and a ready-made way for him to get physical exercise under her supervision, to say nothing of the stimulation of being around other people. He disliked the apartment as much as she did. The training cabin was now furnished, complete with a working bathroom and kitchen appliances. She and Dean could live there.

The question she wasn't ready to answer was whether she'd be able to find the breathing room she believed she needed when it came to Scott. It was possible that being around him twenty-four hours a day would break down her fragile defenses before she'd made her peace with the past. She doubted her ability to see him constantly and not be drawn into the gentle web she already felt encompassing her. It was hard enough to avoid surrendering to him physically as it was. If he was always there—

Rani put an end to her whirling thoughts. The reality was that Dean would be much better off living at the ranch instead of cooped up in an apartment with two long drives each day. She wouldn't have to get him up so early. Scott had already offered her the training cabin to live in. She'd take him up on it, but only if he agreed to let her set the rules. She wasn't going to become his live-in lover. He had to understand she needed breathing space even if she couldn't tell him it was because she had already botched up one relationship.

"Do you really think you can get that contract to stick?" Scott asked her late that night after Dean was asleep and Chad was curled up in the living room watching TV. Scott and Rani were up at the training cabin talking about how to move her furnishings into the rooms and still allow training of the dogs to go on during the day.

"What do you mean?" Rani asked. "Aren't you going to honor it?"

"That's only half of the question." Scott closed a window to shut off the occasional yapping of the dogs housed in the nearby kennel. "It takes two people to make love. It takes two to decide to put on the brakes. And when that happens, there isn't much of a relationship left."

"Scott, I don't know what I mean," she relented.

"The other night, with you—I'm not going to try to tell you it wasn't a beautiful experience. But like you said, we aren't a couple of kids. We have children to consider. I don't want to simply become your lover."

"I'm not asking you to. I never said that." He was staring at her across the length of the living room with its still-unfinished floor. "I'm willing to explore this relationship of ours. I happen to believe it can lead somewhere good. You're the one who's afraid to give it a chance."

"Can you blame me?" she asked. "I need to learn more about myself. I wasn't walked out on that long ago. Things—things happened that I haven't learned to deal with yet, let alone tell you about."

Scott's eyes smoldered. "I'm not Zack. I didn't walk out on my son. I'm not going to bail out on any kid."

"Dean isn't any kid. He—"

"I know what he is. Don't read things into what I say that aren't there," Scott pressed. "Damn! Look, we're not going to get anywhere tonight. You need to set up housekeeping for yourself and Dean. I want to help you. We'll figure out what this means in terms of you and me later."

Rani seized on the reprieve Scott was giving her. She knew she was only postponing the inevitable, but psychoanalyzing herself and her ability to handle a relationship in a mature fashion was not something she wanted to do tonight.

Silently Scott took her hand and led her back through the night to his house. He stopped just outside the door and turned her toward him. He didn't ask, didn't try to explain. His lips found hers in the dark. "This isn't going to hurt anything. It's what we both need. I want you to sleep in my bed tonight," he said, his voice so low she could still hear the rumble from the TV inside. "I'll take the couch."

Rani looked up at him and then dropped her head to the comfort of his chest. "You don't have to do that."

Scott laughed softly. "Yeah, I do. I happen to have a very curious son. He's going to take note of who sleeps where tonight. He's no dummy; he knows something's going on between us."

"I don't see how," Rani protested. "We were at my place when it—" She stopped.

"When we made love," he finished for her. "True. But there's no way we can hide certain sparks that seem to be set off every time we get next to each other. Rani, that colt in there is an adolescent. He'd have to be blind not to notice that his old man is attracted to a certain woman. He knows what usually happens when two people are attracted to each other."

"Oh." The thought worried Rani. She'd been concerned enough as it was trying to determine how much potential pain, to say nothing of embarrassment, Chad might have to assume if he continued to be around Dean. That concern was multiplied now that she realized Chad knew two adults as well as two young people were involved. "We have to be careful."

"Because of Chad? Or because you're afraid to let your emotions have free rein? I just wish you trusted me enough to tell me what has you tied up in knots. I think it'd be a lot easier for all of us."

Rani drew away from Scott's probing question, or at least as far as his arms allowed her to pull back. "You won't leave that alone, will you?" she challenged. "I thought we were going to drop the subject."

"I tried, honestly, but it isn't easy. I can't help but think about where we're heading. Or could be heading when you're in my arms like this."

"Then maybe I shouldn't be in your arms," she shot at him, her voice at odds with what she was feeling inside. "Maybe I should have never gone to work for you."

"It would be safer for you, wouldn't it?" His challenge was equal to hers. "But it's too late for that now. You can't walk out of my life because I'm not going to let you. Do you understand that? You've done things to me that can't be easily undone. You mean too much to me for that."

Do I? Scott, if only you knew how much I need to hear that. Rani stopped her futile struggle and settled back against Scott's chest. He might hate her if he knew what a spineless wife she'd been, but she wasn't going to face that possibility tonight. "I don't know what you're doing to me," she whispered. "I've never felt this confused about anything in my life."

"That makes two of us." He laughed. "But it's too late to try to hassle that out. We've both had a long day. It's time we went to bed."

"Bed?" she repeated from the circle of his arms.

"Separate beds," he whispered. "Although that isn't what I want, and I don't think it's what you want."

She wouldn't answer him. As he opened the door and let her inside, she surrendered to the warmth of his body close to hers, grateful that, complicated as their relationship was, they already understood what those complications were.

At least there were only two adults and their children involved.

Chapter Eight

The phone rang as Rani, Scott and Chad were loading her bedroom furniture from the apartment into the ranch pickup. Rani paused, puzzled. Her phone was unlisted and almost the only calls she received were from her parents. They knew she was in the process of moving and wouldn't call unless it was an emergency.

"Hon," her father began. "I got a phone call for you last night. He wanted to know where you were living. I didn't want to give out your phone number until I'd checked with you."

"Who?" Rani interrupted. Since her father's heart attack he'd shown signs of slowing in his mental faculties. She often had to go back over his conversations to piece together what he meant. "*Who* called for me?"

"Zack. He wants to get in touch with you."

Rani felt her legs and arms go numb. She sat down quickly to keep from feeling fainter than she already did. Since the divorce Zack had been sending child-support checks to her parents' address. He'd never asked for her address. "What did you tell him?" she managed around the buzzing sensation that filled her head.

"Nothing," her father reassured her. "It was a short conversation and not a pleasant one for either of us. I told him I'd relay his message and he could call me later to hear your reply."

"Thank you. That sounds best," Rani said, aware that Scott was standing over her but too shaken to acknowledge his presence. "Do you know where he was calling from?"

"Sacramento, I suspect. He didn't say, but the connection wasn't that good. What do you want me to tell him?"

Tell him I've left the country. Tell him I don't remember who he is. No. She couldn't do that. "I don't know," she admitted. "I'm sorry, Dad. That doesn't help you, does it? I have to take a little time to get used to the idea. You don't know what he wants? He didn't say anything?"

"He wants to get in touch with you, but why I have no idea. Like I said, the conversation was strained. If you want, I'll tell him you don't want to have anything to do with him."

Good old dad. When she and Zack were married her parents had shown affection for Zack. Now they were squarely in her camp, listening when she felt like talking but not asking too many questions. But she couldn't agree to her father's suggestion. If she did, she'd have to live with never knowing why Zack wanted to get in touch with her. She turned searching eyes up at Scott, found the strength she was lacking, and told her father to give Zack the number at the ranch. "I'll fill you in on the details when and if he gets in touch with me," she promised her father. "You don't suppose he's having a delayed attack of conscience?'' she asked before hanging up.

"You don't want to talk to him, do you?" Scott asked. He was rubbing the back of her neck, his strong fingers easing some of the tension that had sprung up in her at the mention of Zack's name.

"I'd much rather bury my head in the sand and hope he'd go away,'' Rani admitted. "Does that sound like I'm a coward? Maybe I am. I just didn't expect this. Why now?'' she asked, her question directed more at herself than at the man helping her regain her grip on her nerves. "What could he possibly want?"

"There's one way to find out. Wait for him to call."

"I don't have much choice, do I? Scott, what if he wants to see Dean?" A sudden chill gripped Rani.

"Are you afraid of him?"

Rani turned the question around and around before attempting to answer Scott. "No," she said softly. "Maybe I'm afraid of my emotions."

"Do you still care for him?"

Rani gasped. But the *no* building inside didn't come out. "I've tried not to feel anything for Zack," she said honestly. "When he first walked out on us I felt nothing but hate. And relief. But then I realized that hate wasn't going to help Dean. No matter what happened, Dean still has a father. Zack's a quick-tempered man, but there were times when he truly loved Dean. I don't want Dean's thinking to become twisted because he believes his mother hates his father. Does that make sense? When the time comes, I want Dean to come to his own conclusions about his father."

Scott was rubbing her arms. Another time she might

have responded physically to his touch. Now she felt as if she were a frightened animal in the hands of a caring human. "You say you tried not to feel anything about Zack," Scott pressed. "I don't see how that's possible. The two of you shared a lot, to say nothing of a bond that won't break as long as you have a child."

"I know." Rani laughed with the strength his touch was giving her. "I'm human. I can't help but be bitter and confused—and hurt."

Scott took a deep breath before pushing his point again. From the moment he'd known Rani was talking about her ex-husband, he'd had to fight an ever-tightening knot inside him. He didn't want the past cropping up again, certainly not until he felt surer about his position in Rani's heart. There was something that still bound Rani to Zack that went beyond their child. He didn't know what that something was, only that it might surface before any of them were prepared to deal with the ramifications. "What if he wants back in your life? How would you feel about that?"

"Oh, no, he can't want that!"

"It's a possibility." Scott leaned toward her, his words coming out despite his heart's desire to deny them. "He's had time to come to grips with what he did. Maybe his thinking has changed. After all, he is Dean's father. Maybe he wants more than just sending support checks."

"I won't let him!" Rani knew her words were irrational, but she couldn't help the way she was feeling. When it came to protecting her son, she could become a wild animal in her determination to protect what she held dear. Rani felt her muscles go taut, her head fill almost to bursting. After what he'd done, Zack had no right getting in touch with her. How dare he try to march into her new life this way!

"What are you going to do?" Scott pressed.

"Throw him out on his ear," Rani hissed, not caring how primitive she sounded. "Listen to me!" She laughed shakily. "I'd be tempted to go after him with a butcher knife if he dares to show up."

"That doesn't sound like the Rani Lassen I know." Scott kissed her lightly on the forehead. No matter how he felt, her emotions took priority. He had to remember that. "You're overreacting. You weren't ready for this. It has you pretty shaken up. You'll handle things when and if he wants to see Dean."

"I'm glad you have so much faith in me." Rani couldn't help but smile at the image of her standing in the doorway, huge knife poised over her head while Zack backed away. Smiling eased a little of the tension. She was no longer married. The old pecking order no longer existed. "I can't really order him off with a shotgun, can I?"

"Not if you don't want to wind up in jail. All I can say is, he has damn poor timing."

Poor timing turned out to be the order of the day. Last week Rani had decided that one of the dogs was simply too excitable to work out. Because the last thing she wanted to do was to have to return the little female to the humane society, she'd called the local newspaper to see if they would help her find a suitable home for it.

She hadn't even started unloading her belongings when the first of three families came out to the ranch to see the dog. "I'm sorry," she apologized to Scott as she was getting ready to take the people out to the run where the dog was. "I didn't know we'd have such a quick response."

Scott touched her playfully on the nose. "You go play adoption worker. I'll get Chad and a couple of the men to help me with the truck. Lilly would never forgive you if you didn't send her off with a family that likes a lot of energy in their dogs."

Choosing among the three families wasn't easy. All of them assured Rani that they had the room for a dog and would provide Lilly with the love she deserved. One family's three children simply couldn't keep their hands off Lilly, with the result that she was rushing between them in a frenzy. The second family admitted that they lived next to a street that was used as a truck route; Rani could just see Lilly losing her mind trying to decide which truck to bark at next.

In the end, the tail-wagging little dog was sent off with a couple who ran their own business from their home. Rani decided that since they would be around but occupied with their own activities, Lilly would have enough but not too much attention from humans. She still felt badly that Lilly hadn't worked out, but in the long run the adoption would probably be the best solution for everyone concerned.

"I think I'd like to take the phone off the hook and go hide somewhere," Rani said, sighing, hours later as she and Scott were setting up her bed in the bedroom of the training cabin. "From now on, I'm going to leave social work up to those who are trained for it. At least Lilly was too excited to give me the evil eye. Do you think she cares that she didn't make it through boot camp?"

"Now you sound like Chad worrying about the first

day of school," Scott pointed out. "Weren't you the one to tell him that everything was going to turn out all right?"

"All right." Rani held up her hands in surrender. "I'm not going to argue with you." She sighed. "Today was busy enough as it was." At least she was no longer asking herself whether she was making the right move by bringing Dean to live at the ranch. She liked being with Scott, liked it more than she wanted to admit.

"I won't argue that with you. I doubt if you've had time to notice, but the telephone company was here while we were at your place this morning. They're put in the amplifier for the telephone. Now we can give the dogs a taste of the real thing."

Rani nodded. She'd negotiated with the telephone company to get them to donate an amplifier system designed to let people with some hearing communicate over the telephone. Not that there would be any hearing-impaired people using the phone, but the dogs needed to get used to hearing loud voices coming from the instrument. "I'm glad. You would have approved of my approach. By the time I was done with them I think they thought they were giving us Christmas in the middle of summer." Suddenly, unexpectedly, she laughed. "All I need now is for Zack to reach me through the amplifier."

Scott walked around to the side of the bed where Rani was standing. "You could have gone all day without bringing his name up again. I hope you don't expect me to shake hands with the man."

"That's the last thing I'd ask of you. Just be behind me to prop me up if my legs turn to rubber."

"I'm going to be beside you, not behind you."

Rani turned toward Scott. "I'm sorry. I didn't mean for it to come out like that."

"I know you didn't." Scott smiled and winked. "But you understand what I'm saying, don't you? I'm not going to step out of the picture if and when what's-his-name shows up. You mean too much for me to do that. I hope you realize that."

"I do. Thank you. Scott, I wasn't looking for any-one—I'm not even sure what I'm going to do with you—but I'm glad you're here. What would I do without you?" The words came from the depth of her being.

"Probably starve," he teased, effectively erasing her dark mood. "I can see you now, selling pencils on a street corner. No, I don't think that would work. You just don't strike me as the type."

"Why not? You don't think I'd made a good pencil pusher?" she challenged, instantly enjoying the switch in conversation. "You don't think I could make my fortune as a salesman?"

"Tall, willowy women with enough hair for two people don't belong on street corners selling pencils. Besides, I think you have to wear dirty ragged T-shirts to get the job."

"Then it's a good thing you hired me."

"I know it was good for me."

As instantly as it had begun, the teasing quality left Scott's voice. He touched her on the cheek, a gentle contact. His eyes held her in the powerful net that now felt as natural as breathing. "Do you know what I've been thinking about today? I've done just about everything there is to do in a lifetime. I've met people most of us see only in the movies. None of that has brought me as much pleasure as helping you move out here."

"Do you mean it?" Did she really need that reassurance from him? His eyes were letting her see deeper than maybe even he realized.

"Don't ever doubt it." His hand moved under her jaw and gently pulled her closer. "Rani, from the first time I saw you I felt there was something special, something different happening. It isn't something that can be translated into words. It was simply there. I haven't changed my opinion."

"I'm honored," she returned, wishing she could duck her head to hide the color rising in her cheeks.

"I'm serious," he went on. "And it isn't just because you jumped into the middle of this job and started handling things I didn't even know were going to come up. You're not the kind of woman who backs down from anything. I admire that."

But I am backing away from what you want me to say about a commitment, Rani admitted to herself. His hand holding her face was strong. His green, probing eyes were just as strong. There was only one way she could sidestep the answer he wanted. Rani closed her eyes, reached out and found Scott's mouth. She let herself be pulled into the circle of his arms, knowing how quickly her body would respond and block out the need to think.

There was risk in surrendering to Scott, but tonight physical contact was what she needed. She'd told him she could only handle one day at a time. In this case it was one night at a time. Tonight she needed his strength and masculinity.

"Are you sure this is what you want?" Scott asked. "If you're turning to me because of that phone call—"

"Is that wrong?" she moaned. "Scott, I'm not as strong as you think I am. I don't always want to stand alone."

"You don't have to." His gentle kisses along her temple and down the side of her neck were his way of telling her he understood. "Everyone needs someone."

And I need you. More than I dare admit. Rani didn't use words to let Scott know what she was thinking. She offered him her mouth and later her body as proof that she'd gone as far as she wanted on her own. What they shared on the newly set-up bed in the training cabin was more than lovemaking. It was the joining of the two hearts into a single unit. Rani didn't ask if those two would continue to beat as one past this night. The answer was important, essential to her future, but now wasn't the time to ask for the answer.

She wanted to make love to Scott and spend the night sleeping next to him. That was what her heart and body craved. What her mind wanted was something she couldn't answer. She could only pray he would be satisfied with that evening's pleasure.

If he wanted more, Scott didn't mention it. This time Rani woke before he did, quickly slipped into her clothes and was already tending to Dean when Scott joined her. "I'm going to leave now," he said. "I don't know if Chad noticed that I didn't sleep in my bedroom last night."

"Oh, Scott, I'm sorry. I didn't think—"

He stopped her. "That's my problem, not yours. I made a decision to stay with you last night. I don't regret it." He cupped her right breast, pulled her against him and continued. "But I am going to have to sit down and have a talk with my son. Explain to him that his old man has certain needs."

Rani let him go. She wanted to tell him that he didn't need to have such a conversation with Chad because there wasn't going to be another night like last night. But she knew she couldn't say that. Last night had been as essential as breathing itself. The morning held a glow she'd never experienced before. It came, she knew, because the woman in her was satisfied.

She also knew she wasn't going to get away with telling herself that she was going to stay out of Scott's bed. "He's a very special man," she told Dean as she prepared their first meal in the new kitchen. "I don't know of any other man who would put up with someone as confused as your mother."

"Scott can make Gas lie down," Dean announced. "He's going to show me how."

"Oh, no, you don't, young man," Rani warned. "I don't want you ever to forget that Gas is off-limits. You'll spend a week in your room if I catch you near that big cat." At the sight of Dean's crestfallen face Rani relented. "When you get older, maybe you'd like to help train the dogs. Would you like to do that?"

Dean nodded vigorously. "I know how to make them bark."

"I don't doubt that," said Rani, laughing to herself. Dean looked brighter-eyed already. Thank heavens she hadn't delayed getting him to the doctor. The decision to act had been made with Scott. That was even more proof, as if she needed it, that more existed between them than simple physical attraction.

Scott was already at work on the ranch by the time she and Dean entered the office. He'd left her a note to the effect that their volunteer fund-raiser had arranged to have a photographer take some pictures in a few days and would Rani think about what kinds of shots would be the most effective. Chad was busy cleaning the dogs' kennels, which meant she wouldn't have to face him for a while.

She jumped every time the phone rang that morning, but none of the voices at the other end of the line belonged to her ex-husband. Because Dean was still acting a little weak, she spent extra time attending to his needs and skipped the morning session with the dogs. It was lunchtime before she'd done half the paperwork she'd wanted to accomplish that morning.

She was in the kitchen feeding Dean when the phone rang. "I'll get it," Chad yelled from the office. Rani held her breath but when Chad didn't immediately call for her she relaxed. She didn't notice Chad entering the kitchen until she sensed his presence beside her elbow. "It's for you. A Mr. Lassen."

Rani turned stricken eyes in Chad's direction. "Oh," she managed, her hand fluttering to her throat.

"Are you going to answer it?" Chad reached for Dean's sandwich and pretended to eat it, which brought a howl from Dean and a hearty bite when he rescued the sandwich.

"I don't want to. Talk about unwanted voices from the past," Rani said shakily. When Chad's eyes asked too many questions, she turned and left the kitchen. Chad knew who it was. There was nothing she needed to say.

The office, which she'd always considered cozy, seemed to have shrunk. The air was too thick to fill her lungs. Rani stared at the phone, hating the black monster. But there was no putting off what had to be done. She picked up the receiver and spoke into it.

"Where were you?" Zack asked. "I thought maybe you weren't going to answer."

"What do you want, Zack?"

"I want to see Dean."

"No!" The strangled cry escaped before Rani could hold it inside her. "What do you want to see him for?" she asked with as much self-control as she could muster.

"What do you mean? He's my child, too. Rani, don't be like this. Do you think this is easy for me?"

If Zack expected her to apologize for her outburst, he was going to be disappointed. Rani had handled too much on her own to think her ex-husband's feelings came first. There were no longer guidelines to their relationships. "I'd like to know why this sudden change in you," she said boldly now that she'd gotten used to sound of his voice. "I find it hard to understand why you were content with no contact for months and now you're getting in touch with us."

"Come on, Rani. I'm not as coldhearted as you'd like to make me out to be. Sure, I felt like I'd been punched in the stomach when I heard about the—you know. But I've had time to adjust to the idea of what's wrong with him. Dean still needs a father. If that sounds like I've done some growing up, maybe that's what has happened. I'm talking to you, aren't I?"

Rani gripped the receiver so hard that it became a physical pain. She shrank from the sudden attack on her nerves. She didn't want Zack around. She and Dean had a life without him. "How generous of you!" she spat out. "It's a shame your maturation was delayed so long. I hope you understand if I find it hard to believe you."

"I should have known you'd be bitter," Zack said. "You're going to hold my leaving over my head, aren't you?"

"It's possible. Do you blame me?" She hated sounding like a shrew but didn't know how to stop herself. "Zack, you walked out on us. Your actions told me you wanted nothing to do with your own child."

"I was in shock. Those attacks he was having— Damn it, I had so many dreams for my son. When I found out what was wrong with him—"

"You couldn't handle it. Zack, do you realize that I've never heard you say the word *epilepsy*. You took the easy way out. You were gone *before*—before the bad part was over. You never would admit your responsibility. I don't think it ever occurred to you that I might need someone to help me during that period."

"I'm sorry about that. I want to try to make it up to you."

Rani wasn't at the point of being able to believe him. She could handle an argument; his contrite tone threw her off balance. "How?" she managed.

"By coming to see you and Dean. He has a right to know who his father is."

Rani shut her eyes in an attempt to shut out the emotions assaulting her. Having Dean to herself was a routine she was settled into. Her world would be turned around if Zack reentered it. "I don't know," she stalled. "I've just moved. I have a new job."

"Rani, don't put me off. I'll come anyway. There's nothing you can do to stop me."

"I'm not going to run away from you, Zack," she said, her emotions firmly held in check. "But I'm not going to welcome you with open arms, either. Dean and I have made a new life for ourselves."

"And I'm not welcome in it. Is that what you're trying to tell me? Don't answer that. I already know what you're going to say. Rani, give me a chance. I made a mistake by bailing out the way I did. I want to make it up to you. When can I see you? Please.''

A minute later Rani was hanging up the phone. She glanced in the kitchen to make sure Chad was busy with Dean and walked outside. She felt totally numb, her thoughts going no further than each step she was taking.

Without thinking about it, Rani made her way up the hill to Gaspar's run. She wrapped her hands around her upper arms as if trying to rock herself and stood staring at the dozing mountain lion. Maybe Gas had to live behind bars, but his life was a simple one. He didn't have to hunt in order to keep his belly full. How peaceful life would be if she could change places with the mountain lion, be the one Scott brought food to. Gas never felt as if his head were going to burst.

Rani heard footsteps behind her but didn't turn around. She sensed it was Scott and accepted the warm feeling of relief that washed through her numb body. When his arms went around her, she leaned back into his chest. "Do you feel like talking about it?" he whispered. "You look like you've been run over by a steamroller.''

"It's Zack. I don't know what he wants. I said things I probably shouldn't have," Rani moaned, trying to pull together the fragments of emotion generated by the telephone conversation. "I don't think he's the same man who walked out on me.''

"When is he coming here?''

Rani took a deep breath before saying the word that had made her flee. "Tomorrow. He wouldn't be put off. I couldn't refuse to let him see his son.''

"What if I won't let him set foot on the property?"

Rani pulled back from Scott's embrace. "What! You can't mean—"

"Of course not." Scott sighed. He could tell she was upset by the conversation with Zack, but nothing in her actions made him think that she might be looking forward to seeing her ex-husband. Scott took comfort in that. "At least not in a deliberate way, but what if the bison happened to get loose about then? You don't suppose that might scare the character off, do you? Rani, I don't want that man around. I'm not just thinking about Dean. I happen to want you all to myself."

Rani admitted that she felt flattered, but Scott's words were also a trap. Two men and a little boy were tugging at her. The only one she could give herself to without reservation was the child waiting for her to return. When she thought about making love to Scott, Rani could easily forget everything except the emotions that took her out of the everyday world. But denial and desertion and divorce had made her gun-shy when it came to men. She'd let Zack dominate her. His temper had marked the boundaries of their relationship. Possibly Scott had a similar flaw of his own. She needed more time than she'd had to determine that.

"You haven't said anything," Scott whispered after they'd been standing for several minutes watching Gas's restless movements within his run. "What were you thinking when I said I'd like to have you all to myself?"

"Scott, don't do this to me." She couldn't take her eyes off the big cat. It couldn't feel any more confined than she did at the moment. "I feel as if I'm being torn into a thousand pieces. I'm scared of what's going to happen tomorrow."

"And that's all you can think of. Is that what you're trying to tell me?"

"I don't know what I'm trying to say," Rani moaned, no longer able to take warmth from Scott's embrace. "You haven't been through what I have. You don't know what it was like." Of course he couldn't know. She hadn't told him everything.

"I know more than you give me credit for. Rani, I think I've been a hell of a lot closer to you than your ex-husband ever was."

"How can you say that?" Rani forced herself to meet the anger in Scott's eyes. "Zack and I were married."

"Marriage isn't everything," Scott pointed out. He knew he was being hard on her, but as much as that bothered him, he also knew she had to work her way through certain emotions if she was ever going to be free. What he didn't know was where they would stand with each other once that was accomplished. "So you were bound by a piece of paper. Big deal! When the going got rough, the marriage fell apart."

"So did yours," Rani said without thinking. "Don't tell me what a failure I was."

Scott stopped her with a look that tore through her and stripped the strength from her legs. "Oh, yes, I know all about failed marriages. About not enough commitment to make things last. But I also know what commitment is." He stopped and waved his hand over the landscape, his forefinger jabbing at the training cabin and dog runs. "I'm not doing that because I need a tax write-off. I never stopped being a father."

"I know that," Rani whispered. She had gone from rage to emotional exhaustion in the space of a breath. "I didn't—"

"Let me finish." Scott was no longer touching her, but the bond between them was just as powerful. "I don't know what the hell this ex-husband of yours is up to. All I know is, if Dean had been mine, I would never have walked out on him—no matter what. Look, we're going to have to continue this another time. There happens to be a bison with a gash on its leg I have to tend to. That's what I mean by responsibility."

Before Rani could answer, Scott turned away. She hadn't known about the injured bison, but there was always one animal or another on the ranch that needed Scott's attention. In the summer they had to have water and shade. In the winter feed had to be brought in to supplement what was in the pastures. In the spring there were new lives and occasional medical emergencies involving those new lives. Scott accepted all that as part of his job. Missing animals, middle-of-the-night emergencies, frightened wild animals who needed calming—he handled them all.

Rani could have called after him, stopped the relentless steps taking him away from her, but she didn't. The words coming from her heart died in her throat.

Not even the restless, watchful mountain lion heard what she wanted to say. "I know you'd never walk out on someone you love."

Chapter Nine

Thursday was one day Rani needed to be alone with her thoughts, but in the morning some members of a local organization considering sponsorship of one of the dogs came for a tour of the place. Fortunately the group, retirees belonging to a travel group, were both enthusiastic about the program and actively in search of a local project to get behind. As she introduced them to the dogs she found herself getting caught up in questions and answers, which gave her the opportunity to forget her personal problems.

In the end the white-haired man with the cane who was president of the club polled the members. It wasn't a question of whether they would sponsor a dog, but of which one they would choose. "It looks like the women win. As usual," the man informed Rani. "How about putting our name next to the one that looks like a big cotton ball." He shook his head in mock disapproval. "If it were up to me, I'd hold out for a greyhound, something that lets people know we're interested in the open road."

"No purebreds here, I'm afraid," Rani pointed out

as she mentally gave the dirty-white cotton ball of a dog the name Rambler. "We really appreciate this," she added. "We hope other organizations will also do what you have."

When Scott's accountant stopped by an hour later he gave the nod to what the group had done. "Publicity isn't my line," he said as he handed Rani some IRS forms to fill out concerning the nonprofit organization. "But whoever is handling your publicity should capitalize on that. Get service groups thinking sponsorship. Scott can't underwrite the entire program."

"I know." Rani's thoughts turned to Scott. She'd barely seen him today, and then from a distance. She couldn't blame him for avoiding her. After all, unless she was distracted by business she seemed incapable of speaking without snapping and jumped whenever anyone so much as talked to her. "Can you tell me something?" she asked the accountant in an attempt to keep her mind on business. "Is what he's doing going to hurt Scott financially?"

"Not if I have any say in the matter." Unexpectedly the accountant smiled. "We have to keep an eye on that man. Sometimes he gets so carried away by this new project that he forgets he has to pay the same bills he always has. But I might have something brewing myself that will help the program."

Rani cocked her head and stared at the accountant until her curiosity was satisfied. "I probably shouldn't say anything yet, but I'm about ninety percent sure that a dog-food company is going to cover the cost of feeding the dogs. Of course they'll get double their money back in the publicity angle, but we don't care as long as it works to the program's advantage, do we?"

"That's great!" Rani said excitedly. "I had no idea you were working on something like that."

"I'm a devious person," the accountant said, winking. "Actually, getting the company president to put his name on the dotted line has been the most stimulating thing I've done in weeks." The accountant picked up his briefcase and headed toward the door. "What Scott's doing is contagious, I guess."

Scott's contagious, at least with me, Rani thought before her mind unwillingly went back to thoughts of Zack. She'd given him directions out to the ranch but had no idea what time to expect him. One minute she was berating herself for not asking, and the next she was raging at him for being so inconsiderate as to leave her up in the air like this. She finally realized that Zack's behavior today was a continuation of what had taken place while they were married. Zack had come and gone as he pleased. She had demanded no accounting of his time and as a result received none. A divorce wasn't going to change the established order.

After Dean's nap, Rani kept him with her while she observed the afternoon training session. She knew Dean would rather be off with Scott while he got the male llama accustomed to carrying a pack for an upcoming movie, but she wanted her son with her when Zack showed up. She tried to distract Dean by having him keep track of how many times she had to ring the doorbell before a dog named Spring responded, but because Dean had yet to show a real interest in learning to count, she was meeting with limited success. At least she could share Spring's trainer's pleasure when the gray-black dog finally received a dog biscuit as reward for running to the door, cocking his head back and forth several times and then trotting to the trainer, whining nervously. Spring still had to learn to make physical contact with the trainer instead of whining, but at least the dog was starting to get the idea.

Spring was being taken back to his kennel for a rest and another dog had been brought in when the sound Rani had been keyed up for all day reached her. A car was pulling into the drive, and the other anticipated visitors for the day had already come and gone. Rani took a deep, gulping breath, took a confused Dean by the hand and walked out of the cabin into the afternoon sunlight.

Zack was getting out of his car, sunglasses shading much of his face. Rani took two steps and stopped. Zack was the one who had wanted this meeting, so let him come to her.

Rani wondered if he was walking more slowly than usual or if her nerves had turned everything into slow motion. She thought about saying hello. This was, after all, the man she'd been married to not long ago.

No. Hello sounded too...friendly. Let him accept her silence. It was all she was capable of.

As he came close enough for her to see that he was sweating from the heat, Rani caught a movement out of the corner of her eye. She turned briefly to see Scott standing by one of the corrals. He didn't move, and from where she stood, there was no way she could read what might be in his deep-green eyes. She was still looking at him when he walked away.

"It's hot out here," Zack said by way of greeting. He ran a hand over his upper lip and bent his back as if to relieve kinks in it. Zack, she now remembered, had problems with his spine despite his slender, well-muscled build. "I had no idea the place would be this isolated."

"The operation needs a lot of room," she explained briefly, wondering at her ability to carry on a civilized conversation. "And the air out here is fantastic for Dean. That's why we're living here."

"In the ranch house?" Zack pointed at the building that housed Scott's living quarters and the office. "You're doing well for yourself. That's a lot bigger than the house we had."

Rani shook her head, unable to resist a smile as she pointed at the training cabin. "I'm afraid not. That's where Dean and I hang our hats. It's our home. The place does double duty as our quarters and training space for the dogs."

"You live in that? It isn't even finished on the outside."

"It doesn't need to be," Rani replied, clamping a lid on what was nearly a sharp retort. Had Zack always worn sunglasses that didn't permit her to see his eyes? She couldn't remember but knew she didn't like it. It forced her to admit how little she knew about the man whose emotions showed only when they exploded. She couldn't be sure, but she didn't think he'd more than glanced at the little boy staring silently at him. "Don't you want to say hello to your son?" she asked, not caring if she was asking Zack to do something he wasn't ready for.

"Sure, of course," Zack said too quickly for the words to be natural. "He has grown, hasn't he? And it looks like he's put on weight." Zack held out his arms, but Dean squirmed around behind Rani until he could shield his head behind her arm.

Rani looked at Dean. For a moment she considered turning Dean over to Zack, but that wouldn't be fair to her son. He hadn't seen his father in months. To him the man in the sunglasses and the sweat-stained shirt was a vague memory from the past. Besides, maybe Dean could sense the tension between the two people who were his parents and was reacting to that tension with unaccustomed silence.

"There's nothing wrong with Dean's growth rate. He doesn't need physical therapy anymore," Rani said, picking up the threads of the conversation. "He had some problems with his medication earlier this week, but other than that he has been fine. That's going to happen from time to time as he grows."

"That's good." Zack sounded as if he was having trouble holding up his end of the conversation. "You've found a good doctor for him here?"

"Of course. I'm using one the doctor in Sacramento recommended. That's my job, isn't it?"

Zack sighed. "I knew we were going to get into that. You have to get your digs in, don't you?"

"What digs?" If Zack wanted to argue, she wasn't going to back down from a confrontation. In the past she might have, but she no longer needed to temper what she said. They wouldn't be going home together, sharing the same bed.

"You know what I'm talking about." Zack lifted his glasses enough to wipe moisture off the bridge of his nose. "You can hardly wait to tell me how you've been sacrificing while I got off scot-free."

Rani turned partly around and draped her arm over Dean's shoulder. "This isn't a sacrifice. Everything I do for Dean is because I love him."

It might have been the heat, but Rani thought she saw Zack's shoulders sag for just a moment. "Forget I said anything," Zack said when the silence threatened to continue indefinitely. "What if you show me around the place? That might give the boy time to warm up to me."

The boy. Rani shrugged off the question of why Zack couldn't call his son by his name and turned her attention to a guided tour of the ranch. She took Zack to see the exotic animals and explained their purpose, but most of her conversation centered around the Dogs for the Deaf work being done. She didn't try to temper the enthusiasm she knew was in her voice. This was her work. Zack had a right to know how content she was with that aspect of her life.

"I never know what I'm going to wind up doing on any given day," she said. "This place has, I think, turned into the in place in the county. Everyone and his third cousin has a reason or excuse to see what we're doing. There's even a college student coming out here in a couple of days to incorporate our program into a term paper he's doing. A local writer is putting the final touches on an article for a dog magazine. Of course there's also the ASPCA, the health department and the CIA, for all I know. Those years of training guard dogs paid off," Rani admitted, hoping to find some part of her past as Mrs. Zack Lassen that was pleasant. "I didn't know I had such marketable skills until I applied for this job."

Zack stopped walking. His rigid posture brought her to a halt. "Don't get started about having to work. I don't know any divorced women these days who don't work."

"What did I say?" Rani countered. She'd been able to relax a little during the tour, but Zack's quick words were briging all the tension back.

"You had to make some crack about having to support yourself, didn't you?" Zack pressed. "Where's this boss of yours? He sounds as if he makes everything go his way. A real Midas touch. Not everyone is well enough off financially to underwrite a nonprofit organization."

"He is well off," Rani said, taking pride in being able to say that. "But he doesn't go around tooting his own horn. He's committed to helping deaf people. I admire him for that."

"I bet you do. What does he think of having an attractive single employee around? I think it's just too wonderful that he's letting you live on the ranch." Zack's tone left it clear that *wonderful* was the last thing he was thinking.

Rani chose to ignore Zack's crack. "What are your plans?" she asked because it looked as if Zack wasn't going to offer anything on his own. "Are you still living in Sacramento?"

"I don't know what my plans are. A lot depends on what happens in the next two days. Can't the kid walk without you holding his hand? You've been pulling him around for a long time."

Once again Rani reacted negatively to Zack's avoidance of Dean's name, but his comment exposed something she'd been ignoring. Yes, she didn't usually take Dean's hand much anymore, especially around the ranch. Maybe she was now because she wanted to be the one touching her son. She let go of the boy, noting, as she was sure Zack had, that Dean continued to stick close to her. "Zack, I have work to do this afternoon," she said. "I really can't take any more time showing you around."

"Is that so? We don't have to make nice conversation anymore?" Zack glanced at his watch. "I'll tell you what. I'm staying at a motel in town. What if I take Dean with me? It'll give him a chance to get used to me without you around."

Rani's breath caught in her throat. This she hadn't expected. "No! Zack, he doesn't remember you. He's going to think I'm letting him go off with a stranger."

"I'm no stranger. I'm his father."

"I know that," she relented, momentarily feeling sorry for the man who had nothing while her life was made complete by the presence of their son. But she sensed the tension in Dean. He didn't want to go with this man who had barely glanced at him. "Zack, can't you understand? Dean's going through a shy stage. Besides, he just got started on a new dosage of his medicine. I'm not sure how well he's going to tolerate it."

"Can't he get along without it for one night?"

"No."

Rani jumped. She wasn't ready for the deep voice behind her. She didn't have to turn around to know that Scott had joined them. Just as she was trying to gather her thoughts to reply, she realized that Dean had turned eagerly toward Scott and was being hoisted onto broad shoulders. "Where have you been, Scott?" Dean asked. "I've been looking and looking for you." Stammering, Rani attempted to introduce the two men.

The attempt failed. Neither Zack nor Scott stuck out a hand. Instead, Scott was insisting on continuing with what he'd started to say before. In fact, at the moment he couldn't care less whom he was making uncomfortable by his presence. He'd tried to tell himself that he'd stay in the background while the meeting was going on. But he had too much at stake. His future with Rani and Dean was on the line. He had a deep-rooted need to see what made Zack Lassen tick. "I happen to have a son of my own," Scott said. "He's not a shy three-year-old anymore, but I can remember how uncomfortable he was in new situations. I can't believe you'd want to force him into something he's not ready for." Scott stopped long enough to make it clear it was Zack he was directing his criticism toward. "If I wanted to make sure a little boy loved me, I sure as hell wouldn't push myself on him."

Rani could see Zack's jaw muscles working, but instead of sympathizing with him, she was on the verge of siding with Scott. She wasn't used to seeing Zack at a loss for words. Finally Zack managed to say something about not wanting to do anything to hurt Dean. Rani couldn't shake the sense that his voice held a note of relief.

"Scott's right," she said softly. "Dean is at a stage now where he's slow to reach out to other people."

Zack's eyes narrowed into the slits Rani remembered all too well. His temper was coming to the fore. That was one thing that hadn't changed. "Of course. And he's the boss, isn't he?" Zack spat out. "Aren't you lucky to have found a boss who's so solicitous of the kid."

Rani bristled. She wasn't going to knuckle under the way she used to. "The boy's name is Dean. It's the one we chose when he was born."

"I know what his name is." Zack ran a hand across

his face. "I don't want to fight with you, Rani, especially not with your bodyguard around. I think the best thing for me to do is to go back to the motel tonight. I'll be back out tomorrow," he finished decisively.

Rani didn't stand around long enough to wave Zack off. Using work as an excuse she took Dean from Scott and started back toward the cabin. Her legs felt strangely numb and her mind caught in the past. She had always hated Zack's temper. Now she refused to think about it. She wasn't aware that Scott was so close until she stumbled on the rocky ground and he steadied her. "It didn't look to me as if you two mended many fences," Scott observed.

"I don't like being that bitter. I don't like being forced into the past." Rani concentrated on the ground partly because she didn't trust her legs and partly because she didn't feel strong enough to meet Scott's eyes. "I don't know what I want," she moaned. "Maybe I was hoping for more from him than he's able to give. I hoped he'd changed some, become more like I wanted him to be. I won't ask for that anymore. Why can't he call Dean by his name?"

"Who knows? My guess is that's his way of keeping distance between himself and Dean. He probably wasn't even aware of what he was doing until you jumped him about it."

"Did I jump him?" Rani stopped and turned toward Scott. "Yeah, I guess I did. I sounded like a shrew. I don't like Dean hearing me talk like that. Oh, Scott, why do relationships have to be so complicated?"

"Because people are complicated. And the more intense the relationship, the more intense the backlash." Scott held on to Dean with one hand. He placed his right arm protectively around Rani's shoulder. "He's gone. You don't have to think about him anymore today."

Rani groaned and made a face. "I wish I could believe you. When I was a little girl I used to think that if I wished hard enough I could make the bad things go away. I tried to run my marriage that way." She laughed a little. "It didn't work then, and it isn't going to work now."

"I'm not so sure about that. I might be able to think of something that would take your mind off Zack Lassen." Scott winked, kissed Rani briefly and started the three of them back toward the training cabin.

Rani surrendered to the sensation of Scott's arm around her. She was no longer a child capable of believing in happily-ever-after endings or a wife hiding her head in the sand, but there was something about Scott—or maybe it was her reaction to him—that made it possible for her to believe he could take her mind off her ex-husband. They were at the door of the cabin before he said anything. "I'm taking Chad to the high school tomorrow. Football practice is getting started and he's decided to try out for the team. Would you like to join us? We could tour the school with Chad, watch practice and maybe go out for dinner. How's that for a hot time in the big city?"

Something warm spread through Rani and brought her to the edge of tears. That was the sort of thing a family did. Did Scott think of them as a family? After the way he'd held her at arm's length earlier today, she couldn't be sure. "Can you take the time from work?" she asked, wondering if her vulnerability to his warm gesture was as obvious as it felt.

"Chad's still uptight about school. This is something I want to make sure he follows through on now that he's made the decision to try out. I'd like you to be part of it."

Rani answered by putting her arms around Scott and pulling his head down to where she could reach his mouth. "Thank you," she whispered. "I didn't think you wanted anything to do with me after our words yesterday."

Scott shook his head. "That's yesterday. What I want to know is, how do you feel about watching football practice tomorrow afternoon?"

Rani grinned. "I'd love it." Then the thought hit her. "Zack. He's going to be back again tomorrow."

"So let him ask what time's convenient," Scott said through suddenly taut lips. "Why should you have to sit around all day waiting for him like you did today? He can't expect you to put your life on hold whenever he decides to play part-time daddy."

"Scott, I'm sure Zack doesn't expect that." In the space of a breath, they'd come close to an argument, but it wasn't something Rani could back away from. "I think he needs time to work through his feelings. He's never been very good at expressing them."

"What feelings? Whether he gives a damn about his son?" Scott was still holding Rani lightly, but he was staring at the ground, his tennis shoe absently kicking at several pebbles that a line of ants was marching around. "You're letting that man get away with murder. Either he wants to be a father or he doesn't. That's one decision he's a little late making."

"I don't want to argue," Rani warned, proud of herself because she'd never had the courage to tell Zack

that. "Why can't you and I talk about Zack? Every time
his name comes up, we wind up at odds with each
other."

"We do, don't we?" Unexpectedly Scott laughed.
"Well, I know how to avoid that." Despite the sounds
of activity coming from inside the cabin, despite the
possibility that Chad might come upon them at any moment, Scott took Rani in his arms and held her so close
that they were both lost. It was impossible for Rani to
think of anything except what Scott was doing to her
senses, her heart. His lips on hers were both sweet and
taunting. Could she keep their embrace from becoming
more than it was already?

Scott was asking himself the same question. He in-
haled the scent of her freshly shampooed hair. When
he had married Chad's mother he hadn't known that it
was possible for a woman to have an appeal greater
than the physical one. But he'd been much younger
then. Now he wanted to link his life to that of a woman
with responsibilities, opinions, commitments. *Strange,*
Scott thought, *how much we change over the years.* The
boy becomes a man. A girl takes on the yoke of
womanhood and the result is fascinating. "Hiring you
was the best thing I've done in a long time," Scott said
when they parted. "This certainly beats the usual
employer/employee relationship. True, it's complicated, but I can live with that."

Rani wondered if there was something in his observation that she should take offense to. No, her heart
answered as she surrendered to the emotions awakened
by his second kiss and the forbidden quality of what
they were doing. There was something terribly exciting
about sharing an intimate moment with the possibility

of being discovered by any one of a half-dozen people. "You never know when there's going to be a photographer around this place. You don't suppose we're going to be blackmailed, do you?" She clung to Scott, gathering strength from his.

It was Scott who finally reminded her that they were standing in the middle of a ranching and training operation, not locked off from the world in a darkened bedroom. "I hate to point this out," he whispered in her ear, "but there happens to be a very interested young man who is getting a kink in his neck from watching us."

Laughing, still feeling as if nothing bad could ever touch her again, Rani bent down to kiss her son's hand. "What do you think of your mommy kissing her boss?" she asked. "That's funny, isn't it?" For an instant she sobered. Tradition said it should be her son's father she was kissing. But that wasn't possible, and it served no purpose to dwell on that fact. "I wonder what Zack will think if he shows up as we're getting ready to go to the high school?" she observed. "I imagine he'll figure that there's something personal between us, if he hasn't already. Do you think that'll become a factor in how he feels about his son?"

"I don't know." Scott frowned. "It shouldn't, but then, I don't have any idea what that man is thinking about anything."

"That makes two of us," Rani admitted. "Why did I ever marry him?" Rani stopped long enough to gaze down at Dean. "At least one good thing came out of it."

"Two," Scott said softly. "It wasn't the way I would have wanted it for you or for Dean, but you obviously did a great deal of growing up as a result of that relationship. We all learn from experience," he went on as he reached for the cabin door. "Unfortunately, young lady, I promised to show my face at this particular training session. You know how it is. The boss has to show interest in his projects once in a while. Nose to the grindstone and all that."

Rani stopped him. She tried to keep her need for him out of her eyes but didn't know how well she succeeded. "It would be a lot easier if neither of us had any responsibilities, but—"

"But that isn't the way life is," Scott said before the activity born of a dog, a trainer and a malfunctioning oven timer took him away from her.

Rani trailed after him, with Dean pushing to get through the door before her. The poor dog, a long-legged mutt with small pointed ears, was going crazy because the oven timer wouldn't stop buzzing. He kept jumping up and planting his front paws against his handler's legs, whimpering until Scott finally disconnected the timer.

"That wasn't fair, was it, old boy?" Scott asked the dog. He was being careful not to touch the animal, who was being comforted by its trainer. Scott turned to Rani. "Here Rex has been trying so hard to do what we want him to, and now that he's made the connection between the oven timer and letting his trainer know about it, he can't get anyone to shut off the annoying sound. It's enough to make a self-respecting dog go on strike."

Rani linked her arm through Scott's, not caring that the trainer saw. "I think I'll join the club," she admitted, her head heavy from both the sound of the timer and the prospect of Zack's visit tomorrow. "I think I'll go on strike."

Rani's desire to go on strike hadn't completely disappeared when twenty-four hours later she was distracted from work because she was again listening for the sound of a car pulling into the drive. Zack hadn't called to let her know when he'd be back, but because that was the way Zack operated, she wasn't surprised. As a result Rani spent too much of last night vacillating between anger and confusion whenever she thought about Zack. She tried to tell herself she could understand that Zack needed time to come to grips with yesterday's visit and wasn't crazy about having to talk to his ex-wife, but it wasn't always easy. There was no denying that she was looking forward to the outing Scott had suggested. From watching Chad around the ranch she felt he had the coordination and strength it took to play football, but she wouldn't know for sure until she'd seen him next to the other high schoolers. Having Zack cling to the corners of her thoughts cast a damper on her enthusiasm.

Zack appeared while Rani was getting out Dean's medication. She was alone in the ranch house when he knocked on the door. She let him in and went back to what she was doing. She could feel his eyes on her, but she didn't look at him.

Finally: "He doesn't give you a hard time about it. You know what you're doing."

"It's something I had to learn," Rani said unemotionally.

"What are you, a nurse? I'm sorry. I don't know why every word you say winds up being about Dean and his problem."

"It doesn't and you know it," Rani pointed out, anger clawing its way up from her belly. "I could talk about the inflation rate if that's what you wanted to discuss." Rani looked up at Zack. He wasn't wearing sunglasses now, but his eyes were hard and unreadable. Something about the way he was clenching his jaw told her that he was holding something inside.

"There was a goose in the driveway when I came in," Zack said out of the blue. "I thought I was going to have to kick it before it would let me out of the car. Are the animals always allowed to run around loose?"

Rani had no idea why Zack was attacking the ranch's animals, but she wasn't going to let him sidetrack her that way. She put away Dean's medicine. Zack had never been able to admit that Dean's accident was a result of his temper. He wouldn't even stay in the room when the tests that identified Dean's epilepsy were taken. "What did you want to do today?" she asked, skirting around touchy words and emotions.

"You won't let me take Dean with me. I guess the next best thing is for him and me to spend some time together here. Do you think that's possible?"

Rani had a pretty good idea what Zack was doing. He was trying to make her feel guilty for being protective of Dean, and in some measure he was succeeding. She had refused to let her son and his father be alone together yesterday, and Zack had that simple right when it came to his son. She took a deep breath in order to hold at bay the instinct of a protective mother. "Of course," she said with forced lightness. "But he's going to need a nap sometime this afternoon; otherwise the world becomes more than he can handle. Please don't keep him out too long."

"Well, thank you. Are there any boundaries of this ranch you don't want me to cross over? Are you going to tell me to stay out of the corrals, not throw rocks at the bison?" Zack's clipped tones left no doubt of his anger. "I'd hate to do anything you don't approve of."

"Stop it," Rani warned, keeping her voice low because she was afraid Dean would be frightened if she allowed her emotions to show. "You're a father. I shouldn't have to tell you what's safe and not safe for a three-year-old boy on a ranch full of animals."

If Rani thought she could dismiss Dean and Zack from her mind as they went for a long walk and she returned to work, she was mistaken. Both Scott and Chad were tied up working with the monkeys Scott had brought to the ranch the other day and couldn't provide her with any distraction from her thoughts. She kept telling herself that her uneasy feeling was unreasonable and came about only because she wasn't used to turning Dean over to someone else. But that wasn't true. When Dean was with Scott or Chad she was able to concentrate on her work. The last time she entrusted Dean to his father's care they'd run into the back of another vehicle. No, that wasn't strictly true. She'd let Zack's insistence win over her own unease. She hadn't stood up to Zack.

An hour passed. Two. She was white-lipped because Zack was obviously ignoring her reminder that Dean needed his nap. Even if he wasn't in danger she knew her sunny little boy could turn into a cranky baby if deprived of his sleep. He might look worlds better than he had in the hospital, but his recovery wasn't complete. Rest was an essential element in his treatment. Years ago she might have chuckled at the thought of

Zack trying to cope with a boy who was so tired that nothing pleased him. But maybe Zack wouldn't recognize Dean's mood for what it was. Maybe he was getting angry at a whining boy. If Zack snapped at Dean. . . .

Rani almost cried out with relief when she finally spotted the two of them through the office window. Zack was holding Dean by one hand while Dean hung back, feet dragging, his face tear-streaked. Rani dropped what she was doing and raced outside. "What's going on?" she gasped as she freed Dean from his father's grip and pulled her son close. "Why is he crying?"

"You tell me!" Zack snapped back. "You've got that boy tied so close to your apron strings that he's an absolute baby around anyone else. You're going to really mess him up if you hoard him all to yourself that way!"

"What are you talking about?" Rani knew she shouldn't be yelling. Her mood was being matched by more sobs from Dean. But she was so upset at Zack that she couldn't stop herself. She wasn't married anymore. She didn't have to tiptoe around his temper. "Dean's no different from any little boy. He's okay with strangers after he's had time to get used to them."

"I'm no stranger, I'm his father. Do you know what he did the whole time we were together?" Zack snapped over the sounds of Dean's sobs. "He kept talking about his mother and Scott and some kid named Chad. He wasn't interested in a damn thing I had to say. I finally got him to stop yakking, but then he started whining and carrying on like a spoiled brat. I swear, I couldn't do anything right with that kid."

"He's tired." Rani buried Dean's head against her breasts, trembling in response to the shaking little body pressed against hers. "You can't drag him all over for a couple of hours without letting him rest."

Zack's head snapped back. "I thought there wasn't anything wrong with him physically."

"There isn't. He just needs a nap. Can't you see that?"

"I can't see anything. I can't think with all that yelling going on. It's ridiculous."

Rani turned on Zack. Obviously he had no idea what it was to be three years old. "Ridiculous? You're the one who isn't making any sense. Your son wouldn't be crying if you were capable of reading his body language. I *told* you he needed a nap. You can't expect him to run a marathon."

"I didn't say anything about a marathon!" Zack shot back in a tone Rani knew all too well. "I want to spend some time with my son. If he's going to become a man he's going to have to toughen up some."

"I don't believe I'm hearing this." Rani didn't care whether her face became contorted. She was fighting for something too essential to let conventional behavior get in the way. She'd always given in to Zack before. But not today and not ever again. "You want to make a man out of a little boy? What about all the necessary steps along the way? It wasn't so long ago that you were afraid to touch him because you thought he was going to break. Now you're rattling on about making him into a man. Can't you at least be consistent?"

Zack seemed surprised that Rani was continuing the argument. It took him a moment to respond. "You're expecting a lot out of a man who hasn't seen his son for months."

"That wasn't my doing," Rani pointed out, ignoring

the fire in Zack's eyes. His temper couldn't touch her anymore. "Look, I'm not going to go on arguing with you anymore. I've got to try to get Dean to settle down."

"It's about time." Zack started to turn on his heel, then whirled back around. "I'll be back tomorrow. I'll come after his nap so we don't have to go through this again."

Rani had started toward the house with Dean, but now she stopped. "No, you don't." Her voice was deep with warning. The time for standing firm was now. "You want to see Dean, but it can't be at your convenience and only when he's on his best behavior."

"Is that so? Then what do you want me to do?"

Rani stared at the man who had once been her husband. His question was too close to something she'd tried to block out of her mind. Just before Zack had walked out on her, there had been days when he had tried to dump everything in her lap. To his way of thinking, Dean's injuries couldn't really be considered his fault. Dean had made a terrible mess with the chocolate. Zack had a right to be upset. It wasn't his fault that the car ahead had been going too slow, that his brakes didn't grab in time, that Dean wasn't in his car seat.

It was starting again. Zack was trying to slide out from under responsibility. Maybe he'd never change, never be capable of making essential decisions, accepting responsibility, gaining control over his temper.

"I don't care what you do, Zack," she said in a voice so dead she wasn't sure it came from her lips. "I have one child. I don't need another." She didn't wait for him to reply—if in fact he was going to. Instead she clutched Dean to her and marched away. A minute later she thought she heard Zack's car pulling away, but she didn't look back to see.

She and Dean were inside the office before either of them spoke. Rani had gone directly to the desk and was moving papers about on it without being aware of what she was doing. Finally she became aware of her son's steady eyes on her. Forcing a smile, Rani looked down at Dean. "Do you think you'd like to take a nap?" she asked. "It's been a pretty big afternoon for you."

Dean was no longer crying, but his eyes were still red and too big for the rest of his face. "Mommy's mad," he observed solemnly.

"You know me pretty well, don't you, sport?" Rani asked as she scooped Dean back into her arms. "You were pretty mad out there yourself, you know."

Dean nodded but didn't say anything more about his earlier outburst. "Are you mad at me?"

"Oh, honey, of course not." Rani covered her son's nose with Eskimo kisses. "I get mad when you wear your shoes in the bathtub, not because you cry when you haven't had your nap. I'm sorry. You don't like seeing Mommy mad, do you?"

Dean leaned back in Rani's arms. His eyes were still solemn, but the frantic quality that had been in them when Zack had been there was gone. "I don't like Daddy."

For a moment that stretched on for too long Rani honestly didn't know what her response was going to be. Finally she said, "Honey, Daddy's doing the best he can around you. He just doesn't know how little boys think, what they need. I feel sorry for Daddy."

"Do you like him?"

Rani shook her head like a punchy boxer. There seemed to be no end to the probing questions her tired son was capable of. "I like what he gave me," she said by way of explanation. "If it hadn't been for Daddy I wouldn't have you. And I love you more than all the puppies in the world."

At last Rani was rewarded. "All the puppies in the world?" Dean asked, a smile tugging at the corners of his mouth.

"Better than all the puppies and kittens and baby goats that were ever born. In fact"—she paused for a moment in order to dramatize what was going to come next—"if you'll lie down on the couch and let me take off your shoes, I'll tell you a story about a man who tried to take care of all the cats in the world."

Dean let his mother stretch him out on the couch. "Tell me about puppies. I like them best."

She had done it. Dean was starting to put the scene with his father behind him, or at least Rani prayed that was what was happening. "Okay, puppies," she agreed, making a quick switch in the story's plot. "Tell me something," she went on as she was unlacing his shoes, "what would you do if you had to take care of all the puppies in the world?"

"Play with them." Although Dean sounded sure of his ability to accomplish that, his voice was starting to drag. "And feed them lots and lots of food."

"And break up a lot of puppy fights," Rani pointed out before launching into her naptime story. As she talked, she kept her eyes on her son, watching the slow blinks, the increasingly heavy lids. She hadn't even filled the man's living room with puppies before Dean gave up the struggle.

Rani rocked back on her heels, mother love washing over her in a familiar, beloved wave. She tucked the covers around Dean, closed the office door and slipped into Scott's living room.

It wasn't going to work. Zack was no closer to understanding his son or himself than he'd been when they were living in Sacramento. In a way it was terribly sad, because Zack might never enjoy the rare, perfect experience of watching his son fall asleep.

She wasn't sure she wanted to share Dean with anyone—not even Scott.

Chapter Ten

"It didn't go well, did it?" Scott asked. He was vaguely aware of the stiff breeze coming from the west that sent occasional flurries of dust up from the ground to settle on his hair, but his nerves were primed for a reaction from the woman sitting on the bench next to him. He'd tried to keep himself busy with a surprise he was planning for Rani and Dean, but not for a second had he been able to forget that Dean had spent time with his father today.

Rani didn't take her eyes off the teenage boys on the football field of the local high school. She blinked repeatedly in an effort to keep dust particles out of her eyes and tried to tell herself she was interested in keeping her eye on Chad, but that wasn't the truth. Not only did all the players look alike from this distance, but her mind was a thousand miles away from the confusing activity that held Dean's attention as well as Scott's. "You might say that," she replied vaguely.

"I thought I heard Dean crying. I was thinking of charging in like the White Knight and rescuing him, but I didn't think you'd appreciate it if I came barging in like I did yesterday.'"

Rani allowed herself a short laugh. It hadn't been as bad as it could have been; Scott deserved to know that. "I doubt if you could have said anything I hadn't thought of or said myself. Trying to talk to Zack was a disaster. I came off rather like a mother hen protecting her chick from an attacking fox."

"Do you want to talk about it now?" Scott asked. Because she'd been able to joke about it, he was relaxing enough to ask the question.

Rani was grateful that Scott was asking for instead of demanding an answer. "Not now. I hope you don't mind, but I don't think I could put a coherent sentence together without my blood pressure skyrocketing again. Poor Dean. He was so tired and ill-tempered, but Zack didn't or couldn't see that. That's what the tears were all about. That should give you some idea of how successful the visit was." Rani sighed and rubbed her right eye to dislodge a dust particle. "Are you sure Chad's out there? I don't see him."

Scott glanced at her, but Rani chose to ignore the opportunity to lock eyes. She was aware of other parents sitting alone or in groups. There were men in business suits and women in blue jeans or dresses. It was late afternoon on a workday, but these parents had taken time from their routines to spend an hour or so sitting in the dust to watch their teenage sons sweat and grunt under the watchful eyes of a handful of coaches.

Scott was here for a reason no more complicated than father love, and that's why she wasn't sure she was ready to meet his eyes. This afternoon her heart was full of respect and understanding and love for a man who put his son before a number of telephone calls still to be returned. The contrast between what

Scott felt for his son and what little relationship existed between Zack and Dean, while no longer painful to admit, struck her as terribly, terribly sad.

After a comfortable silence Scott spent a few minutes trying to explain the various football drills the boys were going through, but Rani finally had to admit that although she knew offense from defense, she wouldn't recognize a tight end if he threw a football at her. They slipped back into silence. They sat side by side, not speaking, until Dean grew tired of the distant action and wandered off to explore a pile of unused helmets left near the bleachers. Rani laughed when Dean placed one of the helmets on his head.

"Think he'll be a football player?" Scott asked.

"Do you think I'd be able to stop him?" Rani groaned with a mother's acceptance of her child's will. "Something tells me his friend out there is going to have him so hooked on the sport that I'd better get used to padding and helmets cluttering up the place. But not—not until I've talked to the doctor. I'm not going to risk another injury."

"Life holds risks, Rani. Don't you think I've thought about that with Chad? But we can't protect our sons from everything."

"Don't you think I know that!" Rani's sudden outburst surprised her.

Scott smiled and for the first time that afternoon touched her. "You're on edge, aren't you?"

"I can't help it." Rani started to pull away and then stopped herself. It wasn't Scott's fault that she and Zack had argued again. "I'm sorry," she groaned. "I feel as if I've been through the wringer today. I think

I'd be better off if I just took Dean and crawled away somewhere for a while.''

Scott tightened his grip. "I won't let you."

"Scott, I'm not fit to be around anyone."

"Why don't you let me be the judge of that?" Scott insisted. "I'll admit you're not the most pleasant company today, but I'm excusing you because I know you're going through a lot with Zack around."

"Oh, Scott, what would I do without you?" Rani moaned and collapsed, sagging against the strong shoulder to her left. She rested her head on his shoulder, eyes on Dean, thoughts of how easy it would be to surrender everything to this man. Scott was strong. He could handle anything that came his way in life. He wouldn't turn his back on Dean, leave her alone the way Zack had. He'd pull her up short if she started overprotecting Dean and help make that future decision about football.

"That's an interesting question," Scott was saying. "It happens to come pretty close to something I've been asking myself. Chad hit the nail on the head earlier when we were talking about you."

Rani cringed but didn't lift her head off Scott's shoulder. "What did Chad say? I'm afraid of what he thinks of me now that he knows."

"Knows what?"

Rani took a deep breath. "About the other night. In the cabin."

"Are you still worrying about that?"

"Do you blame me? Scott, he's old enough to know what happened."

To Rani's surprise Scott laughed. "I should hope he

does. I'd hate to think I was raising a son who didn't know that there's a certain attraction that takes place between men and women. In fact it's probably on his mind more than he's willing to tell me. He called you a foxy lady, said I knew how to pick them."

"Scott!" Rani grew hot with embarrassment. "He said that?"

"You bet he did. Believe me, coming from a fifteen-year-old that's a compliment. I told him that I wasn't going to try to hide anything from him. I told him that you were special and that there were times when I might not leave your room at night."

"You didn't!"

"What did you want me to do?" Scott challenged. "Lie to him?"

"Of course not," Rani stammered, confused. "But—he's a boy. Are you sure he's ready to hear something like that?"

"Boy, do you have a lot to learn about teenagers!" Scott laughed. "Kids these days know what the score is long before we did. He'd know I was lying if I told him we were playing poker in your bedroom all night. I believe in keeping the lines of communication open with my son. After all, he's almost a man."

Something about Scott's tone stopped Rani. There was no denying the pride Scott felt at admitting his son was approaching adulthood. He had a son he could be proud of, a healthy, active teenager who would probably make the football team, find a girl friend and make friends with others who shared his interest in cars, animals, sports. No man could help but be proud of a son like that.

"I was thinking of something," Rani said softly.

"What are you going to do with yourself when Chad grows up? It's going to mean a major change in your life when you don't have him around anymore."

Scott gave Rani a quick wink, but she was sure she saw a sober look in his eyes. "I have that all figured out," Scott said, his eyes going back to the action on the field. "I figure I'll make him a partner in the business so he won't be able to afford to leave. Then I'll hook him up to a nice fertile farm girl and surround myself with grandkids." Scott laughed at the picture he was drawing. "Can't you see me doddering around on my cane being attacked by grandchildren and peacocks and too happy to know the danger I'm in? I'll probably get in Chad's way and drive him crazy."

"I doubt that," Rani pressed.

"Hey." Scott turned on her in mock severity. "Don't rain on my parade. The dream of every parent is someday to have his revenge. I suffered through Chad's growing up. Now he'll have to keep me surrounded by grandkids or I'll never give him any peace."

"You're a devious man." Rani laughed. There were worlds between Scott and Zack, but because there was nothing to be gained by that, she refused to let the thought continue. She leaned forward with her elbows on her knees, her hands shielding her eyes from the dust.

"You're awfully quiet," Scott whispered. "What if I told you I was planning a secret for that son of yours?"

"What kind of secret?" Rani tried to turn in Scott's direction, but the wind wouldn't let her.

"Oh, no, you don't, lady. I'm planning on milking that little surprise for all it's worth. If you won't tell me about your day with good old what's-his-name, then

I'm not going to tell you about what I've been up to, either."

Ignoring the wind, Rani threw back her head and laughed. It felt good! "You're a devious, underhanded man. What am I going to have to do, beat it out of you?"

Scott absorbed Rani's mood. He hadn't known what she was going to be like this afternoon, had worried that she might change in a way he wouldn't like. But this determination of hers to keep her life on an even keel warmed him. "I bruise easily. I think what I'm going to have to do is find a way of distracting you so you won't resort to violence."

Rani risked looking at Scott to see if he was making fun of her, but his eyes reassured her. His hands did the telling. The other parents were sitting higher in the stands. There was no way they could see that Scott's hand was trailing closer and closer to the front of Rani's blouse. She held her breath as his hand made its way beneath the opening and explored the soft flesh around her bra. "What was that about wanting to do bodily harm to me?" he asked, his fingers dipping between her breasts, light whispers of feeling radiating out from the teasing contact.

"You're crazy." Rani giggled, her eyes still on Dean. Her mind was elsewhere, clinging to Scott's fingers and making the journey with them. "What if someone sees?"

"No one's going to see. And if they do, I'll tell them it's part of your therapy. It works, doesn't it?"

Rani had to admit that it did. Life was so complicated. What she felt for Scott, what she was trying to sort out about Zack was more than she wanted to think about. Scott was giving her the perfect diversion. She felt her cheeks grow warm, and then the warmth spread deeper, flowing into her veins and filling her body. "You're driving me crazy," she admitted as fingers tested velvet flesh.

"That's my plan," Scott whispered back. "I don't want you to think anymore. Just react."

The automatic part of her that was a mother kept an eye on her son's exploration of the sidelines, but the part that was a woman surrendered to Scott's penetrating if limited search of her body. She felt no shame at what he was doing. She needed this contact, this reminder of her womanliness, too much. Her earlier feelings that she would be safer without any man in her life evaporated. She wanted—needed—Scott. Her heart might move in another direction tomorrow, but she willingly accepted the journey it was taking today.

She was entertaining no thoughts of changing direction by the time the teenagers started leaving the football field. Scott was the one with the presence of mind to return his hand to more conventional territory. "We'll take this up again tonight," he promised as Chad joined them.

Rani needed help getting to her feet. Her legs were numb and her head still pounded. She wondered if there was anything about her that might reveal her inner feelings to Chad, but since there was nothing she could do about it, she didn't dwell on the question.

Instead she forced herself to concentrate on the animated conversation that was taking place between Chad and the man who still held on to her. Chad was feeling good about his performance on the field. He wasn't ready to stick his neck out, but he thought his chances of making the team were good. "A couple of the guys asked where I came from. When I told them, they asked if it was true about the women in Hollywood."

"What did you tell them?" Scott asked.

Chad laughed. "I said that women are trouble no matter where you live."

"Listen to the expert." Scott rolled his eyes upward as Rani stifled a laugh of her own. "Fifteen years old and he's a cynic."

"Just being honest, Dad. You know how it is with women." His wink for Rani's benefit was too bold to be misinterpreted. Chad was a long way from giving up on the feminine sex.

"Yes, I know how it is with women," Scott answered. "Once they've got hold of you they don't let go."

What did Scott mean by that? Surely he didn't think she was trying to get her claws in him. "I don't know whether to take offense at that or not," Rani said as the four of them headed toward the parking lot.

"I'm just speaking the truth, lady," Scott said. "Look what you've done to me. Here Chad was thinking he was going to live with a swinging bachelor, and what does he get? An old man willing to foot the bill for a family-size pizza."

The thought that Scott might be thinking of them as a family warmed Rani. The alternative was to shy away from the commitment that went with the picture he was painting, and that was something she was unwilling if not incapable of doing.

Scott and Chad were still talking football by the time their pizza had been ordered. Rani sat back, content to listen to a conversation about offensive and defensive positions and coaching techniques. Dean had wandered off to explore the bright lights from the various video games with another little boy about his age. Rani watched them for a few minutes, noting that there was no real difference between Dean and his new friend. Once she might have wondered if Dean would ever be able to take his place with other boys his age; thankfully that period of questioning was over.

At length Chad decided to show Dean how to rack up points on a pinball machine and left the two adults alone. "It's good to see Chad so excited about football," Scott said. "I don't think the first day of school is going to bother him so much now that he's met some of the other students."

"I thought you weren't worried about that," Rani pointed out. "Didn't you tell me he was going to do all right?"

"Did I? I lied." Scott gave her a sheepish grin. "That's my son. I want things to go smoothly for him. I can't help but be concerned."

"They will," Rani said softly. She'd had good vibes about Chad from the moment she had met him and had no hesitancy about letting Scott know that. "He has a lot of his father in him. He's outgoing."

"You think so?" Rani could tell that Scott was taking her comment as a compliment. "I guess you're right. I mean, who am I to turn down a positive stroke where my kid's concerned? Don't tell him, but I'm damn proud of that kid. He's going to turn out all right."

Of course he is. He's always had a father around to guide him.

Scott was still speaking. "I've been thinking," he

said over the sound from the piped-in radio station. "It doesn't really matter how much a man accomplishes in his life. It's how he succeeds as a father that measures his true success. How's that for a double dose of philosophy? I might be boasting, but I think I'm going to give myself that gold star."

"You should," Rani said from the depths of her emotions. At the moment she loved both Scott and Chad with a love so strong it was constricting her throat. "Chad is a son any man can be proud of." Then, before she had a chance to check it, the bitterness she'd been suppressing all afternoon came out. "What makes me want to scream is the simple fact that emotionally Zack is a million miles from his son."

Scott leaned back in his chair and fixed his eyes on Rani. He'd been playing the afternoon her way, letting her speak about Zack when she wanted to and not because he was pressing her. Now that the opportunity was presenting itself, he wasn't going to let it get away. "Now we're getting down to the nitty-gritty. Did you really think that a separation of several months was going to change Zack?"

"I don't know what's wrong with that man!" Rani said, surprised at the anger she was feeling. "I hoped he would want to get to know his son, be excited because a baby is turning into a little boy. But it's as if he's incapable of reaching beyond himself in order to discover that."

"The fool! I'm sorry. I didn't mean to lose my cool," Scott relented. "In a way I can understand where he's coming from. At least I'm going to give it my best shot. Listen to me and tell me if this makes any sense. Parents want a lot for their children. Men look at their sons and want to see themselves all over again. Maybe it's a case of wanting a second childhood, the chance to do it right the second time. There are a lot of unfulfilled hopes and dreams tied up there."

Rani spoke through clenched teeth. "That's not fair to the child. Oh, I know what you're saying, and I can't argue that it doesn't happen. But what you're saying is that Dean has failed in Zack's eyes because—because he went through a period of being flat on his back. Why should Dean be a failure in Zack's eyes simply because of that one setback? Why can't Zack let Dean be who he is? He's a beautiful little boy who still needs naps but may be out on a football field one of these days. Listen to me." Rani's eyes shone with the light of her discovery. "I never used to allow myself to get angry at Zack. I stood up to him today. Did I ever! Do you think I'm finally developing a backbone?"

Chad arrived with the steaming pizza before Scott could respond to her question. Although Rani's hands were busy pulling off a piece of pizza for Dean, her mind didn't leave the unfinished conversation. She could accept that men—parents—had hopes and dreams that hinged on their children. She could see that in Scott's open pride concerning his son, in her own desires for Dean's future. Never, even right after the accident, had she given up her dreams for Dean. The thought had never entered her mind that his future wouldn't be everything he was capable of making it. It hurt and angered her to know that it wasn't that way with Zack.

That's what she was going to tell Zack the next time she saw him. Either he'd decide what he wanted in the way of a relationship with his son or he had no place in

Dean's life. Rani had knuckled under for the last time.

Rani's determination to have it out with Zack once and for all made it possible for her to dismiss him from her mind and concentrate on the conversation which had once again settled on football and school. She felt like a fifth wheel as Scott and Chad continued the topic during the ride back to the ranch. She sat near Scott with a sleeping Dean on her lap, but said little. The relationship between Scott and his son was so natural. True, there were times when they snapped at each other, but the strong fiber of love was always there. That was how she felt about the sleeping child in her arms. Was Zack the one on the outside, the one being cheated out of a loving parent/child relationship?

Scott hadn't come to the cabin by the time Dean was asleep. She could have stayed where she was, but Rani was in no mood to form more questions without answers. She needed someone to talk to. Closing the door softly behind her, she started toward the brightly lit ranch house.

Scott and Chad were watching TV in the living room. "He's asleep already?" Scott asked. "I thought it would take longer than that."

"He didn't have much of a nap, and that was a pretty big evening for him." Rani sat down in one of the unoccupied chairs and stared glassy-eyed at the TV. "What are you watching?"

"Nothing." Chad got to his feet. "You two pick something. I'm going to check on the animals one more time."

Rani was still looking in the direction Chad had gone when Scott spoke. "Perceptive kid, don't you think? He knows when the older folks need to be alone."

"I don't know," Rani stammered. "I didn't mean to interrupt—"

"You didn't interrupt anything. We had finally said everything there was to say about football. Besides, I said we needed to be alone, not wanted to."

"There's a difference?"

"In this case, yes." Scott got to his feet and came to take Rani's hands. "Come on. We're going for a walk of our own. I think better on my feet. Besides, if we stay in here much longer we might wind up doing other things."

Because she agreed, Rani went with Scott. She'd left the cabin because she wanted to be near Scott, and yet lovemaking wasn't the only thing on her mind. The day had been one of sweeping contrasts. What it had taught her was that she was coming closer and closer to an understanding of the man she was sharing the dark with. She thought of those other parents who had taken time away from their workday to sit on hard bleachers and watch their healthy young sons. Needing to be part of that ritual of young manhood wasn't an emotion that translated well into words. It was simply . . . there.

Scott linked his hand with hers and led her in the direction of the more distant pasture, where the sheep were bedding down for the night. This late in the year there were no infant lambs bleating when they became separated from their mothers. The sounds coming from the pasture were sleepy, contented. "I told Zack I was tired of having him act like a little boy," Rani said softly. "That's how the visit ended."

"I don't want to talk about Zack." Scott didn't turn toward Rani, but there was no misinterpreting his tone. "That's not what I asked you out here for."

"Oh? Then what are we doing here?"

"We're going to count sheep. I'll take the black ones. You're responsible for all the white ones."

Rani let her breath come out in a long sigh. "I can't keep up with you. I really think you like throwing things out at me just to see if you can catch me off balance."

"I wouldn't do that." Scott's voice was all innocence.

"Oh, yeah?" Rani stopped walking and faced the tall shadowy figure in the night. "What about that business of having a surprise for Dean? You love that sort of thing."

"Oh, that." Scott shrugged elaborately before pulling Rani close so she could see his face in the dark. "Well, I may have a few quirks like that, but I'm basically lovable."

"The best distraction I could ask for tonight," Rani admitted softly. "After my day—"

"I said I didn't want to talk about him. It's you and me I'm interested in. Answer me something, Mrs. Lassen. Where are we headed?"

"What? Oh, Scott, I don't know." That wasn't strictly true. Rani would have had to be blind and deaf not to have sensed the direction their relationship would lead them if it were given free rein.

"I believe that's what the kids call a cop-out." He leaned toward her until she was forced to arch back. "You're on the witness stand tonight. Everything you say is supposed to be the truth and nothing but the truth. You've never told me how you feel about me. Did you know that?"

Of course she did. The word *love* had bloomed within

her from the day she met him. But Rani was afraid. Telling Scott that she was in love with him could lead to marriage—something she'd already failed at once. She was dedicated to her son and his future. If Dean's own father couldn't commit himself to that kind of dedication... "What do you want me to say?" she managed.

"I have no idea what I want you to say." Scott laughed at himself. "I feel like a kid asking a girl out. There's physical attraction. I just don't know how much further it goes than that."

"Scott, please. I've made one whale of a decision already today. You're asking so much. We haven't had much time—"

"How much time do you need?" Scott released her and took a backward step that left her in danger of collapsing.

If Scott left her alone in the dark she might shatter into too many pieces for anyone to be able to put her back together. Finding the courage to confront Zack was nothing compared to what it would take to go on without the man beside her. Blindly Rani reached for him, both hands gripping his right arm. "Don't do this to me, Scott," she begged, unmindful of the tears glistening in her eyes. "I'm tired of being alone."

A groan from Scott's lips were her clue that her plea had been heard. He leaned forward and drew her to him, his lips seeking hers. "Don't cry," he whispered. "I don't want it to be like that."

Rani's response came from her heart. "Neither do I. You said you wanted us to be alone. Why?"

"No," he whispered back. "I said *need*. We need to be alone. Every time we talk, it's about our sons or Zack. We need to talk about each other."

Rani didn't ask him to explain further. His arms were around her, his strength holding them together. It was as if she had never been in the arms of a man before. The wildly lonely creature kept in check by responsibilities was responding to a masculine body with the strength to take on some of that responsibility. Scott was more than her employer and a man who didn't flinch from what life dealt out. He was what a tall, slender woman had been seeking to bring her private femininity to life.

A chill coursed down Rani's spine, in vibrant contrast to the heat pulsing in her temples, wrists, thighs. Like a fish caught in a current racing toward a waterfall, she could do nothing but surrender. But unlike the fish, Rani was possessed of a woman's needs. She didn't fight the strength washing over and around her. She pointed her body in the direction of the waterfall, responding to the current that was Scott Barnett's masculinity.

Rani was no longer holding on to Scott's arm. He had pulled her against him until her breasts were compressed against his chest. She reached for his neck as her way of telling him that she needed the contact as much if not more than he did. Fighting and families were forgotten when she opened her lips and explored his mouth with her tongue. Rani's eyes were closed against reality. She wanted nothing more than this embrace, demanded nothing less than to engulf Scott totally and be engulfed in return.

The night breeze against her temples did nothing to cool the flame. Her mouth was parted, her body pressed tightly against Scott's, legs spread to balance her swaying frame. Rani released Scott's neck and gave full rein to the desire to run her fingers up the strong line of his jaw into the thick mass of his hair until they were completely covered. That accomplished, Rani freed her mouth and started an exploration of Scott's eyelids, cheeks, and chin with lips that hungrily absorbed every inch of him within her reach.

Scott ran his hands down the small of her back until they reached her waist and slowly lifted away the fabric that separated his fingers from her. Rani trembled convulsively as night-cooled fingers touched warm flesh at the base of her backbone, but nothing could force her to ask him to stop what he was doing to her skin, her total being.

"Let's go to your cabin," Scott whispered.

Because she'd lost the power of speech but hadn't surrendered enough to allow him to know of the moan of desire pressing against her throat, Rani only nodded. She leaned against his side as he led her toward the cabin and the soft but adequate bed. His arm was around her shoulders blocking out the world beyond his warmth. For the first time in her life Rani was feeling like a partner and not just a participant in lovemaking.

Rani had only scant knowledge of having entered the cabin and being led into the bedroom. It was all she could do to will her legs not to collapse under her. She reached for the top button on her blouse, but when her fingers refused to respond, she let Scott remove the confining garment. Scott was a good teacher. He showed her what she needed to do to free him of his shirt. Finally her hands were able to roam delightedly across his chest, where the fine but curly hairs tantalized her fingertips.

Scott was doing some intimate exploration of his own. He had pulled her close enough to reach behind her and unhook her bra. Now he pushed her away and cupped her breasts in his hands. A faint smile showed in the dark as he examined his possessions. "I told you we should take this up again later tonight," he teased.

Rani flushed, her emotions beyond wanting to play word games. "I need you," she whispered, surrendering to him.

Although Scott took the lead in their lovemaking, Rani had no objections. *He knows I need to feel treasured*, she thought as he removed the rest of her clothes and slid her under the cool sheet. She wasn't being expected to run a nonprofit organization, care for her son, confront her ex-husband. Tonight nothing was asked of her except to respond as a woman responds to a man.

That Rani did well. She gave herself fully to the flames in her veins. When her lips parted to receive Scott's deep penetrating kiss, she allowed a small animallike moan to be released. The sound, she knew, represented total surrender. Surrender was in the form of a body that surged toward the masculine one engulfing her and a mind that no longer existed as a separate entity. She'd never lost control like this with Zack or even known it was possible to blend her soul with that of a man. Now that it was happening, she could only revel in her total delight. How good it felt to trust a man to this extent!

There was no existence beyond tonight and the twin hungers that were fed in the darkened bedroom of a cabin.

Chapter Eleven

Rani and Scott woke at the same time. It was early—
not quite six. Rani turned onto her side, the sheet slip-
ping off her shoulder, and reached out to run her hand
over the flat surface of Scott's stomach. "I had a
dream," she whispered, her voice still heavy with
sleep. "I was alone in bed and then someone came into
the room. I lifted the blankets and he joined me. I was
naked, but it was as if that was the way it was meant to
be, as if I had no other reason to exist except to be
there when you climbed into bed with me."

"How can you be sure it was me?"

Rani smiled. For this moment in time her world was
as perfect as she could want it to be. "I knew," she said
before accepting his kiss.

They had fallen asleep without putting on any clothes.
That made it easier for their bodies to find each other, to
fulfill needs and desires that had become even more mature and full-blown since last night. Rani gave herself
willingly to Scott. If she had any existence beyond his
hands, his body, she was unaware of it.

The joining of their bodies, the common journey to a
world without form or responsibility lit by flashes of

emotional light lasted until the sun reached the bedroom window. Finally Rani opened her eyes and noted
the way the sun was filtering through Scott's tangled
curls. He needed a shave and his hair reminded her of
something that had been caught in a windstorm. But
that was Scott, the man who had reached out and
brought her into the sunlight with him.

"I love you," she whispered, feeling the words coming from every pore in her.

"You're sure?"

"I'm sure. I think I've been waiting to say that for
weeks."

Scott raised himself up on his elbow and trailed his
free hand over her eyelids, her cheek. "I love you."

The words spoken in a small cabin as the day was
beginning stayed with Rani all morning as she went
about her work and made the decision that would quite
likely fashion the direction her life would take. She and
Scott hadn't said many of the things they needed to
say, but that time would come. Right now she had to
force a confrontation with her ex-husband.

IT WAS LATE in the afternoon before she managed to
reach Zack at his motel room. His explanation for his
failure to contact her bothered but didn't surprise her.
"I wanted to take a look at the country around here. I
got up, ate breakfast out and then went for a ride. I
can't say much for the city itself, but there's some impressive country around here."

"Why didn't you get in touch with me? Don't you
want to see Dean?"

"If you'll remember, you were pretty damn mad
yesterday. I decided to give you time to cool down."

"Isn't that considerate of you!" Rani snapped and then forced herself to stop. She wasn't going to sound like a fishwife. "We need to talk. I'm not going to put up with being kept in limbo anymore," she pointed out calmly. "The ranch isn't the best place. What if Dean and I come into town this evening? Maybe we can have dinner together."

"So you want to start calling the shots, do you? Are you sure your macho boyfriend will let you out of his sight?" At Rani's snort of disgust, Zack changed his tactics. "Dinner will be fine," he said. "That way we'll have to act civilized around each other. But do you think bringing Dean is such a good idea?"

Rani's newfound determination allowed her to speak. "Don't you want to see him?"

"Of course," Zack said too quickly for the answer to be genuine. "I was thinking of having him around a lot of people. He still eats with his fingers, doesn't he? A restaurant really isn't the place for a little kid."

"That little kid is what you came all the way here to see, isn't he?" Rani pressed, wishing she could see the look on Zack's face. She mentioned a restaurant that included outdoor tables in a picnic setting. "It's a relaxed place. One more thing. Don't lose your temper. I won't stand for it."

Scott wasn't delighted to learn that Rani was going to be seeing Zack, but because he was tied up in a meeting with the director of the local preschool center for deaf children, he didn't have the opportunity to do much more than frown in Rani's direction before getting back to plans to bring the children out to the ranch for a demonstration of what the dogs could do. Rani listened in awe while Scott reassured the man that he'd have no trouble communicating with the children because he knew sign language. Of course he did, Rani reminded herself. A child growing up with a deaf father learns sign language as easily as other children learn to print their names. Scott's father must have been a remarkable man, Rani concluded. Not only was he able to support a family but he'd also raised a son who certainly knew how to stand on his own two feet.

HER OWN LEGS were more than a little rubbery under her when she joined Zack in the parking lot of the restaurant she'd chosen. Zack was dressed casually and his shoes were somewhat dusty, as if they were the ones he'd been wearing during his explorations earlier in the day. Rani had put on a cool cotton sundress and carried a light sweater. She'd washed her hair and used a taming conditioner to get her hair to settle softly around her face. Dean was wearing a denim coverall outfit that let him wriggle around without her having to worry about his shirttail hanging out. Zack's quick glance before starting toward the restaurant told her that her effort had been wasted. He wasn't interested in what people were wearing.

For some reason Rani found it impossible to concentrate on anything except choosing a meal that Dean would eat instead of being distracted by the butterflies flitting around the canopy of roses that served as the background for their dinner. Rani, who couldn't trust her stomach to more than a single glass of white wine, settled on a chef's salad. Zack ordered steak and potatoes and then started playing with his own glass of wine. "You said we have to talk," he said as Rani was fighting her way through a lengthy silence.

She took a deep breath. "I've been doing a lot of thinking," she began, her head pounding from an accelerated heartbeat. "Maybe I haven't been fair to you. I'm expecting a lot from you where Dean is concerned. I want you to tell me where he fits in your life while you're getting used to the idea that he's hardly the same boy who was still in a cast the last time you saw him."

"So?"

"I don't know what I want out of you. No"—she stopped herself—"that isn't true. I hoped I wouldn't have to ask, thought you'd supply that. Are you here to satisfy your curiosity about how Dean is doing?"

Zack was close to a minute responding. "That was part of it. Look, will you just listen to me for a bit? Don't make any judgments and don't tell me I'm wrong." At Rani's nod, he continued. "Is guilt a terrible word in your vocabulary? Probably. After all, you don't have to feel guilty."

"But I do feel guilty," Rani interrupted. "I was part of what happened to Dean. That day I—"

"We'll get to that later," Zack said, his eyes glued to his wineglass. "The past needs to be buried. It was another kind of guilt that brought me here."

Rani waited. Her nerves were strung so tight she wouldn't have been able to speak if she had wanted to. The fact was, she couldn't look at him without feeling as if she were standing at the edge of a cliff with Dean in her arms.

"I sent those child-support checks every month," Zack said bitterly. "For a long time I tried to fool myself into thinking I was meeting my responsibilities that way." Zack took a sip of wine. "Finally I decided that the time had come to face both you and Dean. Until I'd done that, I couldn't get on with my life."

Rani waited, barely aware that their dinner had arrived. She couldn't believe that Zack was able to attack his steak. It was all she could do to show Dean how to hold his chicken leg. When the silence went on until she thought she was going to scream, Rani broke it. "Have you done that?"

Zack appeared reluctant to turn his attention from cutting up his steak. "Yes."

Another silence. "What is it?"

"You're not going to give up, are you?" Zack laughed between narrowed lips. "I've never known a dog more tenacious than you."

"Don't compare me to a dog," Rani said with much more calm than she felt. "If I'm tenacious about this, it's because I'm planning Dean's future. His and mine."

"That's another of your traits," Zack said around a mouthful of food. "You're so damn organized. Like the day of the accident. Where are you going? Why do you want Dean with you? If you had had your way, we'd still be arguing."

Rani stirred dressing into her salad but couldn't trust herself to take a bite. "You're avoiding the issue," she pressed.

"Yeah." Zack bit out the word. "Do you want to know why? Because you're asking me to admit things about myself I didn't think I'd ever have to admit."

"Raising Dean has forced me to admit a lot of things," Rani said, for the moment unmindful of any bitterness that might have crept into her voice. "I'm willing to do anything to make sure he gets the best possible shake in life."

"Bully for you." Zack's eyes bored into hers, but Rani refused to back down. Instead, she bit her tongue until he was forced to fill the silence. "I'm glad you're willing to do so much for Dean. I'm not willing to have my life turned around that way."

Rani felt herself grow cold. She sensed that Zack had finally started on the explanation she had to hear. She could say something to help him get started, but she didn't.

Finally he said, "It probably looks as if I haven't spent much time with Dean since I got here. That isn't true. I've been observing a lot. I've tried to see myself as his father, I really have."

"What do you mean? You *are* his father."

"His biological father."

Rani closed her eyes against the emotion that throbbed through her. "You can't be finished," she said behind closed lids. "You owe me more than that."

"Do I? Maybe I do. Look, this isn't easy. Do you have to look as if I've punched you in the stomach?"

Rani's eyes flew open. "You want me to look as if all you've done is turned me down for a date? Zack, I don't know what you're trying to tell me. I have a right to know why I feel as if I've been punched."

For the first time that evening Zack looked—really looked—at Dean. "Do you remember? You were the one who wanted children. It didn't mean that much to me, but I went along with it because I knew it was what you wanted. When Dean was born and I held him for the first time, I started thinking about what it would be like to watch him grow up. I felt like a father then. Dean would be with me while I worked. We would go fishing and camping together. I'd help him with his homework and talk to him about girls...." Zack's voice trailed off. "Look, I was damn proud of the fact we had a son. Sure, a girl would have been nice, but there's something about having a son that does things for a man. There are things I'd never accomplished. I looked at Dean and told myself that here was my chance to have those things come true."

"You wanted Dean because he represented a second childhood?" Rani asked. Now that Zack was finally talking, the terrible tension inside her was relaxing a little.

"Maybe. Don't look at me like that," Zack warned. "I'm not the only father to feel that way. In fact, I'm willing to bet that that's why most men become fathers. They see themselves through their sons' eyes. Why do you think I was hard on him? I wasn't going to let him mess up. I'd always wanted to be a basketball star. Once, just once, I wanted to be the guy who put in the winning basket at the buzzer. It never happened. The night we brought Dean home from the hospital after he was born, I looked at his long legs and told myself he was going to make that winning basket. Now it's probably never going to happen."

"And that's why you don't want to be involved emotionally with Dean? Because you're afraid he isn't going to wind up a basketball star?" She'd heard much the same words the other day from Scott. Scott had said that a man sees himself in his son. A lot of hopes and dreams were tied up in that emotion.

Zack's answer came too soon for her to have time to tie together the loose threads in the conversation. "It's more complicated than that. I put my son in the hospital. Me. I almost killed him. I wanted a son. Instead I learned that I don't have what it takes to be a father. I don't know what it is—immaturity, my temper. All I know is I make a damn poor father."

"What about Dean?"

"Dean has you." Zack put down the fork he'd been playing with. "You're committed to him. I can't make that same commitment. If you hate me for that, I can't help it." Zack again glanced at Dean. "I thought seeing him might change how I feel. It didn't."

Rani watched Zack get to his feet. Her eyes didn't waver. For now at least she felt nothing. "I'm glad you told me," she said dully.

Zack stopped. "I thought you'd call me a coward."

"Maybe tomorrow. I'm just glad this is over. Now I can get on with my own life."

"I hope so." Zack made a gesture as if to touch her and then let his arms drop to his side. "I don't like the idea of you being alone."

"I'm not alone." Rani thought about smiling but couldn't remember which muscles to use to accomplish that. "I'm in love."

"I thought as much." Zack leaned toward her. "But you better face something, Rani. You're heading for heartache. He isn't going to stay with you."

"How can you say that?" Rani asked, wary. "You don't know Scott."

"I'm a man." Zack tapped himself on the chest. "I know how men think. You're too wrapped up in yourself and Dean."

Rani didn't watch as Zack paused long enough to pay their waitress. She pulled Dean's chair closer to her and helped him slide his fork under some mashed potatoes. The deadening quality that insulated her from the reality of Zack's emotional desertion still held her in its grip. But its strength was slackening.

His words had no bearing on what she felt for Dean. Nothing would ever lessen the strength of her love for her son.

"Why don't we go home?" she asked when it became clear that Dean was much more interested in his surroundings than in mashed potatoes. "Do you want to say good night to Gas?"

At Dean's enthusiastic nod she fled the memories that went with the restaurant. If she thought at all during the ride back to the ranch, she wasn't aware of it.

It was dark by the time she pulled into the ranch driveway, but she wasn't thinking about stumbling when she took Dean's hand and started leading him toward the cabin. She wasn't thinking at all.

"Do you need some help?" a voice asked.

Rani didn't start, although she hadn't seen Chad coming toward her. She relented when Dean reached out to get up on Chad's shoulders. She trailed after them as Chad started walking, telling Dean about his day's activities. A thought hit her—not once since he'd learned about the epilepsy had Zack shared such a simple, open moment with his son. A teenage boy— not his father—treated Dean as an intelligent human being.

I want to hate you, Zack, Rani thought as they neared the dark cabin. *I really want to hate you.*

But hate was an exhausting emotion, one she didn't have the energy to indulge in. She'd asked for the confrontation. She could handle the consequences.

"Do you want help putting Dean to bed?" Chad asked.

"I don't think it's going to take much work tonight," Rani admitted. It's been a pretty big day. What do you think?" she asked her son. "Ready to call it a day?"

Rani should have known better than to ask. Dean's emphatic head shake left no doubt that he wasn't ready to put an end to such an interesting experience. "Tell me a story. A long, long story," Dean insisted.

"What is this?" Chad growled in mock severity. "Are you trying to give us a hard time?"

Delighted, Dean nodded, his hair flying forward with the movement. "I won't go to bed."

"Hm." Chad turned toward Rani. "What do you think we should do about this? I was going to ask Dean if he could help me with a project tomorrow, but now he's going to be too tired." Chad shrugged, his face dramatically crestfallen. "I guess I'll just have to find someone else to ride the llama."

Before Rani could think of something to add to the conversation, Dean was through the living room and diving into his bed. "One little story?" he asked once he was under the covers, shoes and all.

Chad knelt beside the bed and reached for Dean's shoes. "I guess I could do that. How about a story about llamas?"

"Tell me Mommy's story about puppies."

With some prompting from Rani, Chad was able to come up with an acceptable plot for a story revolving around a couple of children and a town full of puppies. Rani sat on the floor of the bedroom, her back propped against the wall, as Chad captured Dean's attention. She supposed she should be recapping the evening with Zack, putting together the final pieces of the puzzle that he had laid out in front of her, but the combination of occasional yapping from the nearby dogs and the slow easing of the tension she'd been under for several days combined to make her want nothing more than to listen to Chad's newly deepened voice have the desired effect on her keyed-up but tired son.

"I don't think we're needed anymore," Chad whispered. Rani looked up to see the teenager standing over her, his hand outstretched. She took the offered hand and got to her feet. She slipped over to Dean's bed and touched her lips to his smooth forehead.

"You make a good storyteller," she told Chad when she'd closed the door behind them. "Dean believes he won the argument over a bedtime story."

"He did. I didn't think it would take him that long to fall asleep. I had just about run out of things to say about puppies." Chad started to leave but suddenly stopped. "I'm supposed to give you a message from Dad. He said to tell you he's sorry, but he's not going to be around for a few days. He'll call you as soon as he can."

"Where is he?" Rani had assumed that Scott was in the ranch house waiting for her to join him; she wasn't ready for this at all.

"Hollywood. Where else? He has to provide some peacocks and stuff for some hurry-up retirement party some big-shot producer is having this weekend. As you might have guessed, Dad's ticked off at having to do it on the spur of the moment like this, but apparently the guy's given Dad a lot of work over the years and he can't very well turn him down. Anyway, he's at the airport getting things ready so they can leave in the morning."

"Oh." Rani stopped, defeated. Scott had mentioned

the retirement party, but he'd thought it wouldn't take place until September. The change in plans couldn't have come at a more inconvenient time as far as Rani was concerned, but there was nothing she could do about it.

When he called the next day she told him only that Zack had finally admitted his shortcomings as a father. "I think I understand him better now than I ever did when we were married," she said over the miles. "I feel sorry for him, but maybe I shouldn't. At least he isn't trying to pretend to be what he isn't."

"How are you?" Scott pressed. "You holding up all right?"

"I'm managing." Rani clung tightly to the telephone as if she could pull Scott through the lines to her. "Your son is teaching mine how to ride a llama. We're still short a dog. I called the humane society this morning, but they don't have anything they think is right." She didn't add that there was a knot in her that wouldn't untie itself.

"We'll find something. Don't worry about it," Scott responded. "Look, I'm late already. How about if we go for a long ride when I get back? There are some things we need to talk about."

Rani nodded and then remembered to say good-bye. There were some things Scott needed to talk to her about. She didn't want to think about what those things might be, but it was impossible not to, because Zack had put thoughts in her head that were responsible for the knot inside her. "He isn't going to stay with you," Zack had said.

Scott was gone three days. During that time Rani concentrated on working with a dog that would be going to a man who had to take public transportation to work. With the approval of the local bus company she took the dog with her and spent the better part of a day riding buses and letting the dog get used to the various sights and smells. When she wasn't riding the bus she was on the phone long-distance with staff from a nationally syndicated TV program interested in filming a segment on the training center. Playing the role of a public relations officer and at the same time letting the reporter and cameramen know that they would have to stay in the background as much as possible in order not to distract the dogs gave her little time to think about personal matters. She concentrated on the reaction she knew she'd get from Scott when he learned that thanks to the hard work of their public relations volunteer, the program's work would be recognized beyond their immediate area. It was what both of them knew needed to happen if the program was going to get the wide-based financial support it needed in order to succeed.

Rani didn't hear from Zack, but then she didn't expect to. Despite the way the evening had turned out, Rani knew that finally everything was out in the open. Zack hadn't lost his temper, and she hadn't hidden her head in the sand. He was probably back in Sacramento, maybe feeling a new sense of maturity because he'd owned up to certain things about himself. She could imagine him sighing a sigh of relief now that he'd faced his ex-wife and admitted his inability to give enough of himself emotionally for his son.

But at night, when there were no longer any distractions, she had to face the other thing he'd said.

"He isn't going to stay with you" played through Rani's mind no matter how hard she tried to shove the thought away. Zack hadn't had to spell it out. She knew why the words had been spoken.

Rani hadn't had the backbone, the courage, to stand up to her husband. As result Dean had wound up in the hospital and her marriage had fallen apart. Rani had lived with guilt so long that it was part of her, a parasite that would live for as long as she did. Someday that parasite might feed on what existed between her and Scott.

Scott might love her now, but maybe it wouldn't last. Zack had said she was too wrapped up in herself and Dean. It wasn't healthy, but she didn't know how to shut off the emotion. She could't blame Scott for turning away from a woman haunted by guilt.

Chapter Twelve

The next time Rani saw Scott she was watching Chad's football practice. She'd been driving Chad and Dean to the high school and occupying herself with paperwork while she waited, but this afternoon, like the others since Scott left, her mind had been more on her employer than the job she was doing for him. Actually Dean spotted Scott first. He started running toward Scott even as Rani was trying to convince herself that the tall, casually dressed man with the wild hair really was the one who had been keeping her awake nights.

Rani acknowledged the warmth that washed through her at the sight of Scott, barely keeping tears in check at the way Scott hurried to Dean and lifted him onto his accustomed perch on his shoulders. Scott looked so good! It was impossible to look into those eyes and not believe him capable of giving her future all the security she craved.

"We'll be right back," Scott called out. Before she could speak, he'd made an about-face and was marching back toward the vehicle he'd driven from the airport. A moment later she heard Dean's happy squeal.

She got to her feet and started toward the parking lot.

Coming toward her was Scott, Dean and a bouncing bundle of life with a fluffy tail curled up over its back. "Meet Dino," Scott announced. "I told you I had a surprise for you. Dino is going to become one of our projects. And I told Dean that this is his very own dog."

"What?" One look at Dean and Rani knew that her son was under the blond dog's spell. "Scott?" She reached him and pulled him aside so Dean couldn't hear. "Please don't do that."

"Why?" Scott knew he wasn't being fair. He should have let Rani know from the first what his plan was, but unfolding it was too much fun. It would allow him to see the somber look leave her eyes as she realized what he was up to. He was like a kid at Christmas, he knew, but he'd been planning the moment for a couple of weeks; it had to come out right. "Dean loves Dino."

"That's just the problem," Rani hissed. "Scott, you named the dog after Dean. You're telling him that it's his dog. Don't you know what Dean will go through when Dino's training is over and he's placed with a family? Dean will be crushed."

"Dino isn't going to be placed with a family. He's staying here."

At Rani's puzzled, skeptical look, Scott unwrapped his package. "I've been thinking. We're going to be doing a lot more public relations work—visiting organizations and groups to sell them on what we're doing. We need a demonstration dog, one that can be counted on to always have his best foot forward. Dino will be on staff permanently. There's no reason why he can't be Dean's."

"Oh." Rani barely got the word out. Of course Scott

wouldn't let Dean give his heart to a dog only to have it broken. "Oh." She brightened. "Scott, that's a fantastic idea. Dino can travel with the trainers, with you or me when we put on demonstrations." Her enthusiasm grew. "We could take him to senior citizens' groups, schools—"

"Now you're getting the idea," Scott interrupted. "And I don't see any reason why Dean can't be part of the program. He can let pepople see that even a small child can get a trained dog to respond. Now what do you think of my surprise?"

"I think you liked seeing me jump to the wrong conclusion."

"I confess." Scott draped a big arm over Rani's shoulders and headed back to the seat she'd left a minute before. "What if we let the playmates get used to each other? Do you have any idea how much I missed you?"

But even as he sat beside her, the thoughts and doubts that had been assaulting Rani came back. Scott was looking down the road a long way by bringing Dean and Dino together, but there was no guarantee that anything would last. Someday soon Rani would have to tell him of the terrible secret she carried in her heart. "I thought I might find you here," Scott said after they shared a lingering kiss. "Thanks for bringing my kid here. How's he doing?"

When Rani explained that she wasn't the person to ask about football performance, he laughed. "Stick with me, lady. I'll turn you into an expert yet. Something tells me we're going to be watching a lot of football games before that kid and his sidekick are grown."

He wouldn't leave her. Scott wouldn't be talking like

that if he had any doubts. Rani snuggled against him, unmindful of any other spectators who might turn their eyes from the football field to the couple with the small boy. Scott called her capable, and maybe she was, but right now nothing could feel as good as having him next to her, his bulk shading her from the afternoon sun. She asked him a few questions about his trip and explained about the national coverage they would be getting, but those concerns weren't nearly as important as thinking about how warm and comforting and subtly sensual a man's shoulder rubbing against hers could be. "I'm glad you're back," she whispered when she had him caught up on what had been happening in his absence.

"You aren't the only one. Going to California has never been my idea of fun, but it's been so much harder to leave here since I met you. Next time I want you to come with me."

"I'd like that. But what about Dean? Do you think Hollywood's ready for him?"

"It better be. You're going to be part of my life from now on, lady. I don't think I'd get very far saying your shadow can't come along."

Rani felt a small chill but refused to let it grow. This time was for reunion, not for problems that made sleep impossible.

"Are you going to tell me what happened between you and Zack?" Scott asked. "I know this isn't the long ride I promised you, but it'll have to do. Is he still around?"

Rani shook her head. "He isn't cut out for what it takes to be Dean's father," she said. "I asked for a confrontation. I got it in spades."

"I guess it takes all kinds. But a man who turns his back on his kid— I hope you told him to take a flying leap."

"It wouldn't have done any good. Scott, the other night you said you didn't want to talk about Zack. Now I'm the one who feels that way. He isn't part of my life or Dean's anymore. I have to look forward, not back."

They watched the action in silence for a few more minutes, and then as practice broke up, Scott explained that he'd meet her back at the ranch after he'd gone back to the airport to pick up the animals. "Then we'll have that long ride if we don't wind up in bed," he said, winking.

Chad's animated talk about practice and his pleasure at having his father show up to watch kept Rani from having much time to think until they were back at the ranch. She prepared Dean's dinner and then went outside to watch as Scott and Chad unloaded the animals. She couldn't help but feel warmed by the sight of the tall son and father working side by side at a job they were both competent doing. Scott could have turned much of the ranch's operation over to one of the hired men, but he'd taken the time to include Chad in everything he did so that now the teenager could be trusted to care for the animals in his father's absence. Rani kept Dean close to her, thinking that this was what a father-son relationship was supposed to be. "He isn't going to stay," Zack had said. Zack had to be wrong! He had to be!

Scott and Chad were finishing up when Rani took Dean to bed. She'd finished his story and was listening to his regular breathing when Scott came in. He put his arm around her shoulders and drew her close. "I'm not going to pretend it doesn't hurt when I think of what he's been through," Scott whispered. "I don't want that for the little guy."

"I didn't, either," Rani replied, feeling defensive.

"I know that. It just doesn't seem fair that such things happen to kids. I'm just glad most of it is behind him and he's young enough not to remember any of it. I'm just sorry you have to."

Rani was going to say that was the price she had to pay for being the kind of woman she was then, but she didn't. Tonight, right now, she didn't want to think heavy thoughts. "What was that you said about a long ride?" she asked, looking up at eyes that seemed capable of seeing through her.

"You're going to hold me to that, are you? I thought I might be able to continue with an activity that seems to satisfy both of us."

Rani ducked her head so Scott couldn't see the sudden color rising to her cheeks. "My boss is a slave driver. He has me working twenty-four hours a day. I'd like to see a little more of the countryside."

"Your wish is my command, my lady," Scott said as he opened the front door. "We're going to have to have a talk with that boss of yours. Let me tell Chad where we're going so he can keep an eye on Dean."

"You don't have to do that," Rani said in sudden alarm. "He'll be all right."

Scott gave her a long look. "I know he will, but it won't hurt Chad to know Dean's alone. He'll want to keep an eye on him."

A few minutes later Scott was back. With a flourish he helped her into his sports car. "Now, young lady, this is the guided tour. You want to see Sol Valley at night? Pay attention—I might give you a test on it later."

Rani had been looking forward to spending time with Scott, nothing more. She had no idea that the next two hours would be filled with a detailed travelogue that covered everything from the history of the valley's early settlers to the life stories of the farmers who now raised crops and livestock throughout the sun-blessed valley. They stopped long enough to tour the outside of the small school where the area's children went through the eighth grade. Scott explained that he periodically brought animals to the school and several times had let some of the older students "work" for him during the summer. "I don't know how much work I got out of them," he admitted. "But I felt good about it, so I guess that's the right trade-off. I'm sorry Chad's too old to go to school here."

It was after midnight when they returned to the ranch. "You know what I regret?" Scott said after he'd turned off the motor. "Bucket seats aren't for making love in a car."

"You were thinking about that?" Rani asked, unable to admit that the past two hours had raised her sensitivity to the point where she wasn't sure how much longer she could keep her hands off him.

"How can I help it?" Scott brought his hands in contact with Rani's breasts. "You do crazy things to me. You're just lucky I'm a law-abiding man or you might not have any clothes on right now."

"I wouldn't mind," Rani admitted before ducking away from Scott and scrambling out of the car. She didn't pull away when he joined her, leading her through the dark to the cabin.

"We're going to have to do something about our separate living quarters," Scott said just before they reached the cabin. "You are going to make an honest man out of me, aren't you?"

"I—Scott? What are you saying?"

"Can't you guess?" Scott opened the cabin door and led them into the darkened living room before continuing. "Rani, I don't believe in casual relationships. What I feel for you is something I want to continue in a marriage."

Rani blindly sought the safety of Scott's arms. She buried her face in his chest, his words closing around her and bringing her life. "You can't mean it," she whispered, not caring that her words made little if any sense. "We haven't had much time."

"I've had all the time I need. When I name a dog after my girl friend's son, it's serious," Scott replied, his voice sounding almost as shaky as hers. "I've had a lot of years of dating and the single life. I know when I've found the person I want to spend the rest of my life with."

But what about when I tell you about what I did or didn't do, Rani thought. She didn't have the courage to speak the words aloud. Instead, she drank in the masculine smell of Scott, ran her fingers over the hard cords of his arms. She'd face cold reality another time. Right now nothing mattered except being with him.

"You aren't saying anything," Scott pointed out.

"I don't know what to say. I love you."

Scott laughed. "That's a start. Now, how about saying you'll marry me?"

"Scott. You—I don't know what to say."

Scott grabbed her arms and forced her away from

him. Gripping her firmly, he stared at her. "Is it Chad? You don't want a teenager around?"

"Oh, no!" Rani gasped, astonished that Scott could think such a thing. She loved the lanky, muscular boy. Her sense of contentment in being able to watch him grow up was total. Surely Scott saw that. "There's nothing I'd like more than to be around him."

"I wasn't sure," Scott said as he drew Rani back against him. "A teenager isn't always the easiest person in the world to be around. You're used to a little boy, not a kid who can't decide between girls and earning money and pushing for independence."

"Chad's everything I'd ever want in a son," Rani whispered, knowing how close she was to making a commitment and yet terrified that that commitment would backfire.

Scott was rubbing his hands along her backbone, stirring up thoughts and emotions that had nothing to do with carrying on a serious conversation. She arched her spine, lifted her head and parted her mouth to receive Scott's lips. His fingers toying with the outlines of her ribs as his mouth consumed hers quickly brought Rani totally under the spell the ranch owner was weaving. Whether he was aware of his great power over her she didn't know, but she didn't see how he could possibly not realize that when he took her in his arms she no longer existed outside his all-consuming circle.

Rani closed her eyes in an attempt to absorb everything there was to feel and experience about Scott Barnett. Before meeting him she hadn't been aware of wanting a man capable of total sensual control over her. But as he loosened her blouse from her waistband she surrendered to that power.

They made love, not in the bedroom where Dean was sleeping, but on the hide-a-bed in the living room. Rani giggled self-consciously as they fumbled with the seldom-used bed, but when Scott lowered her onto it she was no longer laughing. "I can't think when I'm around you," she admitted, pulling him down with her. "What were we talking about?"

"Don't worry about that. Right now I'm going to seduce you. After we're done—*if* we ever get done— we'll pick up our conversation again."

To Rani's drugged senses Scott's suggestion made sense. She watched him remove his shirt and admitted that being seduced by this man was the only thing she wanted to concentrate on tonight. He lifted her back into a sitting position and slowly—reverently, it seemed to her—removed her blouse. He was standing, leaning toward her as he unfastened her bra and pulled it off her. "I love doing that." He smiled. "I feel like a kid on Christmas morning."

"Is that what you want for Christmas?" she asked, looking down at herself.

"It's at the top of my list. Of course, it's what comes with the undressing that makes it such an intriguing activity. I don't know what you've done to me," he groaned. "I can't get enough of you."

Rani reached out her arm, begging Scott to join her. He pulled off his slacks and obliged her, shoving her over playfully to make room for him on the bed. Instead of folding her against him, Scott propped himself up on one elbow and teasingly drew his fingers in a slow, mind-drugging line from her earlobe down her neck and finally to her breasts. Rani lay on her back, trembling, lips parted so she could draw air into her lungs. She longed to pull Scott close to her, and yet the pleasure he was giving her as he took her nipples between his fingers was enough to keep her ignited body quiet.

"Do you like that?" he whispered. "I want to make it good for you."

"Do I like it? You're making me crazy." She was surprised to find she could talk at all. To her delight he was in no hurry to leave her breasts. First one mound and then the other was subjected to an intimate probe that left them throbbing. By now Rani's hips were squirming on the bed, her fingers curled into tight knots to keep them still. When finally he dipped his head to cover her left breast with his mouth, Rani could contain herself no longer. She wrapped her arms around Scott's neck, forcefully pulling him against her.

"You're pretty strong," he muttered from where his face was nestled between her breasts.

No, she wasn't. If Scott hadn't been ready to turn from play to more intimate contact she would never have had the strength to draw him to her. But this touch that extended from lips to feet was what they both wanted. Even as she was drowning in Scott's presence she wondered if there wasn't something of the artist in her. She wanted to memorize every inch of Scott, imprint him on her memory and paint him someday.

The thought was a fleeting one. It was replaced by the sensation of being pulled beneath the surface, floating somewhere in a silent, cushioned world with Scott. They were underwater, but since there was no need to breathe, the experience was totally joyful with no thoughts of drowning. Whether Scott's strokes matched hers she didn't know, but when their bodies joined it was as if no more perfect union could exist. She laughed with the joy of it, cried in relief and release. If anything, their lovemaking, which had been all she'd ever wanted, was getting better.

Scott fell asleep first. Rani sat up, pulled a blanket over both of them and lay back next to him. She gave herself a mental reminder to awake at dawn so that all signs of the night they'd spent together could be removed before the day's work began. She let her mind drift off, not thinking, not wanting anything more than the warm body next to hers, the slow, deep breaths brushing against the side of her face. *I love you, Scott Barnett,* she thought as she drifted off. No matter what happens, nothing will ever change that.

Dean, who was the first to wake up, was a little disoriented without his mother around. When Rani heard him calling for her in the next room she jumped out of bed, placed him on her lap and whispered baby talk. She was telling him some nonsense story about a puppy and a giant green man when Scott came into the room. For a minute he leaned against the doorjamb, arms folded across his chest, watching. "What do you think of the name Dino?" he asked Dean. "You can change it if you want to."

"No. Dino's mine forever and forever. He's going to go to school with me."

"He is?" Scott pretended surprise. "I didn't know they let dogs ride school buses."

Dean gave Scott a look that plainly said that Scott had a lot to learn. "My dog can do anything I want."

"Well." Scott winked at Rani. "I guess that settles that. I take it Dean isn't interested in falling back asleep for a few minutes."

"I'm afraid not."

"Too bad. I was looking forward to a little more experimentation concerning what can be done in a hide-a-bed."

"Certain things have priorities," she pointed out. "Like breakfast."

"I've been a parent long enough to be aware of that," Scott said as he turned on his heel and started to leave the room. "You're so sensitive when it comes to Dean. Try to relax. It colors everything you do and think about."

Rani turned back to her son, blinking to halt the pressure of unspent tears. Maybe she had overreacted. It was possible that Scott had been joking and had meant nothing by pointing out that Dean was responsible for their being out of bed. But Rani still had things to make up to her son, her own private way of easing her guilt. The time she spent with him wasn't something she could make a joke of.

And it was more than that. Last night Scott had asked her to marry him. Their lovemaking had gotten in the way of what her answer would be. Now it was morning and Scott hadn't repeated his question. Instead, he'd watched as she chose her son over him.

Maybe last night's question was something he already regretted. She could understand that a romantic night ride and the promise of lovemaking could lead to Scott saying things, asking questions he now wanted to take back. But that didn't make it any easier for Rani to face.

"What am I thinking, kid?" she asked Dean as they were picking out his clothes. "Do you want a father?" She choked on the words, closed her eyes to fight back the tears, and when she dared went on. "Maybe it isn't in the cards. I can understand. I really can. I have so much to make up to you. That—that could take precedence over other things, change what Scott feels for me." She stopped, then continued. "If only I'd kept you with me that day. Maybe I'd still be married to your father. I wonder what our life would be like."

She didn't try to answer her own question. If Scott walked out of her life, she wouldn't hate him. At the same time she knew she'd never be able to forget what they'd shared. That was the part that hurt so much, that finally won over her determination not to cry.

Rani loved Scott in a way she'd never loved Zack. It was a combination of his competence and compassion: the way he handled a complex business, made sacrifices to make Dogs for the Deaf a reality, and still found time to be a full-time father. But maybe that was as much as he was capable of.

Staying married to a woman with an imperfect child was more than the child's father could contemplate. Why should Scott be any different?

Rani finished dressing Dean before going into the training room. She took a chair in a corner of the room, beyond caring whether her now-dried tears had left their mark on her face. Scott was engaged in working with one of the dogs and barely glanced at her before turning back to the dog to make sure the animal's attention didn't wander.

Rani knew she had work to do, but she couldn't bring herself to stand. When Dean climbed up on her lap she used his rare desire to be snuggled as an excuse to put off returning to the work routine. Holding Dean, pretending to be absorbed in the training, gave her time to study Scott. As she watched him kneel to bring his face close to one of the dogs, she couldn't remember what she'd snapped at him about earlier. His movements were so fluid, so innately sensual that she found it hard to believe any woman had been able to ignore him. It was obvious that their female trainer was taken with Scott and in subtle ways tried to get him to pay attention to her. Rani wouldn't blame Scott for responding to her teasing remarks and open smiles. After all, she was young and single, not trying to make up for past mistakes.

Rani watched Scott as he took a moment from working with one of the more advanced dogs to give the somewhat restless Dino a pat on the head and a reminder to stay where he was observing the action. He was giving Dino more attention than he was giving her, and that made her face the possibility that he might be sorry that he'd said anything about their getting married. Rani would have given anything not to have that thought come back to haunt her, but the question had a life of its own. There was no way she could keep from having to face it. Last night they'd been lovers. This morning she'd been a mother—a totally different creature. Her decision to leave Scott and go to Dean had to have been interpreted as a decision on her part to choose her child over her lover.

But she really didn't have any choice in the matter. She'd wronged her son once before. She wasn't going to make the same mistake again, even if it spelled an end to her own chance at happiness.

Rani surged to her feet. She couldn't face that possibility! Before Scott could say or do anything to stop her, she hurried from the room and trotted back to the office with a confused three-year-old clinging to her hand. She tried to face the never-ending paperwork, but in her distracted state, handling correspondence was beyond her. After half an hour of wasted effort she turned off the typewriter and got to her feet. Dean looked up from his building blocks, obviously excited at the prospect of being able to leave the office. "Are you all done working, Mommy? Can we go and play with Dino?"

"Your mommy has cabin fever," she told her son. "How about if we get a little fresh air? I think Scott wants Dino with him right now. Think you'd like to say hello to Gas? He misses you."

At the mention of Gas's name Dean shoved his blocks into a corner and raced to the door. Rani laughed, sharing her son's joy. It was time to let heavy thoughts rest. She opened the door, letting the sunshine kiss her cheeks. As they made their way to the mountain lion's run Rani thought about the changes that had taken place in her life in a few short weeks. A mountain lion was now someone she didn't mind her son being around, as long as he was careful.

Dean seemed to have understood what everyone had told him about staying away from the cage and observing Gas from a safe distance. Only when Chad or Scott was around would he venture close enough to touch the animal's thick, glossy coat. Because Rani hadn't spent much time with Gas, she kept the same respectful distance from him that she expected her son to observe. "I wonder if Gas likes me?" Rani asked absently. "I'll have to ask him that."

Because she was trapped within herself, Rani was barely aware that Chad was outside Gas's cage but reaching in doing something to the big cat. When she became aware of the teenager's concentration on his job, she stopped, keeping a distance between herself and whatever was going on. She didn't want to startle Chad or Gas by coming up unexpectedly. It wasn't until Chad gave a grunt of disgust and stepped back that Rani spoke. "Is something wrong?"

"Not really," Chad said without turning away from the mountain lion. "Gas caught his shoulder on something. He has a cut here I'm going to have to treat."

Rani stepped forward and looked where Chad was pointing. The gash on the mountain lion's shoulder was about four inches long and not very deep but filled with dirt or some other foreign material. "What can you do about that? You can't put stitches in him, can you?"

"I could, I guess, but that cut isn't going to need stitches. I've got to clean it, though, so it won't get infected. He won't stand close enough for me to get to the wound. I'm going to have to go in there."

"Chad, isn't that dangerous? I mean, Gas is in pain. He isn't in a good mood. Let me get your dad." Rani started off, but Chad stopped her.

"I've treated animals before. Gas and I understand each other," he said shortly. "I don't have to run to Dad."

Rani understood Chad's desire to prove himself, but she couldn't help feeling uneasy about having him treat what was basically a wild animal. "Let me help," she offered. "What can I do?"

Chad looked dubious but didn't turn her down. "I'm going to get in there with him. If you'd hand me the disinfectant, it would be a help. He isn't going to like it because it stings, but I don't think he'll take his bad mood out on me."

Rani took her place where Chad had been standing before and waited while he unlocked the door to Gas's run and slipped in. Rani was impressed by Chad's calm, self-confident manner. Yes, Gas had been handled by people all his life, but he had to be uncomfortable. If Chad had acted nervous, Gas might have become edgy and short-tempered himself. As it was, Chad was able to work himself around to the mountain lion's side and started cleaning out the wound while Rani handed him pieces of cotton dipped in disinfectant. She was concentrating on Gas's eyes, ready to warn Chad if he showed any sign of impatience. Because her eyes were on the mountain lion, she didn't see Dean push against the large door and enter the run.

Chad spotted the little boy first. "Rani." His voice was low and calm but with a note of warning Rani couldn't ignore. "Get him out of here."

Rani jumped, her maternal instinct instantly in full gear. She'd dropped the medication and was nearly to the opening when the mountain lion spotted the new presence in his domain. He took a step toward Dean, head lowered and mouth slightly open. Just as Rani was gauging whether she could jump and throw Dean to the ground under her, Chad punched Gas squarely behind the ear. The move was enough to distract the mountain lion. He turned toward Chad and with a blurred motion reached out with his right paw, a slashing contact that knocked the teenager back against the cage.

"Chad! My God! Scott!" Rani screamed as she grabbed Dean and hauled him out of the cage.

Chapter Thirteen

Rani acted out of instinct. She took a second glance at Dean to make sure he was safely out of the cage and aware of the necessity to stay where he was. Even as she heard feet running in her direction, she slipped back inside the enclosure.

Rani almost collided with Gas's rear end before she swerved to the left and came alongside the mountain lion. Sprawled on the ground was Chad. He was holding his left arm and staring fixedly at the narrow-eyed lion. Rani froze, knowing without being told that any sudden movement could be their undoing. She whistled low and off-key until the animal's ear and then its head turned in her direction. "Move slowly," she whispered to Chad, her eyes boring into Gas. Was it possible to hypnotize a meat eater? She didn't know, but she was determined to hold his attention through force of will until Chad was out of danger.

She sensed movement from the cage entrance but didn't dare turn away from the mountain lion. It wasn't until the form came closer that she realized it was Scott. "Don't move," he said as calmly as if he were ordering dinner. "If you stay frozen you're all right. I have to get Chad out first."

"I know," Rani replied without moving her lips. She saw Gas's eyes start to slide past her and whistled until she once again had his full attention. She sensed rather than saw Scott help Chad to his feet and lead him out of the cage. Not until she heard the low, confident command from Scott urging her to leave did she slowly back out of the cage. She thought she would scream from the tension when Scott's hands reached her shoulders and she sank backward into them. The moment of intimacy lasted only a second. As soon as she'd gained control over her feet, Scott released her to lock the cage door firmly in place.

"How is it, son?" she heard him ask and turned attention to Chad. The teenager was still holding his arm, his eyes deep with pain.

"How is Dean?" Chad asked through tight lips. "Is he hurt? I'm sorry. I forgot to lock the door."

"It isn't your fault," Rani reassured him as Scott started lifting away the torn fabric of Chad's shirt. "You had to leave it unlocked so you could get out. I should have been watching Dean."

Assessing blame, if there was any, would have to wait until later. As soon as Scott had exposed the claw mark it was obvious Chad would need stitches as well as a thorough cleansing of the injury to protect him from infection. While Scott stayed with Chad and a whimpering Dean, Rani ran for Scott's sports car and drove it up to where they were waiting. Her legs still trembled from the shock of her close call, but her emotional state was pushed into the background as she tended to Chad and her own frightened son.

"I can take him in," Scott said as he was settling Chad into the back seat of the car, a large towel wrapped around the wound.

"I'm going, too," Rani replied in a voice that left no room for argument. Not accompanying Chad would be as illogical as letting her own son go to the hospital alone. She and Dean slid into the front seat next to Scott so Chad could have the back seat to himself.

Once they were on the road Scott asked how the accident had happened. Chad once again tried to take all the blame himself. "I wanted to treat Gas by myself," he said between deep breaths designed to maintain control over the pain he was obviously feeling. "I was sure I could do it without getting into trouble. I forgot about the door and Dean. God, I'm sorry!"

"Don't be," Rani reassured him. "Dean's fine. You're the one we're worried about."

"Yes. But if anything had happened to that little guy..." Chad's voice trailed off.

Rani continued to look back over her seat at Chad, but for several minutes she couldn't bring herself to speak. Chad had risked so much to protect a child who should have been watched by his mother. The teenager had acted out of instinct and as a result had endangered his own life. She'd known for some time that the bond between Chad and Dean was strong, but until today she hadn't seen how powerful it was. Knowing that Chad loved her son that much left her weak.

Months ago Dean had almost died because she wasn't responsible or strong enough. Now another boy was paying for her irresponsibility and weakness. She'd been bearing the burden of guilt from the accident she'd already had a hand in. It was starting all over again. God! Of course it was!

Rani couldn't meet the green eyes of the stern-faced man driving well over the speed limit. Scott dearly loved his son and was reaching out toward Dean, too. She didn't need any more proof than a curly-tailed dog named Dino. He was a good, caring man. He deserved better than she was able to offer. She couldn't blame him if he hated her right now.

But now wasn't the time to allow such thoughts to consume her. The prospect of losing Scott, as Zack had said she would, was more than she could stand. Because she needed to touch and be touched in turn, she reached out and rested her fingers on Scott's neck. She had to find out.

Scott responded by grabbing her fingers and bringing them to his mouth for a light kiss before turning his attention fully to the road. "Are you all right?" he asked. "Thank you."

"For what?"

"For maybe saving my son's life."

There didn't seem to be anything else to say during the ride to the hospital except to reassure Chad that the wound didn't look serious enough to keep him away from football practice for more than a few days. Chad was still blaming himself for his lack of foresight, but Rani couldn't blame Chad. Chad was fifteen, swimming his way toward manhood but not quite there. She couldn't burden him with adult responsibilities. Besides, who was to say that an adult would have handled the situation with any more wisdom than Chad had? She had to accept the blame herself. She could have insisted that Chad leave treating the mountain lion to his father, but she hadn't.

Scott went into the examining room with Chad while Rani stayed at the emergency-room desk to fill out the forms and keep an eye on Dean. The wait seemed endless, especially because Dean kept trying to go into the room where he'd seen his friend being taken. Once Scott came out to report that Chad's arm had been numbed and the repair should begin soon. "He's feeling pretty cocky now that it doesn't hurt anymore. He wants to make sure we count the stitches so he can tell the guys on the team."

Rani rolled her eyes skyward. How quickly young people bounced back! She kept her own nervousness concealed from Scott. She was still shaking from the aftereffects of something that could have turned into tragedy. But the knots in her stomach and her pounding head came from more than that. Nothing would have happened if Chad hadn't been trying to keep a mountain lion away from Dean. Chad's quiet action might have saved Dean's life. She owed the teenager so much!

It was that thought that forced her into the examining room despite the disapproving glare from the nurse assisting the doctor. Rani tried to hold Dean so he couldn't see the stitches being taken, but it was impossible. Dean was fascinated by the angry wound and the black thread bringing the ragged flesh back together. If Rani thought Dean would be upset by the sight, she was wrong. Instead, Dean made little clucking sounds as if reassuring Dean. "I had stitches," he announced. "And a broken arm. I hurt my head bad. Did you hurt your head?"

"Hey, kid," Chad said, "I'm going to live. As soon as these stitches are out I'm going to show you a thing or two about staying out of Gas's cage."

"That's a good idea," Rani managed. God, she loved Chad! The emotion was so intense it overwhelmed her. "Maybe you better include his mother in that lesson, too."

"Maybe. Maybe not. Those things happen," Chad said, shrugging. "We just have to make sure it doesn't happen again."

Chad's words reached Rani, hard. Chad saw today as a learning experience, nothing more. She needed to take what she was learning another step, but this wasn't the time or place to say anything personal. Instead, she stepped back so she wouldn't be in the way and formed the words she needed to say. "I want to thank you for what you did. Dean should never have been in the cage. That was my fault," she said softly, ignoring everyone in the room, even Scott, as she concentrated on the teenager on the examining table. "You saved Dean's life."

"Yeah?" Chad flashed her a grin. "That's me, the hero."

"I'm afraid I can't agree," Scott broke in. "Chad, I've told you about handling Gas. He's okay as long as you're alone with him, but when there are other people around, he gets distracted and nervous. That was a dumb move. When I think of what could have happened—"

"Nothing happened!" Rani snapped, a mixture of hospital smells, tension and her own unanswered questions of the past days exploding in sudden temper. "I'm sorry Chad was hurt. I blame myself. I'd give anything for that not to have happened. Don't you think he's gone through enough?" When Scott glared at her, she glared back and went on. "Do you think blaming him will change anything? Give him credit for having learned something on his own today."

"Listen to the expert!" Scott snapped. "You think you have perfect insight into the future. Well, you're wrong, and you have no business jumping on me."

"Don't I?" Rani held what else she might have said in check because it was obvious that their argument was sending sparks flying through the room. She grabbed Dean and stalked out of the room, only half comprehending what the argument was about.

Scott was right behind her. He grabbed her right elbow and dragged her forcefullly into the waiting room adjacent to the emergency complex. He shoved her unceremoniously into a chair and stood leaning over her, his eyes shooting daggers. "I will not have you contradicting me when I'm talking to my son!" he thundered. "That's my child. Not yours!"

The words hit Rani like a blow to the stomach. She recoiled visibly, mouth sagging in shock. "Your son? Is that what it would have been if we'd gotten married? Your son, my son. What happened to sharing?"

"That's not what I meant and you know it," Scott managed. He barely remembered what he'd said to make her look sick like that. He'd been so caught up in the accident and the emergency-room scene that he honestly didn't know what was coming out of his mouth. He'd had his share of injuries in his life, but seeing his son's arm torn like that did things to his insides that he wasn't doing a very good job of dealing with. He wanted to tell Rani how he felt, that he was wondering what he could have done to have prevented the accident, but the right words simply wouldn't come. "Look, it isn't every day I see my son with a mountain lion standing over him. My reactions were pretty primitive." He couldn't add that he believed that it was somehow his fault.

"Mine were, too," Rani pointed out. She put Dean down, watching him out of the corner of her eye as he wandered off toward a TV set in the room. "Love is a primitive emotion," she whispered, feeling suddenly drained of her former anger.

To her surprise Scott's face underwent a total transformation. She watched, fascinated, as the rage she'd shrunk from was replaced by a look of deep concentration, of tenderness even. "Funny we should be talking about love right now," he whispered and sat down beside her. "That's what brought all of us here today. Do you realize that? That also reminds me that we were having a discussion on that very subject the other night. We didn't finish."

Rani longed to touch Scott, to bring back some of the feelings that she had for him, but she was afraid. Simmering inside was unresolved anger over his attempt to tell her she had no say in Chad's life. What she felt for the boy in the emergency room was too fierce and protective and maternal to be dismissed. "I don't think this is the time to change the subject," she pointed out. "We were talking about his and hers and ours."

"I thought we were talking about marriage."

Rani turned quickly away from Scott, but it wasn't enough. She needed more distance from him. She gathered her feet under her, rose and walked swiftly to the window, where she could stare out at the rows of parked cars. For almost a minute she said nothing, grateful for Scott's silence. Her emotions were pounding through her brain with such intensity that she felt in no condition to hold up her half of any conversation. She couldn't understand his bringing up his proposal at this time. He could have done that this morning when Dean took her from his side, but he hadn't. Now, after an argument in a hospital, was hardly the time or place.

Besides, the answer she would have to give was destroying her.

I can't marry you, Scott. Even if you say you love me, I'm not worthy of you. I don't deserve it. Not after my role in bringing two boys to hospitals. I'm not good enough for you.

Love. Once, a thousand experiences ago, she had thought it was a magical word. True, she loved Scott, loved his intense devotion to everything that he touched, the way he turned her body into a musical instrument. When she left, she would miss Chad and the work for the Dogs for the Deaf program terribly.

Saying no, which she would have to do to save herself from even more agony later on, would cost her dearly now. But she wasn't worthy of Scott and his son.

When she could no longer go on wrestling with her thoughts, Rani turned slowly, blinking feverish eyes in order to concentrate on Scott. Without her being aware of it, he had come up behind her and was now standing a foot away in the deserted waiting room. "Can I touch you?" he whispered. "You look as if you're going to fall apart."

Dully Rani shook her head and shrank from him. "Please don't do that to me. Scott, marriage wouldn't work for us."

"Why?" He might not have been touching her, but his eyes were reaching her like hot strands of molten fire. Scott felt as if he was standing on the brink of disaster. If he could touch her she might not turn away from him, but if he made the wrong move, said the wrong thing... "Give me some reasons that make sense."

"You—you'd leave me later."

"No, I'd never leave you. I'll never stop loving you."

"Love has nothing to do with it. You don't know what I—I owe Dean so much."

He didn't know what she was talking about. Or maybe he was starting to and didn't know how to help her say the words. "I want to be Dean's father. Rani?" He reached out, and when she didn't shy away, he took her icy hands. "What I said a few minutes ago in the examining room—I was wrong. I was hurting because Chad was hurting. I felt somehow responsible. Parents aren't all-knowing. We aren't filled with some great wisdom. We make mistakes. One of the biggest I've made today is calling him *my* son, shutting you out."

"Why did you?" Rani whimpered, the pain of his words striking her again.

"Because I didn't want to be standing there watching some doctor put stitches in his arm. I wanted to be anywhere but where I was. I kept thinking, *if only I could take us back in time.* I—I wasn't thinking." He wasn't sure whether he'd said enough to make it up to her. He could only pray she'd understand.

"Oh, Scott!" His words reached something in Rani's core. Now she could understand a man who lashed out in pain and in the process said things he didn't mean to. "I understand," she whispered, for the first time returning the pressure of his hands with pressure from her own. "It hurts so much to see our children hurting. I've felt guilty for so long."

Scott nodded, pulling her closer. "I'm not going to tell you it doesn't hurt when I think of what Dean went through. I love that little guy. Rani, darling, it was an accident. You can accept responsibility for your part in what happened, but don't let it prevent you from enjoying life. Put it in the past and go on from there."

"You—you mean that? Scott, it happened again today. I was responsible for another accident." There was more she wanted to say, but the tears were getting in the way. How long had it been since she'd cried? If something drastic didn't change, the drought would be over.

"It's over. Chad's going to be okay. We've all learned something from the experience. It's time to go on from that point."

"You don't understand. I know I shouldn't have let Zack take Dean that day. He was already angry about something I'd done. I—I didn't want Dean to go. But"—she dropped her head—"I didn't want to argue anymore. I let him win. I was gutless, and Dean paid the price."

"You aren't gutless. At least I haven't seen that side of you. You didn't back down when Zack was here. I wouldn't be surprised if he's still thinking about that."

"I've been thinking about the accident, how I could have prevented it, for so long. It wakes me up at night—"

"Don't let it! What are you going to do, make a career out of guilt? You want me to blame you for Chad's accident? Sorry. There's no percentage in that."

"You don't blame me? I don't need to feel guilty?" Rani opened her mouth, but only a wounded animal whimper came out. She'd needed to hear those words for so long! Until now, here, she'd given up ever hearing them from another human being.

Rani collapsed toward that human being and buried her hot face in his chest. Sobs born of mother love and fear and pain and hope broke past the dam she'd spent months erecting. Now that they were free, there was no holding them back, no holding herself erect against the tide. Rani sobbed brokenly, released an endless torrent. Scott had said she could put guilt behind her. She needed to hear that, maybe more than she needed him to proclaim his love for her.

With Scott's arms around her, Rani gave way to her pent-up tears and admitted there were times when independence could give way to sharing. This man, this truly remarkable man was offering her what she'd denied herself during her battle to bear her guilt alone. She didn't have to stand alone. There was a man who would share the journey with her. Scott loved Dean. It was as simple as that.

How long she remained locked in Scott's warmth and strength she had no idea, but when at last her tears subsided, she felt as if a great weight had been lifted from her shoulders. Rani blinked to clear her vision and struggled against the arms that held her to Scott's wet shirt.

Scott was looking down at her with tears in his own eyes.

Trembling, Rani reached up and touched his tears. She'd never seen a man cry before. "I love those boys," Scott whispered by way of explanation. "And I love you."

"Oh, Scott, what's happening?" Rani moaned. "I didn't think I was going to cry. I didn't when I learned what was wrong with Dean and I didn't when Zack walked out on us. This—I don't understand this."

"Who says we have to understand every emotion?" Scott asked before kissing her wet face and trembling lips, stilling their movement with a power that came from deep inside him. Another time Rani would have responded to Scott's kiss as a woman responds to a man, but this time the embrace was for forging a bond between two people who had committed themselves to their children and were reaching out to share that commitment.

"Rani?" Scott was talking around lips that were still tasting her. "I love you. You know that, don't you?"

She nodded, blinked back any tears that remained. "I love you."

"I think we better go back to Chad," Scott pointed out. "But first"—he held her so there was no turning away—"I don't want you to ever doubt the way I feel about Dean. That has to be part of what exists between us."

"I understand," Rani whispered, trembling from the intensity of the moment.

"I think you do," he whispered back. "I wasn't sure until what happened today. You risked your life for Chad. If we have that kind of commitment for each other's sons, then the word *ours* applies."

"It does," Rani agreed. She wanted time to think about the instinct that had pulled her into the cage to protect Chad, but before the thought had time to form, she realized she couldn't see Dean.

She turned worried eyes in Scott's direction. "Dean? Where is he?"

Instead of panicking, Scott turned her in the direction of the examining room. "My guess is he got tired of this adult talk and went back to check up on his big brother."

At first glance it seemed as if Chad was alone in the examining room. He was propped up on his good arm, back toward the door. That was when she noticed Dean perched cross-legged on the table next to Chad. Silently she reached out to wrap her arm around Scott, the gesture telling him that this was a private moment and that their role was as observers.

"It hurts like fury at first," Chad was telling Dean, who was reaching toward the bandaged arm but not quite touching it. "But I guess you could always bite the bullet if it gets too bad. What am I telling you for? You know all about hospitals, don't you?"

"I hate hospitals. I'm never going to one again," Dean proclaimed.

Chad's voice dropped an octave. "Don't make any bets. Something tells me you're accident-prone. I just hope it isn't catching. I'll tell you what. Maybe I'll become a researcher and find a cure for accidents. You could be my assistant. Would you like that?"

When Dean didn't respond, Chad leaned forward, nibbled Dean's nose and then watched him laugh. "Yeah, that's not a bad idea," he went on slowly. "After all, I figure the old folks are going to tie the knot one of these days and we're going to be brothers. What do you think of that? Your big brother the medical researcher. Accidents can be a real pain, can't they? People are always getting uptight because they think they're supposed to have a crystal ball to see when an accident's going to happen. Think of all the finger-pointing that wouldn't happen anymore if we found the cure."

Rani didn't argue as Scott pulled her out of the room. She let him back her against a hospital wall and place one large hand on either side of her. His wild curls were damp with sweat and his face looked almost as ravaged as she knew hers was. But in his eyes was a kind of peace that gave her strength.

"He just might do it," Scott said. "Anything's possible."

"If he can just find a cure for guilt, I'll be happy," Rani whispered. "I let it eat me up for so long."

"No more being uptight. Is that what you want Chad to accomplish through his research? He's right, you know. Accidents happen. They get over. Something tells me we haven't seen the inside of an emergency room for the last time. What do you think?" Scott asked in a lighter tone. "Do you think the old folks should tie the knot?"

Rani answered by bringing Scott's hands off the wall and placing them around her. She clung tightly to his neck and reached for his lips. He had asked her a simple and yet complex question. She no longer had any doubts about the long-term outcome. There was a tremendous amount of strength in love. It could accept less than perfection. It could forgive and go forward from that point. But love was more than acceptance, more than forgiveness. It was also commitment.

And commitment was forever.

Rebecca had set herself on course for loneliness and despair. It took a plane crash and a struggle to survive in the wilds of the Canadian Northwest Territories to make her change – and to let her fall in love with the only other survivor, handsome Guy McLaren.

Arctic Rose is her story – and you can read it from the 14th February for just £2.25.

The story continues with Rebecca's sister, Tamara, available soon.

HARLEQUIN *Love Affair*

Now on sale

OPEN HANDS   *Rebecca Flanders*

Joe Ella was like a hummingbird that brought shimmering beauty into Cameron's world for a moment, then vanished. Over the years, their paths had crossed and recrossed, and though Cam understood Jo Ella's restless spirit, he couldn't stop hoping any more than he could stop loving her.

Cam's offer of temporary shelter was a balm to Jo Ella's soul, which had been battered and bruised by an ugly scandal. Jo Ella knew it wasn't fair to stay with him in Dallas, but for the first time in her life, she had nowhere else to go. . . .

THE HEART'S REWARD   *Vella Munn*

It was unlikely that Noah's Ark had contained a better menagerie than that which brayed, barked and roared on Scott Barnett's ranch in Oregon.

Rani found the ranch an exciting place to work and Scott an exciting man to work for, but she balked at Scott's suggestion that she and her three-year-old son, Dean, live there. For Dean did not mix well with assorted camels, llamas and cougers. And while Scott's teenaged son clearly enjoyed his duties as babysitter, Rani did not believe that he, or anyone else for that matter, could provide the constant attention and gentle care that Dean so badly needed.

FROM TWILIGHT TO SUNRISE   *Martha Starr*

To a man, the English Department of Minnesota's Fielding College objected to its newest staff member. Spearheading the opposition, Chairman Alec Thomas made it clear that he had no quarrel with Lilly's excellent credentials—it was her gender he minded.

Alec paraded his dislike of women at staff meetings, at social functions and in the plays he wrote. Lilly had no choice but to dig in and fight. First, she had to find the woman responsible for Alec's hostility. Then, Lilly had to find out whether Alec was still in love with that woman. . . .

Next month's titles

HEART'S JOURNEY *Cathy Gillen Thacker*

Gwen Nolan looked at the face she had not seen in twelve years and heard echoes of all their breathless promises and whispered dreams. Memory stretched across the chasm of years and bridged the distance between them. Daniel Kingston spoke her name, as he had done so many times in her daydreams, and Gwen felt a fluttering in her heart.

But then the familiar pain came rushing back, the ache of all the secrets she had had to bear alone, and Gwen found she could say nothing at all to this man—the only man who had ever mattered!

PERFECT COMBINATION *Sandra Kitt*

Dale Christensen was a visionary, pioneering medical advances that would some day restore happy, normal childhoods to sick and injured children. When Dale decided to take her first break from work, it was only because she hoped to exchange ideas with kindred souls at the convention in New Orleans. . . .

Damon Christensen was amused to discover that the hotel had mistaken his bags for those of another Dr. Christensen. The problem was speedily resolved, as were most problems in Damon's life, but this time a new problem replaced it: the distracting image of the other Dr. Christensen had lodged itself firmly in his mind!

THE WELLSPRING *Pamela Thompson*

The town of White Rock was dying. Standing between life and death was Brent Archer, city manager of neighbouring Joplin. If Brent didn't find the cause of White Rock's malfunctioning water line, built by and running from Joplin, more livestock would perish, tottering businesses would collapse and the citizens would be bankrupt.

As White Rock's mayor, Jennifer Lyon knew it was not just a duty to see that the town had water—it was a moral obligation. Her course of action should have been simple but for the unforeseen complication that arose—one that risked her heart!

These two absorbing titles
will be published in January
by

HARLEQUIN
SuperRomance

MOONLIGHT ON SNOW by Virginia Nielsen

Diane Armstrong would never forget the terror of having to land a small aircraft after her husband suffered a fatal heart attack at the controls. Nor would she forget her wanton reactions to the kindness of the man who helped save her life.

A well-bred girl, she was deeply distressed by her behaviour with Jim Forbes. But she determined to rebuild her shattered life without the help or comfort of the San Francisco executive with the alluring Southern drawl.

This self-sufficiency was dictated by her pride. But Jim Forbes demanded more of her soul than she had ever put to the test before.

WHEN ANGELS DANCE
by Vicki Lewis Thompson

Angie Nichols, public-relations consultant, needed Ben Scheaffer to make her promotional campaign a success. She was prepared to do almost anything.

Ben Scheaffer, computer genius, devoted himself to his floppy disks in a secluded Colorado cabin. As a retired Olympic skier, he knew the cost of fame and fortune—he wasn't prepared to stand in the spotlight again.

Their problems snowballed when they found themselves falling in love.

Harlequin ◈

Accept 4 gripping Love Affair titles absolutely FREE

Share in the bittersweet passions of heartbreak and joy in Love Affair romantic novels.

Here are stories every woman will understand, stories that explore the hearts and minds of men and women caught in the tender trap of love. By becoming a regular reader of Love Affair romances you could enjoy six thrilling new titles every two months and a whole range of special benefits too:— your very own personal membership card, a free monthly Newsletter packed with exclusive book offers, recipes, competitions, a monthly guide to the stars, plus extra bargain offers and big cash savings.

And by way of introduction we will send you 4 superb Love Affair romances free — turn over the page for details.

**Complete the coupon below and send it back today
and we will send you 4 Introductory Love Affair
Romances, yours to keep FREE.**

At the same time we will reserve a subscription to
Harlequin Love Affair for you. Every other month you
will receive six of the latest novels by leading Romantic
Fiction authors, delivered direct to your door. You don't
even pay for delivery. Postage and packing is
always completely Free. There is no obligation
or commitment — you only receive books
for as long as you want to.

**What could be easier? Just fill in the coupon below and
send it to:—
HARLEQUIN READER SERVICE, FREEPOST, P.O. BOX 236,
CROYDON, SURREY CR9 9EL**

**Please Note: READERS IN SOUTH AFRICA write to:
Harlequin Ltd., Postbag X3010, Randburg 2125, S. Africa.**

FREE BOOKS CERTIFICATE

To: Harlequin Reader Service, FREEPOST, P.O. Box 236, Croydon,
Surrey. CR9 9EL

Please send me, free, and without obligation, four Love Affair romances, and reserve a Read
Service Subscription for me. If I decide to subscribe I shall receive, following my free parcel
books, six new Love Affair titles every two months for £7.50 post and packing free. If I decide not
subscribe, I shall write to you within 10 days. The free books are mine to keep in any case.
understand that I may cancel my subscription at any time simply by writing to you. I am over
years of age.

Signature _____

Please write in BLOCK CAPITALS.

Name _____

Address _____

_____ Postcode _____

SEND NO MONEY — TAKE NO RISKS.
Please don't forget to include your Postcode.

EP16